A Recipe for Love
Addison James

Addison James

To my cat, who is always my first listener and my number one fan.

Contents

Series Note

This book is the second book in the "A Supernatural Christmas" series. These books are all interconnected but fully stand on their own. Although Max and Luc from the first book, *A Werewolf for Christmas*, appear in this book briefly, it is not necessary to have read that book first. If you are interested in learning more, Max and Casey's story is out now.

Content Notes

*On-page, descriptive sexual scenes

*The FMC being in a relationship with someone who is not the MMC at the start of the novel (no sexual scenes)

*An emotionally manipulative relationship between the FMC and her ex

*A relationship between the FMC and her ex that grows to be physically abusive

*Some on-page violence and implied, off-page violence

CHAPTER 1

Marcus

B ecoming my own great-great grandson is a colossal pain in the ass.

Or am I missing a great? It honestly is impossible to keep track of my fake lineage. I should check the family tree I made for these types of moments.

It's too much work. It's the normal amount of work that any person would go through when moving cities, of course. But then it's also miles of faked paperwork, creating an entire life story for myself, fleshed out with paperwork for fancy boarding schools and colleges and jobs and legal government documents. Then it's creating a plausible cover story for why the old me is gone.

And now, I'm left in a new city, sitting on a couch I already can't stand, thinking of the too-long list of things I need to get done before the day is over.

First off, the company. I have to assure the employees and the board that I can be a competent, controlled leader, which is galling because I've been running this company for generations now. Not that they'd know it—I've worked a lot of different roles, in a lot of different offices, and sometimes move around between any of four companies I hold a major stake in—but still, it's the principle of the thing.

Moving straight across the country will help with the risk of being recognized. Add in a few months of working almost exclusively online—supposedly to wrap up work at the office I managed prior to this one—and practically no one will put the pieces together later.

Humans. It's amazing what their brains will conjure, just so they don't have to face the facts of what's out there.

The company is a big drain on my energy, but I squared away most of it before my prior self "retired." The bigger issues facing me right now are the day-to-day things.

Namely, this stupid couch.

The penthouse apartment I'd purchased had been furnished. I suppose wealthy humans like that kind of thing, a place filled with luxury furniture that takes no thought whatsoever. For a dragon, it's practically obscene to have this place, my new nest, filled with someone else's possessions and taste. Still, the pre-chosen furniture was worth it for the view this place has.

That doesn't mean I'm tolerating this furniture long term, though. The couch I'm sitting on is as stiff as a board, and apparently whoever bought it never sat down. It needs to go, along with every gray-scale sharp right angle glass and chrome inch of this place.

And then there's all the mundane things that need to be done. I need to hire staff for this place, like a cleaning service to come in once or twice a week and a chef to prepare a few meals I can re-heat. I need to go buy a new suit, something appropriate for the supposedly now younger version of myself. There's a local charity event meant to raise money for clean water, which is a worthy enough cause. And as much as I'd like to consider cutting them a check and being done with it, it's a see-and-be-seen type event, and I, sadly, need to be seen in my new role. Humans always believe their eyes first, and I need them to see me as who I present myself as now.

I need to find a tailor too, then.

The list keeps getting longer, and I let my head rest against the back of the truly awful couch, exhausted.

Not all dragons live like this.

These days, my father lives permanently in his dragon form in a cave on a big old mountain, and he's not the only dragon I know that lives like that, even in this modern age. And I know at least a few dragons that live lives where they blend in with the most ordinary of humans, but can never quite explain their hoards.

At my last count, there were maybe a few dozen dragons left. The world isn't like what it used to be, and blending in is taking more and more work to where too many of us have just given up.

But I like my life. I like humans. There's an energy about them, a liveliness. Where most dragons go stagnant with age, humans are always moving. It must be the short lifespans.

Plus, they make beautiful, beautiful stuff.

I can't count all the stuff I've acquired over the years. Some of it belongs in museums. Some of it would probably belong in a rubbish heap, if I was some human who didn't see the delight in such ordinarily wonderful things. Either way, it's all mine.

Humans make stuff. Humans are lively and innovative and always moving in ways I'd never expect. It makes living among humans more than worth it, and I remind myself of this when the tailor pricks me with yet another pin.

The suit will need to be a rush job, and I assume my name is making him nervous. Marcus Golde might be a pseudonym that no one knew about before last week, but the money that comes with the name opens doors.

And, unfortunately, makes unsuspecting tailors clumsy with pins.

He promises me the suit will be ready in two days, and I reiterate it can't be a moment later, then hand over a wad of cash to emphasize the point.

Paper currency. One of the best inventions humans ever had, only ever surpassed by putting all that money on a little plastic card. No dragon will part with actual treasure without a great deal of pain, but cash and credit don't bother the dragon inside of us. They see it as absolutely worthless, and we can reap the benefits from it.

Like rush-ordered new suits, and promises from an over-eager furniture salesperson that the new couch I chose will be delivered to the penthouse by tomorrow morning, and of course, they'll carry the old one away.

Two things off my to-do list are enough for one day, I think. Time to go test the new bed in the penthouse.

The next day, I have an interior designer come look at the apartment. I emphasize my love of maximalist spaces, of comfort and practicality and streaks of opulence, and I just don't think she's getting it.

She hates the new couch. She looks like sitting on it is dirtying her clean, freshly pressed cream pants.

I like it. It's soft as butter, overstuffed and perfect for afternoon naps in the sun. Not that I often have time for afternoon naps, but the idea is nice. Something the dragon in me likes, perhaps.

It's also a deep, forest green, which seems to be anathema for a woman allergic to color. She hasn't shown me one design not done in cream and gray and, occasionally, a splash of black.

After forty-five minutes of her showing me pictures of things I hate, I politely but firmly tell her the meeting is over, then search for the next interior designer to call in. Just because a human is famous and expensive, doesn't mean they're the right fit. I know what I want. I've been alive a dozen human generations or more, and have had plenty of time to develop my tastes.

And this is my home, or it will be. If everything goes right, I'll be here for a decade or two. And I want to be comfortable while I'm here.

I finally find a website for a designer named Valerie Kim, and I like her style. Classy, and tasteful, but also decidedly maximalist. It's all plush blankets and rugs, soft fabrics, gorgeous colors, and beautiful decor.

Unfortunately, when I call the office, they tell me Ms. Kim is with a client and won't be available until next week. I grit my teeth but don't argue. This woman is the best at what she does, and dragons never settle for anything less than the best. I'll wait. I won't be patient, but I'll wait.

One more thing crossed off my list. I'm making substantial progress at this starting a new life yet again thing.

CHAPTER 2
Elise

"And what time are you getting home again, babe?" Ethan asks me for the fourth time.

I roll my eyes in the mirror as I tie my hair back. "I don't know. Late. Whenever the party is over, I guess."

I hear footsteps getting closer, and then Ethan appears behind me, resting one hand on my shoulder. "Kinda sucks that you're spending the night at some party, and not with me."

"I'm working, Ethan. Not partying," I correct absently, reaching up to squeeze his hand.

It is a party, but I'm the help. I'm part of the catering crew tonight, and while I'm glad to help out the organization for clean water, I'm more glad for the check I'll be getting at the end of the night.

I work as a private chef by day, cooking for clients all across Manhattan. I don't make bank at it or anything. People tend to think being a private chef means I work for millionaires, but mostly I work for busy professionals looking for a few meals to be pre-made for them. That doesn't exactly bring in the type of money that will pay off my student loans, so sometimes I pick up jobs at my friend Lacey's catering company.

I say friend, but, really, we just went to school together. I don't have time to hang out off the clock, so I think friend might be stretching it. Occasional boss doing me a favor is more like it.

Lacey does a lot of fancy parties, but I think tonight's charity dinner might be the most high-profile yet. I'm happy for her, and doubly happy she trusted me enough to bring me in.

Ethan, however, remains unhappy, a frown creasing his brow as he watches me tidy up the counter. "You're working at a party. Same thing."

I'll return home tonight a sweaty mess, worked to the point of exhaustion. If he thinks I'll have even a moment to enjoy the party, then he's never listened to a single thing I've ever said about working these nights.

"I just don't get why you work all day, then can't be home at night with me," he says, sliding up behind me now, wrapping his arms around my waist, hooking his chin over my shoulder.

I try to wiggle out of his hold, but he doesn't let me go. "I don't have time, Ethan. I need to leave now."

"You could stay home. You don't need two jobs, babe."

I need two jobs desperately. I'm paying my half of this exorbitant Brooklyn rent, and I still owe money for my degree. I'm barely scraping by with my current clients. So yes, I'll still take any catering jobs that Lacey wants to throw my way.

But I don't want to argue with Ethan about it. I know my schedule bothers him, and I suppose I get it. Ethan works a pretty standard nine-to-five, providing tech support at a big office in the Financial District. He thinks my gig-economy type of work makes me a bit flighty, but he puts up with me anyway.

He's been with me since I started culinary school, every step of the way. I think he thought things would settle down when I was no longer a student who was also working two part-time jobs, so I understand his frustration when that never happened.

"I have to go," I say again. "I can't be late."

He holds me for another moment, then finally lets me go, not saying anything as I speed-walk out the door.

The train is late, and I run the last few steps into the kitchen at the fancy event space we're in tonight.

Lacey looks at me, eyebrows raised. "You okay?"

"Sorry," I pant, tugging my chef's coat and knives out of my shoulder bag. "Trains."

Her expression clears, the word trains being the language that every New Yorker knows. "You're on appetizers," she tells me. "And I need you to get started right away."

I know exactly what I'm doing, because she'd actually asked for my input on the menu for this one. Most of my ideas got shot down, but between the harsh culling of the event coordinator and ingredient budgets and Lacey's strict standards, I'd gotten to select the appetizer.

I get out the cheese, the flour, the olive oil, and lay them out on the workstation. I'm making saganaki, or Greek fried cheese. It's delicious, with a mild, approachable enough flavor not likely to elicit many complaints, but still seemingly unique enough to feel highbrow for the type of people going to drop five thousand dollars minimum just to be here.

The menu tonight is set. A salad, then my saganaki, then a choice of either salmon or chicken, followed by a sorbet for dessert. I'd argued for a vegetarian meal, but the idea of a third entrée had apparently been one budgetary concern too far, so now we just have to hope that no one complains.

And that gets me re-thinking my saganaki. If someone who's a vegetarian comes, they can at least eat the salad, the appetizer, and the dessert. But if a vegan shows up...

Saganaki is basically cheese, and my version adds honey. And I'm relatively sure there's cheese on the salad, too.

Shit. Still, it's way too late to bring it up.

As I plate my appetizers, I pull out my phone, determined to get a picture or two, but Lacey snatches it out of my hands. "Absolutely not."

"Why not?"

"Because you can't build a profile off of my company."

I bite the inside of my cheek but nod. I just want pictures for my ridiculously tiny little food blog. I have about thirty followers, so it's not like anyone would really see it. But she's right; if anyone who ran this event saw the pictures, they could give Lacey trouble.

Hell, if my bosses saw the picture, they could give me trouble. I'm not, strictly speaking, supposed to be taking jobs that my company doesn't line up for me.

Salads have gone out, and if I get too close to the kitchen doors, I can hear the sounds of a hundred or so guests over the clatter and noise of a working kitchen. Finally, runners come out to bring my appetizers to the tables.

The main course is covered by Lacey and her regular staff, and the sorbet is already prepared, and it's too early to start scooping it. So I clean my station extra thoroughly, drifting closer to pitch in if I'm needed.

"Lacey—"

"Don't mess with my station, El." She doesn't look away from her food, brushing me off.

"I was thinking for next time—" I've always enjoyed pitching food ideas to Lacey. Our tastes don't exactly match up, although that might be because Lacey's always been better at budgets and scaling recipes to size than I have been. Even so, Lacey has always been the person you can talk to, as long as you don't expect social niceties back, and I'm currently bursting with fresh ideas.

"I don't want ideas for next time yet, Elise. Especially not any of your out there ideas," she says so brusquely that I take a step back.

"But—"

"Not. Right. Now." She plates her salmon, looking up. "Where the fuck are my runners?"

Lacey is not known for being especially welcoming while cooking, but she's never brushed me off like that before, either. She also doesn't usually insult my ideas. Sure, I don't exactly plan menus that look like a typical catering menu. I have creativity. Was the original pitch for tonight's appetizer some boring shrimp cocktail? Yes. But I made it better, and Lacey knows it, too, or she never would have let me make it.

I'll leave her alone for tonight, then. For now, I set to cleaning and think about what I'd do differently next time.

CHAPTER 3

Marcus

The conversation is tedious beyond belief. At least the wine is passable, and I sip at it as I stare around the ballroom rented for tonight's event.

This place is a who's-who of New York's old money crowds, and I should probably try harder to make connections. My new identity needs people to make him seem more legitimate, and as I take over my own company yet again, I should really have a network of the New York elite behind me.

I know all this, but it's tedious and I've done it too many times before. I check my watch, trying to calculate exactly how long I need to stay here before it's only mildly offensive for me to leave.

And all thoughts leave my head when I taste the appetizer.

Saganaki is something I've had before, having traveled to Greece multiple times. It's not that the dish is new or especially exciting for me. Still, something about it draws me in.

It's just right. Perfectly made with a delicate touch, and it captures my attention in a way nothing else has, lately.

I flag down the nearest server. "I want to speak with the chef."

The poor man looks instantly terrified, but runs off before I can add that I want to say positive things to the chef. Shit. If he scares off whoever made this meal, if I managed to scare him that badly…

I need to control myself. Dragons tend to terrify humans, triggering long-dormant prey instincts still buried somewhere in their brains, and it takes careful control to avoid scaring the humans. It's not unusual for me to accidentally make a human feel what they perceive as an unexplained but deep sense of fear just by one look in my eyes.

Still, something tells me that this is important. That I can't afford to mess this up in any way, and if the server is too scared to get me the chef, then it will be a tragedy for us all.

A harried chef approaches my table. She's tall, thin, and her light hair is contained in a tight knot. "I was told you wanted to speak to me?"

I frown, looking her over. I still have the undeniable urge to speak to the chef, but this woman doesn't make me feel anything in particular.

"You made the appetizers?"

She straightens. "I'm the head chef here tonight; everything that comes from the kitchen went through me."

I eye her for a moment. She's protective, I think, and that's a trait I can admire well enough. "I wanted to say how good it was."

"Oh." She deflates slightly, defensive posturing dropped when she realizes that I'm not a threat to her staff. "Elise made them. I'll pass on your compliments."

"I'd like to meet Elise."

She stares at me, clearly trying to take my measure. I just look back, trying to keep my expression neutral. "Alright," she says at last. "Give me a moment, then."

She goes back to the kitchen, and three minutes later another chef appears.

This time, my dragon's instincts respond. Yes, this is who I was looking for.

Elise speed-walks across the room towards me. I watch with rapt attention, trying to figure out why my dragon is so insistent on this human.

Yes, she makes good food, but I've known hundreds of humans who do that. She's attractive, too, with clear dark eyes and ample curves, but I didn't come to this party tonight to pick someone up.

I watch her as she gets closer, and I can't deny that she's exactly the type I'd pick up if I was looking. But she's working, and I'm just some rich guy attending a party. I can't ask her to come home with me. The power differential is too weird.

"Hi, I'm Elise. Lacey said you wanted to talk to me, sir?"

15

Shit, she's stopped in front of me now, brown eyes watching me intently, and I have yet to figure out exactly why I want her here so badly.

I know the rest of my table is staring, and I just tune them out. Maybe Marcus Golde will develop a bit of an eccentric reputation, but I couldn't care less.

What I really need is more time, I think. I know a good way to get that. "Your food is good," I tell her.

She flushes, a beautiful pink coloring her cheeks as she ducks her head slightly. Her chef coat is buttoned up to her throat, leaving me to wonder how far that blush goes, then scolding myself for the entirely inappropriate thought.

"You ever work as a private chef?" I ask.

"It's my day job," she admits.

"I'm new to town and trying to establish my day-to-day needs," I tell her, desperately clinging to whatever will get this woman to stay here with me. Although it's true—I'd be more than happy to eat this woman's food every day. "I'd like to hire you. Your food is good and I want more of it."

Her food is good, and I am looking for a chef. I was envisioning someone coming in two or three times a week, making a few things that I can just pop into the oven when I get hungry, but the vision suddenly changes. If I could have her in my house every day, then perhaps I could figure out why the dragon is clawing at me to be around her.

Dragons don't do that. I find humans amusing, at least most of the time, but the dragon couldn't care less about them. He's never demanded one's presence before.

"Do you have a website?" I ask, already envisioning the future I'm creating.

"I work for a service," she says. She's not quite looking me in the eye as she talks, but her voice is clear and confident. "I can be hired through the service." She fumbles for her pocket, then frowns. "I don't have a business card with me tonight."

She's somehow adorable when flustered, and I just want to soothe her worry. "That's okay. Here." I pull one of my business cards from my wallet, flipping it to the blank backside. "You have a pen?"

She produces one from her coat pocket, writing down Elise Wilson, then the name of the service. She adds a phone number at the bottom, then hands the card back to me. "I'm glad you liked your food," she mutters.

Servers come out carrying the main course now, and Elise steps smartly out of the way of the one placing the salmon in front of me. "You make this too?"

"No, that's Lacey."

I nod, taking a bite. Terribly rude when she's not eating as well, but she's watching me intently.

It's good. It's well-prepared, well-seasoned, and the sauce is a good accompaniment. Still, it doesn't spark something inside me like Elise's food did.

Still, I smile. "Please pass on that it's delicious." Let her and everyone else at this table not-so-subtly listening to this conversation think I'm just a passionate foodie.

"I will."

"Expect to hear from me tomorrow."

"Thank you," she says, and then hastily retreats.

I watch her go, trying to ignore how attractive she is as she walks away. She has the type of ass that I just want to squeeze, and it's entirely inappropriate to be thinking that of someone I'm planning on hiring.

I turn back to the table with great difficulty to find everyone staring at me. I look back, forcing eye contact with each and every one of them, and they all return to their entrées quickly enough.

CHAPTER 4

Elise

When I get home, it's almost three in the morning. The trains are a pain in the ass at this hour, and there's a walk between my stop and my apartment building.

No one enjoys walking in the city at this hour, but I'm used to it, mostly. I carry pepper spray in one hand almost the entire way, but I've never had to actually use it, so, all things considered, I'm pretty lucky.

I'm sweaty and tired and my feet ache. I also haven't been able to forget the rich guy insisting he wants to hire me as his personal chef.

He probably won't call. Still, it was nice for him to make such a big deal of enjoying my food.

I expect Ethan to be long since asleep when I get home, and have been debating if I want to risk waking him with a shower. But to my surprise, he's sitting on the couch, waiting for me with his arms crossed.

"What time do you call this?" he asks. It's not a kind question, not a sweet welcome home. His words are short and sharp.

I make myself take a deep breath. I know he worries. I know he even means well. I'm just so tired, and I want him to see that and let me go to bed.

"I've been at the party, Ethan," I tell him. "I just got done with clean up at almost two."

"It's three."

"I had to take the train home."

He uncrosses his arms, looking me over. "You're telling me that you didn't stick around for anything else? Didn't talk to anyone?"

I think momentarily of the rich guy whose name I never got, who liked my cooking and said he wanted to hire me. The image of his intense green eyes somehow flashes across my mind.

I don't answer him quickly enough. "Babe," he whines, shifting from foot to foot in that way he does when he needs reassurance.

I shake my head quickly. "No, no, it's not that," I protest, speaking quickly so he can hear me before he gets more worked up. "I just got a job offer tonight, and was thinking about that."

I hadn't wanted to tell him, or tell anyone, because the chances of the guy actually following through are next to nothing. No sense in getting people excited about what will probably not even happen. Still, I rather that than be this anxious. "It probably won't turn into anything," I concede. "But yeah, a guest at the dinner is looking for a private chef."

He just watches me with narrowed eyes, and I hold very still. Everything I've said is the truth. I didn't mention that the specific guest was a man, and one not that much older than us, to boot. And attractive. I try to push that last bit out of mind.

I have an attractive enough man right here, after all. Ethan's always been beautiful, with blonde curls that would make him look more at home on a surfboard than in a Wall Street office, a strong chin, and a grin that makes people stop and watch him. And, unlike some rich guy who definitely just wants an employee and probably isn't going to call me anyway, this one actually wants me.

"I'm going to bed," I tell him. "And you have work soon, so you should probably join me."

I shouldn't have phrased it like that, because Ethan never really enjoys being told what to do. I wait for him to argue, but instead, his posture relaxes.

"Of course, baby," he says, stepping forward. He pushes my loose strands of hair out of my eyes, looking at me for a long moment before he takes my hand to tug me to bed.

I've had three coffees before eleven am the next day when my phone rings. I fumble the grocery bags into one hand so I can pull my phone out, side-stepping a speed-walking man in a business suit as I try to make it to my client's house to prepare a few dinners.

"Elise Wilson."

"Elise, it's Makayla."

"Hey, what's up?" Makayla handles the scheduling for everyone at my agency, and I can't think of why she'd be calling me in the middle of the day.

My heart picks up speed. Unless my mysterious guest from last night actually called the number I gave him.

I'd spared half a thought this morning to call the agency to let them know they might receive a call asking for me, but I didn't know what to say. I didn't even know the guest's name, and a rich stranger probably wants to hire me sounds ridiculous.

And it's still ridiculous, I remind myself. So that can't be what Makayla is calling about.

Except then she says, "I have a new client for you, if you're looking to take on another one. Except this one is kind of different."

My throat catches. "Different how?"

"He's not looking for a couple pre-made meals a week. He's looking for a full-time private chef. His suggested hours were ten to six, if that means anything."

I stop, heedless of the fact that I'm in the middle of the street, ignoring my arm full of grocery bags. "For real?"

That is absolutely not what I expected. Not that it surprises me that anyone at the party last night is rich enough to consider this a normal expense, but the fact that the guy is willing to hire me off of one appetizer.

"Yeah. It was weird, he asked for you. You been free-lancing or something?"

I bite my lip. I'm very much not supposed to free-lance, and while Lacey's catering company is a bit of a gray area, I'd prefer not to disclose it.

Luckily, Makayla doesn't need my answer. "I told him that you have other clients, don't really do the full-time personal chef gig. Offered him some other names, but he was insistent it had to be you."

Damn, okay. This man really likes fried cheese.

"So then I asked what kind of food he likes, and told him you have a really random approach to cooking—" I flush, wanting to interrupt. It's not random. It's not like I throw random things in a pot and see what happens, like I'm in one of those cooking shows where they get totally random ingredients. Sure, sometimes I see something in a market that inspires me to go in some new direction, but it's still not random.

I like to experiment. I like to dig up people's recipes and try things out. If I had money, I'd love to travel and expand my horizons that way, too.

If Makayla called me to tell me that some rich guy wants to hire me to be his private chef, just to tell me that she scared him away, I'll jump right through the phone and hit her.

"And what did he say?" I ask.

"He asked if you could start tomorrow."

I blink. Then I almost drop my groceries in an attempt to pinch myself. "Really?"

"Yeah. And I told him you'd be there at ten tomorrow, naturally."

Everything about this seems a little too good to be true. A client who wants my cooking specifically, who apparently wants a more eclectic approach, who wants me full time. I'll get to see him eat my food, maybe even get feedback.

I have one concern. "What about my current clients?"

She huffs. "Like I can't rearrange them. I'm sure someone will be happy for the hours. Not a problem, Elise." She stops talking for a moment, and I think I hear typing. "So, finish up with your clients today, then tomorrow you're at the new guy's house. I'll text you the deets."

"What's his name?"

"Oh. Marcus Golde. And I checked the address—this guy is seriously rich, Elise."

Yeah, I could have told her that. Still, I'm glad to have a name to go with the face.

As I walk home from the train after my last ever job for my second client of the day, I realize there's a second issue I didn't think about earlier.

Ethan. He's going to freak.

Me spending a full shift in the house of one man, providing all his meals—it doesn't matter if he's a client and that's the end of the story. Ethan's always so worried that he's going to lose me.

He won't, of course. We'd both been so lonely when we met, two recent transplants to the city who just needed someone else so desperately. We've had each other ever since. But I think Ethan is just so worried that something will happen and he'll be left lonely again, and I don't want to do anything to exacerbate that fear.

I consider the issue as I get closer to our apartment. I could just not tell him, I suppose. My actual schedule won't change that much, not enough to be truly noticed.

It feels dishonest and kind of shitty. But maybe Mr. Golde is married or has a partner. Or maybe he has a maid or a butler or a personal assistant—surely a guy as rich as him has staff. Anyone else who would regularly be present in that apartment. And then, once I know they exist, I can break the change in my job to Ethan, but make sure to tell him I'm never really alone with the guy.

Yes, that should work.

With that resolved, I spend the rest of my walk home thinking about what kind of questions I want to ask Mr. Golde tomorrow, so I can make sure to give him exactly what he needs.

CHAPTER 5

Marcus

E lise gets buzzed up by the doorman exactly five minutes early.

I'd given my best description of her to the doorman, along with her name, and insisted that she have permanent access to my penthouse. So far, she's the only person besides myself who does, although I'm looking to hire a cleaning service as well.

She's wearing a chef's jacket similar to the one she wore two nights ago, a dark gray one that only serves to highlight her curves. It makes me want to peel it off and see what lies underneath.

I give myself a shake at the alarmingly inappropriate thought. She works for me now, and I didn't bring her here to seduce her.

How long has it been since I got laid? The fact that an answer doesn't come quickly to mind is not a good sign. One more thing to add to my still too-long to-do list. Find a partner for a night or two to blow off some steam so I don't eye-fuck my new chef and scare her away.

She runs a mostly discrete eye around the penthouse, lingering on the kitchen. "The place is new," I tell her. "So if there's anything you'd like for the kitchen, please don't hesitate to speak up. A decorator will be coming through early next week, but if you need something urgently, I'll have it here by tomorrow."

I've been told the kitchen is near-professional quality, although I have no way to confirm that other than Googling the appliances. I've never been much of a cook.

"Thank you," she says, and then produces a small notebook and pen from a pocket in her coat. "Do you have a few minutes this morning to discuss what exactly you're looking for?"

She's very professional. I glance at the ugly minimalist clock on the wall. "I have a conference call in an hour, but I'm all yours until then."

She nods, and I gesture her to the dining table with uncomfortable chairs. I wince. "These need to go."

"I thought you said the place was new?" She ducks her head. "Sorry, ignore me."

"No, please—say whatever you want. I don't mind. The place came partially furnished. I hate almost every bit of it and am anxiously awaiting being able to donate it and get something else in here. Something more comfortable."

Dragons like comfort. We're all for soft, well-feathered nests, in both the metaphorical and the literal sense. And this apartment just offends all my dragon sensibilities.

"So, I was told you're looking for ten to six service. Do you work from home?"

"For now. I'll occasionally go into the office, but right now I'm winding down my role managing an office in California, while starting my role here—it's easier to do it all digitally."

She nods, her expression not changing. "So, breakfast, lunch, and dinner at home then?"

"I'm not huge on breakfast. I mean, I'll eat something, but I don't do big hot breakfasts. And I thought I told the woman on the phone that I didn't need you here until it was time to prepare lunch. I consider myself a pretty reasonable employer, and I don't want you working crazy hours."

She tilts her head, considering. "Would fruit, overnight oats, muffins, that type of thing work for breakfast? I could prepare them the night before, so you can eat them whenever you start your day."

"That works."

"And Makayla, the scheduler, said she'd spoken to you a bit about what kind of food you might like…" She trails off, looking at me, clearly waiting for an answer.

I hadn't given the woman on the phone much of one. She'd said Elise could prepare an array of food, that she enjoyed experimenting with different things, and I'd agreed without hesitation. That was partially because my dragon is still driving me to do this; it desperately wants her here, and I still don't know why.

But also partially because having a wide array of always-shifting options sounded damn appealing.

I like food, and I've eaten it all over the world over the course of my long life. After all these years, I tend to get bored easily. Getting a wide variety sounds like something that would keep my interest.

"Surprise me," I tell her, then withdraw the credit card I've prepared for her. "This is for you. Buy whatever you need, go in whatever direction your heart desires. I like things I can eat at a desk for lunch, lighter things, but dinner can be literally anything. Go wild."

She swallows, accepting the card and sliding it towards herself, but not putting it away yet. She leaves it on the table next to her little notebook, which she hasn't put a single note in yet. "What's your budget?"

"No budget. Buy whatever you feel you need to make a good meal. If you need an appliance or some sort of tool, buy that too. No approval needed. Hell, if you're out shopping and need a coffee or something, get that on the card too."

She withdraws both her hands to her lap, hiding them under the table, like she thinks the card is going to bite her. "Expenses like that can stack up fast, sir. I don't want any miscommunication, or any trouble because we're not on the same page now."

I lean forward slightly, but careful not to get too close to her space. I've worked hard to create a generally affable, or at least non-threatening, appearance for humans, but I know how easy it is to slip too close to their space, or say just the wrong thing, or look at them a certain way and let the illusion slip. But she doesn't flinch. "Elise, I have plenty of money, and I like good food. I promise I'm not going to fire you for spending money on a card I gave you. If it somehow becomes an issue, we'll talk. But it won't be an issue."

She just stares at me, nodding.

"Anything else?"

By the time I rush to the office for my conference call, we've finalized a ten am to six pm schedule, with the caveat that she can adjust it as she feels necessary. She qualifies that by saying it's for things like grocery shopping, or if I have dinner guests or a meeting and request a later meal. I reiterate that it's as she feels necessary, and can change her hours for any reason.

We establish that she should have weekends off, and she makes a plan to leave me some food I can just pop in the oven and eat. She asks me about spice levels, allergies, and favorite flavor profiles. She then weasels some of my all-time favorite meals out of me, and nods the whole time, asking pointed questions, clearly trying to discern what exactly I liked about them.

The whole time, she speaks with a scientific approach, dissecting the problem of preparing a menu with precision. At the same time, every word is infused with a clear passion for what she does.

When I need to rush off for my meeting, she tells me she's going grocery shopping, then waits. I think she's hoping I'll tell her what to buy, or at least give her a budget.

I don't.

This woman is very focused on not upsetting me, I've noticed. It's money, I'm sure of it. I don't worry one bit about upsetting anyone, knowing I can buy my way out of anything, and if I can't, then the dragon lurking beneath my skin will assure that no one bothers me.

But Elise Wilson doesn't have money or a dragon. A quick background check had revealed a culinary arts degree she still has loans for, an overpriced and under-maintained apartment in Brooklyn, a long-term boyfriend she shares a bank account with, and a mother who lives out of state. Not quite the same circumstances that I'm in.

I spend half the meeting thinking about her, only vaguely focused on the projections being shown to me. Elise Wilson is interesting, because the dragon in me is very pleased to have her here, and I still don't know why. Dragons do a poor job at communicating in words. It's mostly feelings, sometimes images, and I haven't been able to fully latch onto the feelings surrounding Elise yet.

Half the reason I did the background check was to know if she was someone I'd crossed paths with before. Sometimes dragons can sense bloodlines, so if I knew an ancestor of hers and was fond of them—especially if I owed them something—it would make sense why the dragon would be drawn to her now.

But no. There's nothing in her family tree that I recognize, nothing in her personal history that means anything to me. She's been in New York for almost nine years, and, before that, lived in a small town in Pennsylvania. I haven't even lived on the East Coast in her lifetime.

By the time my meeting is done, she needs to be let back in with the groceries. I need to get her a key, I suppose, and add it to the to-do list.

She immediately sets to making lunch, looking at me over her shoulder a few times. It's obvious she wants me gone, or at least some explanation for why I'm standing here watching her.

If I knew why I couldn't just leave her alone, then my life would make so much more sense.

I watch her move around the kitchen like she's some sort of dancer. It's all grace, and I can't help watching her hips sway.

She slides a plate on the counter in front of me, piled high with two pressed panini, each cut in half down the middle. "Enjoy, sir."

"First of all, call me Marcus," I say before I can think about it. I desperately need to hear her call me by my name. "Second of all, is one of these for you?"

She raises an eyebrow, and that lovely flush comes back to her face. "No, they're for you, sir. Marcus."

"You need to eat."

"I'm not worried about it."

"Well, I am."

She frowns. "I can't eat your food."

"You absolutely can. And should." I say what I know will get me my way. "I insist."

She stares at the table for a moment, not quite making eye contact with me, but then nods. "I guess I'll need another plate." Then, like she wants to avoid looking at me or speaking with me any longer, she turns sharply back to the kitchen on the other side of the island I've been watching her from, and opens a cabinet by the stove.

Where she promptly finds a bunch of cookbooks, and sighs. "I did the same thing twice already," she mutters. She turns to me then, not quite making eye-contact but still looking in my general direction. "Would it offend you if I re-organized this kitchen?"

"Not at all. Set it up however you want." That's big words from a dragon in their nest, but it's not like I use the kitchen. It's new and I don't cook, so surely the dragon doesn't feel especially attached, and that's why I give her dominion over it so easily. "I can help you move things, of course."

"It's fine, thank you," she says, moving to the cabinet where plates presumably are stored. "Did you set it up initially?"

"No, sorry. Those cookbooks are mine; I have quite the collection of books. But all the dishes are new. Brought in by the initial interior designer." I eye the plate under my sandwich critically. It's inoffensively plain, but if she hates it, the new designer can replace them.

I own fine china. I own some plates so decorative that they really ought to be considered art pieces. They're kept carefully preserved, as is a lot of my hoard, but I should dig up the china to present to her.

My mind freezes. To present to her, or to let her use? The difference between the two is astronomical, and my first thought was present to her. Like I would give her the china.

It doesn't matter whether or not I particularly care about the china. It's my china; I have claimed it and taken it into my hoard, and for a dragon, that's enough to never, ever let anyone else have it.

As a little thought exercise—although no thought exercise has ever made my heart beat quite this hard—I imagine the scenario. Bringing whatever fine china I have back to this apartment and presenting it to her one morning, putting it in her hands and telling her it's hers.

My heart just beats faster. But it's not anxiety, or anger, or readying for a fight, all the things I might expect from a dragon thinking of parting with their treasure.

I imagine giving her something more valuable. Something I actually care about.

My mother's necklace, a piece of her treasure that I've been given to remember her by, the only thing I've had of hers for two hundred years. Beautiful, with a heavy sapphire that always catches the light just right. I imagine fastening it around Elise's neck, and that's when I know.

Dragons only share treasure in two circumstances. One, with their young in their earliest, most vulnerable days. Elise is not that, so that leaves option two.

Mates.

Elise, beautiful, blushing, dark-eyed Elise, is my mate.

She slides one half of one of the sandwiches off my plate and onto another perfectly serviceable plate.

My mate should have prettier plates. Plates made of gold, perhaps.

She leaves an entire barstool between us when she sits down, and I try not to lean any closer. She's a human, and she has no idea what I am. What she is to me.

She's my mate, and that changes everything.

"If you could have anything in this kitchen, what would it be?" I ask her, nearly tripping over myself with the urge to provide for her.

She looks around the space, but it's a cursory glance, not the look of someone who is seriously considering what she needs in the space. "This is more than enough. Unless you like certain specific foods, like wood-fired pizza or something—I suppose if we get to that point and you want the food, you'd need to consider those specific appliances."

Frustration surges through me, a quick flash, but I look at her and it's gone again. It's not her fault that she doesn't know what a dragon is offering her, to fill his nest with things for her. It's my job to explain to her what that means, how far I'll go to make this a place where she wants to be so I can keep her here.

How does one even begin to explain that to a human?

"I am interested in those cookbooks, though," she muses. "They look old."

"They are old. I've collected books, and my father collected books. There's quite a collection."

My father does have a collection of books, I'm sure, because he's a self-respecting dragon and would have a collection of just about everything that might lend value or comfort to a home, so I'm not technically lying to her.

"That's impressive. Would it be okay if I read them?"

"They're yours." I say it impulsively, but it feels more than right. Like something has clicked into place, like all my years of collecting make sense.

She raises an eyebrow. "No, no, I couldn't—but they look like they're old, and from all over the world, so I'd be interested in reading—"

"Of course you can read them," I interrupt, trying to quell the frustration at her refusal to take them. It's not her fault, I remind myself. It's mine. I haven't convinced her yet. "You can read them, and take them home if you want. And I'd be honored if you'd try some recipes from them."

"Oh!" Her whole face lights up, and I feel fifteen feet tall. "I would love that!"

I practically preen with having made her smile. The dragon in me is already noting what my mate likes, what kinds of gifts and treasures draw that smile from her.

CHAPTER 6
Elise

This man is not what I expected.

His insistence that I call him Marcus alone is almost laughable. Marcus. Like we're on a first named basis. Like I'm casually hanging out with a man with an apartment that has a prime view of Central Park, or a man who owns a twelve thousand dollar gas range and thinks nothing of it.

I thought the clients I'd worked with in the past had been rich; it's clear that they are nothing when compared to this guy.

And the casual way he throws money around. Offering to redecorate the kitchen, or give me probably really expensive and rare books, or buy me any crazy appliance I asked for. I have a feeling I could have asked for anything, and it'd be here in a few hours, installed and ready for me, with not a single further question asked except perhaps where I'd like it to go.

But he also offered to help me rearrange his kitchen, like he has time in a probably very busy day for that. Even so, the offer felt sincere.

I can rearrange the space, and I'll probably move things two or three times until I find the best flow for this kitchen. Plus, I can't imagine spending my afternoon with this man standing right next to me. It's too... well, honestly, I don't know. But it's like I'm always aware of where he is.

He's a rich guy who owns the type of apartment you see in magazines. On top of being unfairly wealthy, I can admit he's attractive—not that I'm looking—and well-spoken. Of course I feel like it's too much when he's around.

He doesn't make me uncomfortable, or at least not in the way some guys do. Yes, he watched me make him lunch, but I don't feel any malice behind it. Some guys watch me like they're undressing me with their eyes, while others watch like they're just waiting for me to mess up. Marcus watches like he's curious, and I can work with that.

I think about it as I poke around the kitchen, trying to find a new, better home for those incredibly interesting cookbooks. Maybe he's lonely. He just moved here, and while I haven't seen the entire apartment, I don't see a single sign that anyone else lives here. He's certainly never mentioned cooking for anyone else.

Well, anyone but myself, at any rate. But that's just another point for him being lonely—who else would ask the help to eat lunch with them?

Still, it's sweet, and he's not overbearing about it. And, hell, this might be the best job I've ever had, between the stability and the sheer amount of freedom he's offered me. I'm not going to look a gift horse in the mouth.

I check the stew cooking over on the stove. The weather finally turned, and the savory, spicy aroma of the food fills the entire apartment. I'm not above admitting that I chose it for just that reason; Marcus seems like he's set on me being here, but the advertisement of my food filling every inch of his home can't be overlooked.

It would be a great recipe for my blog, too. People like seasonal-appropriate recipes, and this one is just perfect. But I have a policy of not taking pictures of food I cook on the client's dime, so I refrain.

Instead, I flip open the cookbook with delicate fingers, settling in to peruse while I wait.

A shadow falls over the table, and I look up quickly. Marcus has emerged from his office and is standing over me.

I look him over. His shirt has the top three buttons undone, and his dark hair looks like he's been running his hand through it for several hours. Tired, then, and probably wants dinner.

I tense, prepared for aggravation to find me distracted on the job. "I'm sorry," I begin. "Dinner is ready, I just—"

"Don't be sorry," he interrupts smoothly. "I told you that they're yours to read, and I meant it. Dinner smells good." He looks over at the clock on the microwave. "I take it you're about to head out?"

I nod, although I have to admit that I've totally lost track of time. "Yeah, I—yes, dinner is all set. I'll see you in the morning?"

He nods and gives me a gentle smile that makes something go soft and easy in me. Like this man has somehow erased all my worries with a look. "Get home safe."

"Tomorrow, let me know what you liked about dinner—and what you didn't," I ask, grabbing my bag. "I'd like to refine our menu based on your tastes."

"Of course. Have a good night, Elise."

I ignore the shiver I get when I hear my name from him, the soft, sure way he shapes the word. That's an unprofessional thing to think about, and I'm a professional person.

"Goodnight, Marcus," I say, feeling bold, and walk out the door.

The trains are a bit of a nightmare, but I make it home before it's too late.

Ethan is waiting for me on the couch, head tilted back and TV playing. He's changed after work and has a beer in one hand,

and he sets it down to walk over to me and give me a hug. "Hey, babe."

"Hi." I sin into the hug for a moment, soaking up the feeling of home.

"You're later than usual."

"New client," I tell him, kicking off my clogs by the door. He lets me go, which is a real shame.

"You didn't tell me you had a new client."

"I have different clients all the time, Ethan," I protest, moving to the kitchen, thinking about what we have in the fridge so I can make dinner.

"Yeah, but they don't usually fuck with your schedule. Or intrude on our time together."

I poke around inside the fridge. Cooking for people I care about has always been how I show them I care, and even if I don't have the energy to make something especially elaborate tonight, hopefully Ethan feels my love anyway.

I stand up and turn to face him, making myself smile. "Well, I'm here now. What do you want for dinner?"

After dinner Ethan is clingy, holding me too tightly on the couch, like he's worried I'm going to disappear or something.

"Tell me about the new client."

"Not much to tell," I say evasively. "The client is just interested in dinner service."

There is a lot more to tell, and the guilt is an uncomfortable sharp jab in my chest. But Ethan would freak out if he heard me talk about some rich client who wants me in his house eight hours a day and insists I call him Marcus. A rich guy who gives me gifts and says things like I can rearrange his entire kitchen and, well, looks like that. Ethan would lose his mind.

I've never lied to him before. And this isn't the time I start, either. It's not a lie. It's just not telling the truth. Ethan is worried about someone else catching my eye, but this isn't that. This is a financially secure job, and Marcus Golde is just my boss.

He makes a grunting noise. "Well, see if you can get home earlier. I miss having you home, babe."

"Of course," I tell him, the biggest lie I've told tonight.

CHAPTER 7
Marcus

I follow her home.

It's a shame to leave the food just sitting on the stove, but I have to hope it will still be good reheated later. I simply have to see that she gets home. If she's not going to be safe in my nest, then the dragon isn't going to let me rest until I know she's safe somewhere else.

Once she leaves, I go up to my private roof, changing to my dragon form. It's the first time I've done so since I've arrived here, and it's a relief when the roof doesn't crumble under my new weight.

Then I take to the twilight sky. My deep green scales are suited for the night, and it's not quite dark yet, but humans never see us, regardless. With some concentration, I make the mist appear, and no human will ever know the difference.

By the time I'm in the sky, I've already lost her. In New York, that probably means she's underground, in the gross, clogging stench of the subways. I remember her address from my background check, and start flying towards Brooklyn.

I find a building to wait on, feeling like a gargoyle perched up here.

Finally, I can see Elise moving up the street. I don't like her walking around all alone after dark, but she moves with confidence towards her building. They're charging her an insane amount of rent to live in this building, especially considering they do such a mediocre job of maintaining it. I make a mental note to contact someone about purchasing it, if that's what it takes to give her a better place to live.

I picked the right side of the apartment building when I chose this building to land on. I can see a tiny section of her living room through her window, and I see her step in. Then a man walks over to her, drawing her into a gripping hug. I bristle at another man touching my mate like that, even if that's a completely unfair reaction.

Elise isn't mine. She might be the dragon's mate, but that doesn't automatically make her mine in a way I get to be defensive over.

There's a prickle of unease in me as I look at him, but I squash it down. That's the dragon talking, not me.

Elise walks out of view of the window, the man trailing along behind her. I watch for another half an hour, just in case, but I only get brief glimpses through that too-small window.

The most rational part of me knows this is stupid. Not only stupid, but invasive. There is no earthly way I can justify what I'm doing right now.

I force myself to fly home, then eat the delicious dinner Elise left for me while I contemplate what to do next.

The dragon has no idea why we didn't swoop into Elise's apartment, take her from there, and shower her with jewels and cookbooks until she agreed to stay with us forever. The dragon is the reason why there are so many stories of dragons kidnapping princesses in the past.

Fortunately, I am not just my dragon and am perfectly capable of understanding that my mate is a human. And more than that, she's a human very much in love with someone else who's shown no interest in me whatsoever.

My mate doesn't owe me her devotion.

But more to the point, I'm not sure I owe her mine yet either. Oh, there's no question that I've already crossed lines in my head over this woman—being willing to offer her parts of my hoard and following her home show that—but that doesn't mean I'm in love with her.

I wonder if all dragon matings start this way, if the obsession comes first and the love later. I'd ask my father, but he's hard to get a hold of, and even all these centuries later, talking about my mother is dangerous territory. And they were both dragons, so who's to say it works the same, regardless?

I need her here. I think the dragon will lose his mind without her here, but that doesn't mean I need to be the lecherous dragon, pursuing her and pushing her when I'm her boss and she's clearly happy with someone else.

There's nothing that says I can't be her friend, though.

After I clean up the dishes from my dinner, I try to sleep for a few hours, but the dragon isn't having it.

When restlessness drives me from bed, I pace the penthouse, fiddling with my nest. It's a tried-and-true dragon trick; everyone knows having our space just so is the perfect way to calm a dragon. But tonight, it's not enough. I can't force thoughts of Elise from my mind.

What do young human women like, anyway? What can I add to this space to make it a place she wants to be?

She wouldn't tell me a single thing yesterday that she wants, not even for the kitchen. That's fine; I'm older than dirt, and I've learned to be patient. I can coax the information out of her slowly.

She knocks on my door exactly at ten. "Good morning," she says, a beautiful smile on her face. Her smile feels like how the muffins she made me for breakfast taste — I can't explain it, but a warm and homey feeling suffuses my entire soul.

"Good morning." Then, not sure what one is supposed to say to their mate one day after realizing the eternal bond between the two of you, utterly consumed by the thought of them and trying to control it, I tell her, "The muffins were delicious."

"You liked them?" she asks, fumbling with the bag on her shoulder so she can set it down, heedless of where she leaves it, so she can pull her notebook out of her pocket again. "What exactly did you like about it?" She has a pen in hand, poised to take notes.

I consider it for a second. I can hardly say that I love them because she made them.

"The balance," I eventually say. "The sweetness paired with the spices."

She nods her head and scribbles my answer into her little notebook. It only takes her a second, and then she looks up at me, still smiling.

"Sandwiches for lunch again?" she checks.

"That sounds good. Thank you."

"Of course." She moves into the kitchen, putting her bag on one of the stools at the counter. "Any requests?"

"Surprise me."

She raises an eyebrow, and I know she doesn't like that answer. "Elise, everything you've made so far has been delicious. Surprise me. I'll love it."

Slowly, she nods, and I watch her get back to work until I know I'm being creepy.

I retreat to my office, but I keep an ear open for the soft sounds of her working the entire time.

CHAPTER 8
Elise

I don't know any more than I did before about what this man really likes, but the muffins are at least a start. He likes muffins and fried cheese. I realize I didn't even ask about the stew before he left for work.

I'm a little distracted, so I'll have to make a specific effort to remember to ask him later. Ethan had been a clingy mess since last night, and he'd been clingy this morning, even though he's never late to work.

It should feel nice, right? To have a guy that is obsessed with me, who clearly wants me so badly that he dragged me back to bed twice this morning.

I tell myself that a few times as I plan my menu for the day, looking over my groceries.

Tomorrow is Friday, and I have the weekend off. I can give Ethan all the attention he clearly needs this weekend.

I make a quick tomato sauce, making plans for this weekend. A breakfast in bed, maybe. That might show Ethan that I'm still focused on him, if I take the time to cook for him.

I used to cook for Ethan all the time. We were broke, so it's not like I could buy anything too fancy to work with, but we also couldn't afford to eat out, so it made sense that I cooked for us, testing out everything I learned in school on him.

I still cook for us most of the time, but I admit I'm a little lazier about it now. I cook all day, and I'm not always into cooking when I get home.

It'll be a few weeks until I see the check for a steady eight-hour-a-day gig, but I suppose I can take a little advance against it. Pick up something nice on my way home tomorrow, do a nice breakfast and maybe a nice dinner for Saturday too. That'll fix whatever is happening between us, I'm sure of it.

When lunch is eventually ready, Marcus emerges from his office with perfect timing.

When he sits at the counter, giving me that soft smile that makes him look warm and approachable, I finish plating up the food, then walk around to set a plate in front of him.

It's an eggplant parm sandwich. I have to say, when he told me yesterday that he prefers meals he can eat while working, I expected him to, well, work during lunch. Not gesture for me to sit down for a meal with him again.

"So, how's work this morning?" I asked awkwardly, unsure what one says to their probably billionaire boss when he insists on having lunch with them.

I couldn't even begin to guess what he does all day. Meetings? I'm pretty sure yesterday he said something about video meetings and maybe that he was currently managing two different businesses in two different locations.

Not that I know what any of that means.

I don't know what else to talk about with this man. Is it impertinent to ask the man who hired you to cook his meals what his hobbies are?

"Work is fine," he says blandly, not offering any additional information, which I can't tell if I'm grateful for or disappointed by. The conversation has already stalled out, and I have only taken one bite of this damn sandwich.

It's a good sandwich. A simple recipe, but eggplant can be hard to cook in a way that does it justice. I've made better sauces in the past, but this one's definitely not bad.

When he pushes the plate back slightly, I expect him to get up and return to work, but he doesn't move. He tilts his head to look at me and then asks, "What else can I get for you to make your job easier, Elise?"

"I don't need anything else. Thank you," I say it politely but neutrally, wracking my brains. What else does he think I need? "Are you looking for something specific?"

He waves that away. "No, no." He glances around the room, then looks back at me. "Just checking. I want to make sure I take care of you, Elise."

"I'm all set," I say flatly. Take care of me? Marcus seems sincere enough, but I don't know how to take that. He's my boss, not my friend. I'm here to do a job, nothing else.

He nods, taking half a step back. "I should get back to work." He stands, brushing a hand down his button-up shirt to get it to sit correctly on his frame.

"Wait, before you go—" He freezes, immediately turning to me, giving me his full attention. "Muffins again? Or something else?"

He smiles. "Surprise me."

I'm not sure if I'm more frustrated by that absolutely blinding smile, or the fact that this man can never give me a straight answer.

I spend most of Saturday cooking only for Ethan to listlessly pick at all the food.

"Is something wrong with it?" I ask after he spends yet another few minutes pushing his steak around.

Steak and frites. Classic, straightforward, and something that I know Ethan likes. The meat costs a pretty penny, but obviously he's worth it.

Sure, it hadn't exactly taken a genius to prepare this meal, but it had taken time, and on my day off, too, so I thought he'd at least like it.

He'd eaten the breakfast I made this morning—French toast with fresh fruit—but he'd seemed distracted while doing it, paying more attention to his phone than to me.

I do not handle the cold shoulder well. My mom had been too young when I was born, and that clearly affected what she thought was appropriate discipline for her child. The cold shoulder might be great for your high school friends, but it leaves its mark on a little kid, and being ignored makes me twitchy.

Ethan knows this. Ethan knows everything about me. He's been my person for so long now, and I can't figure out what I've done wrong that now is when he starts ignoring me.

"Nothing's wrong with the food," he says simply, then takes a big bite as if to punctuate his point before going back to staring off disinterestedly.

I stare helplessly at my own plate, also more full than it should be. I'd taken a few pictures of it before we sat down, already composing a blog post about a delicious date night meal, but now I can't make myself eat it. I don't have much of an appetite, it turns out.

"Ethan?" I ask, my voice soft and pleading, unable to put up with this anymore. "I know we've both been working a lot. I just thought, some time together, a nice night—"

"I haven't been working any more than usual," he says, voice absolutely impenetrable.

I swallow. "You're right. It's me. I'm sorry, I didn't mean—"

Ethan also feels neglected easily. It's why we work so well together. I take a deep breath. "I'm sorry," I say again.

He stares at me for a long moment. "I deserve better than being passed over for your work," he says simply.

I've been home a little later, because the train between here and Marcus' place is hell. But I've been here to see him off to work every morning, and I try to make time for us when I get home. I haven't even done a catering gig since the one I met Marcus at. I wrack my brains for what I've done, and how I can make up for it, since dinner clearly isn't cutting it.

Maybe if I explain myself, he'll accept it. "I'm sorry," I say again. "I made dinner tonight because I wanted it to be like it used to be. You know, when we were in school? Just us?"

To my immense relief, his face changes to a tender, soft expression. "I remember," he says. "I miss that, baby."

We'd lived in an even worse apartment, and I'd had as much practice making ramen seem gourmet as I did at any of the skills I actually learned in class. I don't mention any of that, not when he finally seems to be warming up.

"I don't work tomorrow," I mention. "I was hoping it could be a day for just us?"

"I'd like that, baby," he agrees. He looks at his plate, then up at me with a smile, and it feels like the sun has come out again.

When he goes to leave for work on Monday, Ethan pulls me into a long kiss and grabs my ass. "This weekend was good," he says, leaning down to suck at my neck, no doubt leaving a bruise. He pulls back and tilts my chin up so I'm looking at him. "We need every day to be like that."

"We'll try," I promise.

He squeezes my ass. "No trying. We're doing it. Just you and me, babe."

"Right," I agree, as he's already turning out the door. "Just you and me."

By the time I finish my grocery shopping for Marcus—using the credit card I practically break out into hives just thinking about—I'm barely in time to start lunch.

It takes a moment for him to open his apartment door, and I'm left juggling the bags while standing outside.

He breaks into a genuine grin when he sees me, and it makes the skin around his eyes wrinkle. "Elise, good to see you," he says, stepping aside so I can enter. He takes a bag from me, walking ahead of me to the kitchen, ignoring my protests that I have the bag. "Sorry it took me so long to get to the door. The interior designer is here."

Interior Designer. Because crazy rich people don't decorate their own places. And apparently this brand-new looking apartment needs to be redecorated.

I admit the place isn't my style, but I know it's certainly an expensive style. And just because I'm not into painfully sharp corners, ruler-straight lines, and washed out colors doesn't mean no one is.

"No problem," I tell him, setting the second and third bag on the counter. "I'm sure you're very busy."

He shrugs. "Never too busy for you. How was your weekend?"

He sounds so earnest when he says it, too, like he really wants to know. Like he wants more than the bland fine, how was yours? He's a considerate guy, I've already learned, and something in me wants to open up to him.

But I'm not telling him about Ethan's weird behavior, or how the cold shoulder made me cave in like an hour flat. "Fine, how was yours?"

"Boring," he proclaims. "Except for mealtime. The meals you left were delicious. Not that I expected anything less; every meal you've made me so far has been delicious."

I busy myself with the bags so he can't see my flush.

Sharp heels click against the floor, and I look up to see a petite Asian woman in a luxuriously soft looking oversized cable-knit sweater and skin-tight leather pants walk in. "Marcus, I'm so sorry to interrupt."

"You're not interrupting. This is the person I wanted you to meet, anyway," he says. I can't stop noticing those eye wrinkles. I'm assuming Marcus is five to ten years older than me, but he's aged well. Those laugh lines just add character.

I make myself look away. Not a thing I should notice about my very rich boss when I'm a very happily taken woman.

I turn away just in time, because Valerie extends a hand capped with long lilac nails. "Valerie Kim. I'm an interior designer, and Marcus says you're the person to talk to about the kitchen."

My throat goes dry. "I'm sure whatever Marcus wants—"

"Marcus has refused to give me a single bit of input on this kitchen until you showed up," she says freely, waving around the space. "I have some ideas, of course. Some luxurious, maximalist trends that will really match the rest of the space. But I—we, really, of course—want this space to be functional for you. And Marcus has made it clear that nothing happens without your approval."

"Dream as big as you want," Marcus says from beside me. His voice is a low, reassuring rumble, like he knows he needs to quiet my racing thoughts. "Nothing is off-limits. Ask for anything."

What the fuck does that even mean? Ask for anything? I have no concept of this.

"You said you had some ideas?" I venture.

Valerie smiles. "I can show you a rough sketch I did of the space an hour ago."

Her rough sketch has more detail than most art pieces hanging in a museum, and I take a minute to take it all in. "I tried not to upset functionality, just aesthetics," she says, heedless of how long this is taking me to absorb. "Of course, you're the expert on that, so feel free to tell me that I've bungled it. Or, as Marcus said, advocate for any changes you'd prefer."

The sketch doesn't have color, just little labels. The cabinets are apparently going to become a deep forest green, and instead of the sleek, minimal lines, some of them are becoming open shelves.

I purse my lips. "I like the open cabinets," I say. "But if you put them right near the stove, you risk the dishes getting greasy. And that's a pain to clean."

"Good note," she says, jotting it down. "Anything else?"

I look over at Marcus, but he just looks back, one eyebrow raised. "She's asking you, Elise."

"It's not my kitchen."

"Well, I certainly haven't cooked in it yet," he says. "I want this place to be functional for you, Elise. The better to keep you cooking for me as long as possible."

I've had clients who liked me before, who considered my cooking significantly above average and specifically requested that I do regular service for them. None of them ever remodeled their kitchen entirely at my request.

Valerie seems to be aware of the tension in the room and tilts the drawing slightly. "This is why you hired me, Marcus. I can make aesthetic decisions with just a little input from you both. I mostly wanted Elise's opinions on the practical elements, and she gave her opinion on that."

Marcus doesn't stop staring at me, but after a moment, he nods. "If you think of something, Elise, let us know. At any point."

Valerie withdraws the drawing and turns away from the kitchen. "We were discussing the bedroom, Marcus."

"Right. Elise, are you all set?"

I smile and try not to think about his bedroom. "Any requests for lunch?" I turn to Valerie. "Will you be joining us for lunch?" It's only after I say it I realize I'm overstepping. Joining us. Like I'm inviting people to this house, like I'm assuming Marcus and I will eat lunch together like we have been.

Marcus doesn't so much as twitch, though. It's a common enough expression, I guess. Probably not out of place for me to be asking if I'm planning the meal.

"Oh, I'd love to, but I'll be out of your hair by then," she says, turning to sweep off to the bedroom.

Marcus doesn't follow her right away. He keeps looking at me.

"Any requests?" I ask again.

He shakes his head. "Whatever you're planning will be delicious," he says. "But I was serious when I said you can make any changes you want."

The worst part is that I know he is.

"I don't need much," I tell him. Then, because I can't keep looking at him while he tries to stare his point into my soul, I turn to my bags of groceries. "I'm fine, really. I promise."

He finally nods, going to follow Valerie and leaving me to my kitchen.

His kitchen. Just because he's confused about that doesn't mean I should be.

CHAPTER 9
Marcus

Valerie is exactly what I've been looking for. Someone who likes bold colors, luxuriously soft things, and plenty of decoration. She doesn't so much as blink when I mention probably a few too many priceless treasures to display around the penthouse, just takes it in stride and adds them to her drawings.

I authorize her to make purchases without any limit, and she takes that in stride, too. And, while I've only known her this morning, I'm confident she will take advantage of that option, ruthlessly running up my credit card statement and buying only the best. I doubt she knows how to live any other way.

If only I could get Elise to buy things with quite so much ruthlessness. I'd even accept a moderate amount of enthusiasm.

"Well," Valerie says, clapping her hands together, her long nails clicking. "I think that's it. I'll be in contact, and I'll start procuring materials. We'll of course put a rush on them, like you asked. Once I have an estimate on that, I'll reach back out to set up a timeline of work here. We'll do our best to be unobtrusive, but I have to admit we might get in your way a bit."

Nothing I hadn't expected. "That's fine. An excuse for me to go into the office, I suppose."

Valerie's eyes cut to the kitchen, where Elise is busy at the stove. "And your friend?"

Friend doesn't feel right, but then again, it would feel worse if she said *your chef,* which is probably how Elise would describe herself, so I let it stand. "I won't die if I eat takeout for a day or two while the kitchen is out of commission. We're not making a lot of changes, so it'll be quick, right?"

"The paint will take the longest," she promises me. "I'll leave you to it, then. Enjoy your lunch." She gives Elise a long look, like she knows something I don't, and then turns to leave.

Lunch is a steak sandwich, paired with a spicy sauce and some caramelized onions. "How was your weekend?" I ask her after I swallow a bite. It's delicious, as is everything she makes for me.

"It was fine." Short, simple. A little evasive, I think, but I don't want to push her. She went home to her boyfriend over the weekend, and I'm smart enough to know what that means.

The dragon vehemently rejects that thought, but I force him to shut up. He doesn't get a say in Elise's life.

"How was the food I left for the weekend?" she asks, changing the subject without any subtlety. "Did reheating it work?"

"It was delicious," I promise her. "Was it too much work for you to make it all on Friday?"

"Not at all," she says, and I know that's a bit of a lie.

"Lunch is fantastic," I tell her instead of calling her out on it.

She smiles shyly at me. "It's actually a recipe from one of your cookbooks. I thought I'd give it a try."

I'm irrationally pleased that she not only read the cookbooks I gave her, but enjoyed them enough to want to try recipes out of them. I watch her for a moment as I continue to eat, considering. She turned down every time I offered to make this place more welcoming to her today. I wonder what it will take to make her feel invested. If she liked the cookbooks, would she like other things for the kitchen?

"My mother's china is going to be delivered tomorrow," I tell her impulsively, which means I'll need to fly out and pick up my nice china tonight. It's not my mother's; my father has most of her treasure, as is right for a widowed dragon. But I can at least say that my mother helped me gather the earliest pieces of my hoard.

"Oh, that's lovely," she says, smiling and putting the remnants of her sandwich down. "Where are you going to store it?"

"Well, I was thinking the open cabinets Valerie talked about would be the best for them, so we can see them. They are rather nice," I say, which is an understatement. Each piece I collected was hand-crafted, often laid with precious metals. "So I'm glad you suggested moving those shelves away from the stove. I want to save these pieces from grease."

"A china cabinet might be better," she muses. "Save them from dust, too."

I nod, considering it. I honestly don't care which way we display it. The china is just as precious as anything else in my collection, and, when everything is precious, by definition, everything loses its value a little bit.

What I do care about is that she seems invested. Got you, I think, a perverse pleasure in having even a fraction of her attention. She won't like me giving her the china outright, but maybe if I make it available to her...

"Is your mother...?" she asks, trailing off, clearly not sure how to ask.

"She passed," I tell her. "A while ago now." That's an understatement, but it still hurts.

Maybe Elise can tell, because she actually reaches out to briefly touch my arm. She pulls her hand back a moment later, but her touch tingles pleasantly, even through my shirt. "I'm sorry to hear that."

"Thank you," I make myself say. "She was great."

"Tell me about her?" she asks.

I should remember what my backstory is, who my mother is on paper. I always craft a background for my family history, and I've never forgotten it before.

I don't want to tell Elise about my fake mother. I don't want to make up a story.

I scramble for a second, thinking of how to describe a dragon to a human without revealing anything I don't want to. Dragons and humans have such different standards for what's appropriate, after all. The fact that my mother never gave me a single thing after I turned ten or so would be appalling to a human. For a dragon, it's absolutely normal, and probably vital to our development.

She must read my delay as reluctance, because she hastily says, "Of course, you don't have to, I'm sorry, I crossed—"

"She was supportive," I interrupt her to say, not wanting her to think that she can't talk to me. "She made a house a home. She pushed me when I needed it. She was kind."

She was also ruthless with her enemies, a shrewd, greedy collector, and stubborn as anything. She loved my father fiercely, and I do believe she was proud of me.

"That's nice," Elise says, smiling softly.

"And your mother?" I ask, although I already know. But I don't want the conversation to end.

She shrugs, looking away now. "She's fine. She lives in Pennsylvania. She's a receptionist at a dentist's office."

Biographical information I already had, and not a single feeling. She must realize that too, because she softens and says, "She loves me fiercely. She would have fist-fought anyone who crossed me when I was growing up. She gave up a lot to raise me."

"You must miss her," I say, although I'm not sure if she does. From everything I read, contact between the two seems to be sporadic at best.

She shrugs. "I'm happy here, though."

I want to respond to that, to tell her I'm glad or that I'm happy she's here too, but my phone buzzes in my pocket. I glance down at it to see the calendar alert for my call in ten minutes.

"Back to work?" she asks lightly, beginning to clear our places despite not having finished her food.

The dragon registers his protest at that, a sharp spike of frustration, and I get an image of feeding her by hand, holding her in my lap and insisting she eats.

I shake my head to dislodge it. Dragons are fucking insane.

I've never felt such a split before, like the dragon and human form aren't entirely the same person. Having Elise here is bringing it out in me, forcing me to see my dragon's instincts and needs separately from my own, and I can't say I like it.

"I'll see you later," I manage to tell her before slipping back to my office.

CHAPTER 10
Elise

This man is definitely lonely. How else do I explain him sitting and eating lunch with me every day, then him softly telling me a bit about his deceased mother?

That doesn't really explain why I told him about my mother, though.

I didn't tell him much, I console myself. I didn't over-share that badly. And anyway, he asked first. And sure, he left immediately after. But he's a busy guy, and he'd already spent longer on his lunch than I expected him to.

For a guy who is supposedly running two businesses simultaneously, I'm always surprised by how much time he spends with me at lunch.

Like I said, lonely.

And also not my business. If the man is lonely, surely he's smart enough to find ways around that. Friends from work, a dating app, one of those fancy parties like the one I met him at. Any of those is a more likely option than me becoming his friend.

I pull out the dried chickpeas I bought this morning and prepare the falafel mix for lunch tomorrow. Then I start a batch of overnight oats, mixing in dried fruit, letting myself sink into work and letting go of everything else.

By the time I start on dinner, I've almost found some sense of normalcy, which goes out the window when Marcus emerges from his office. His sleeves are rolled up and half the buttons undone and his hair mussed, presumably from running his hand through it.

"Empanadas?" he asks, taking an obvious sniff.

"Just finished. You have perfect timing."

He smiles, and it's disarmingly sweet. "I try. Are you heading out?"

A quick, sidelong glance at the clock tells me it is indeed six. I nod and reach for my bag in the corner. I can feel his eyes on me, but he doesn't say anything. "See you tomorrow."

"Get home safe, Elise," he says, and I nod, then head for the door.

The trains seem determined to slow me down in getting home. It's never an easy commute, and the MTA seems determined to make it worse every single year. Fares are ridiculous, trains are slower, and there always seems to be some sort of delay or emergency every time I turn around.

When I finally make it home, my feet are throbbing and my vision is getting fuzzy from exhaustion. I need dinner too, my stomach grumbling as I unlock our door, pushing it open with my hip.

"I'm home!"

"You're late, babe," Ethan says.

"Trains again."

I go to the kitchen, taking the ground beef I left out to defrost this morning, then begin some quick, lazy tacos. It only takes ten minutes to put them together, but considering how hungry I am, that's already too long.

Ethan meanders into the kitchen partway through, already changed out of his work clothes and into sweatpants. "How was your day?" I ask.

"It was fine." He wraps his arms around me, pulling me close. I sink into the touch for a moment, soaking up the warmth and affection. I let my eyes slip closed, relaxing into his warm arms.

How many times have I done this? How many times has Ethan held me when I felt like the world was falling apart, when things were too much? Ethan has always been my safe space, and I let myself completely go in his arms.

"I miss you," he murmurs into my neck.

"I'm right here." I open my eyes again, reluctantly breaking the embrace so I can finish the food. His hand on my belly is sweet, but it's also reminding me just how hungry I am.

"You know what I mean," he pouts. I can't see it, but I can hear it even with my back to him.

I don't, really. I know he feels like I've been working more, neglecting time for us. But besides the trains being late tonight, I honestly don't think it's true.

I don't want to start an argument, though. "I miss you too," I tell him. "Want to eat on the couch?"

"That sounds nice," he agrees, stepping away from me to go to the fridge to grab a beer.

I hastily assemble the plates. Maybe I can sit leaning up against him and have another moment like when he was holding me earlier. It'll probably make him happy, too. Reassure him I'm here.

"What kept you so late?" he asks once I sit next to him, handing him a heaping plate of food. He looks like he's been losing weight, and I want to make sure he's eating enough. He eats methodically, and I wait for him to say something about the food. He doesn't.

Marcus always compliments the food, I think, then squash the thought. It's a totally unfair comparison. For one thing, I shouldn't be comparing my boyfriend to my boss. For another, I spend hours carefully crafting everything I make for Marcus, and I spent ten minutes making tonight's dinner for the two of us. They're not the same, and I shouldn't expect the same reaction.

Ethan used to act like everything I cooked him was magic, some small part of my brain reminds me. But that was a long time ago. He needed me to know he appreciated me. It's not like now, when, of course, I know he appreciates me. How could I not? He's said it often enough in the past.

"Trains," I tell him when he nudges me for the answer. "And I'm doing a dinner service now, remember?"

He starts. "That's a regular thing?"

"Yeah," I tell him, a growing anxiety weighing in my gut. I still haven't told him it's one client now, one full-time gig. That the stability is great, and so is the creative freedom Marcus gives me. I doubt any of that will matter that much to Ethan, though.

He inhales deeply, holds it, and exhales, like he's desperately searching for calm. "Ethan, it's not that big a deal. I—"

"You shouldn't make changes like this without consulting me," he interrupts.

I start. "I didn't think it'd be a big deal."

But didn't I? Isn't that why I didn't tell him?

"Well, it is a big fucking deal, Elise. You're changing things about us."

"I'm really not working later than I was before. The trains, they've been bad—"

"Don't blame the damn trains. You're not prioritizing us, babe."

I open my mouth, then rapidly close it. Was I not prioritizing us when I spent half this weekend cooking to try to impress him? Was I not prioritizing us when I had sex with him this weekend? When I came home to make him dinner tonight, even though I got home later and had been cooking all day?

He heaves a huge sigh. "Listen, babe, I'm sorry. I just—you know how important you are to me."

"You're important to me too, Ethan," I say, thinking back to our early days together, how fundamental Ethan has been to my life since leaving home.

He's quiet for a long moment, then says, "I know, babe."

But it doesn't sound like he knows. The silence before that statement is prickly and uncomfortable, and I wrack my brains for a way to change that. "You mean everything to me, Ethan."

He snakes an arm around me and squeezes. "I love you too, Elise." He looks down at his plate. "Dinner is delicious."

I warm up at that, letting more of my weight slump against him, finally relaxing.

The next day, there are boxes of china when I arrive at work. They're professionally packed. Certainly not the way I wrapped paper towels and tissues around our chipped plates the last time Ethan and I moved.

Marcus is in the kitchen, smiling at me as he looks up from his knees, bending over one of the boxes. "Perfect timing. Come see."

Momentarily disarmed by that smile, it takes me a second to take off my coat and my bag, slinging them in the corner where I usually leave them, neatly out of the way.

"Oh," Marcus says, watching me. "I put in a hook for you last night."

I look up, and sure enough, there's a decorative coat hook hammered into the wall. This man, sometime between dinner and now, went out and bought a coat hook and personally hammered it into the wall for me?

That's because he noticed a problem. People don't take time to do stuff like that unless there's something so annoying it gets stuck in their brain. Which means my stuff not being put away neatly annoyed him. It must be embarrassing for him, I rationalize, to have my stuff strewn around. The rest of this place is so well put together, and my department store sales-rack jacket and my purse that's falling apart probably don't fit the decor.

I should probably be embarrassed, I realize too late. In fact, if the hook wasn't already in the wall, I would tell him to put it in the closet so he doesn't have to look at my stuff.

"Sorry I've been leaving your house such a mess," I say lightly. "And thanks for giving me a way to clean up."

"You've never left a mess," Marcus says, interrupting my thoughts. "I just want you to have space here. Your stuff belongs, you know?"

I freeze for a moment, light and warmth bubbling in my veins. Like champagne, I think faintly. Like his every word is just another bubble, another infusion of that liquid warmth.

Lonely, I remind myself. Surely he's just lonely.

So what does that make me, the person who falls for it so quickly? I'm not lonely.

"Come see," he invites me, gesturing to the space on the ground next to him, and I kneel next to him to check out what he wants to show me.

My first thought is that the money is clearly generational. His mother owned gold-plated serving bowls. Three of them, from what I can see. And while those are the most obnoxiously ostentatious, there's a whole host of dishes that might as well be art. Some of these look like they belong in a museum. They're definitely hand-painted, and the art is stunning.

"These are beautiful," I murmur appreciatively, entirely captivated by one particular plate painted with vibrant cranes.

"Thank you," he says. He opens his mouth as if to say something else, but bites the comment back. "I'm happy to have them here now."

"Your mother was quite the collector."

Bizarrely, he laughs a bit. "Yeah, she definitely was that." He glances at his watch. "I'm going to set these on the dining table until there's a better place to unpack them into. It won't be in your way, will it?"

There's that warm feeling again, that he'd think to ask, even though it's his home. "No, it won't be in my way," I reassure him, moving to stand. He hefts the box like it weighs nothing, and I almost lift the second box before considering the financial disaster if I managed to drop it. I keep my hands to myself.

"I have a conference call in ten minutes," he says. "I'll see you for lunch. Oh, and the cleaning service is starting tomorrow, just so you know. They'll be here once a week for now."

A cleaning service. I probably should have anticipated that from this insanely rich man. "Got it. Should I do anything?'

"Nope," he says. "Unless they do something in a way you don't like. Then let them know to change it."

Right, like I'm ever going to do that.

He sets the second box on the table, then heads to his office, and it's only when the door is shut and his overwhelming presence is decidedly out of the room that I realize I didn't ask him the question I decided I needed to ask on my way over this morning.

CHAPTER 11

Marcus

M aybe this is the influence of the dragon's instincts on me, but I actually think Elise and I might be friends.

Or friendly, at least. I don't usually talk to people who work for me like this. I'm polite, because good manners aren't optional, but I certainly don't tell them about my mother. I don't go out and hammer in wall hooks either, just hoping it'll be one thing to make them feel more at home.

So all in all, friendly. Making progress.

The feelings from the dragon are sour and dismissive, and I don't need words to know what he's thinking. He's not here to be friendly, but it's what he's getting. It's what we're getting, really.

I barely pay attention during the conference call. And while I have more experience running a business than any two other employees combined could hope to match, I really need to give this my attention. After all, it would be a shame to sink the business now, when I've kept it going for so many generations.

I keep myself going until lunch, when I emerge from my office to chase down whatever smells so good today.

Today's meal is falafel sandwiches, and Elise is sitting at the counter, pouring through one of the cookbooks I tried to give to her. The dragon swells in triumph, and I just hope I don't say anything stupid in the next few minutes. "Time for lunch?"

She startles, frantically slamming the book shut. I wince, considering its age, but don't say anything. It's her book now, and she can do what she likes with it. "Time for lunch," she agrees, now much more carefully setting the book aside and standing so she can fiddle with the two plates.

"Anything else good in that cookbook?" I ask, accepting my sandwich. "Yesterday's sandwich was great."

She gives me a small smile. "We'll find out. I'm already planning some more menus."

"Then I look forward to testing it out," I tell her sincerely, my point only strengthened when I bite into my lunch. Delicious, as always.

She smiles at me again. It's small, there and gone, and it's obvious she's nervous, although I can't figure out what she could possibly be nervous about.

"I have a favor to ask," she admits after a moment, looking down. "And I know I haven't been working for you very long, so this might be too much to request, but—"

"What can I do for you, Elise?" I interrupt gently.

"My boyfriend and I are used to having schedules more in line, and with how long the trains can take between here and Brooklyn, I'm getting home kind of late."

"I see," I say neutrally. Is she looking for a car service? I can set that up. That wouldn't be too hard.

"So I was wondering if I could change my hours slightly," she continues, speaking fast now like she needs to get it all out in one breath.

"That's all? Of course." I told her from the start that her hours were at her discretion. "What hours would work better for you?"

"Are you sure?" she checks.

"Yes, I'm sure. What hours, Elise?"

She swallows. "Nine to five, maybe. But I understand if that's too early. It would make for a rather early dinnertime."

It will make for a rather early dinnertime, but I know without even thinking about it for a moment that an early dinner is a sacrifice I'm more than willing to make to keep her around. Would she quit for the boyfriend? Probably. From what I know, they've been together a long time. And if I'm an inconvenience, then she could probably easily walk right out of my life forever, and I can't have that.

"Nine to five works fine," I tell her.

Some tension in her I didn't even realize was there eases. "Thank you," she breathes, like I just gave her some sort of magnificent gift.

"Of course, Elise," I tell her, taking another bite of my sandwich.

"You know, I've been making sandwiches because I was under the impression you'd be eating one-handed at your desk," she says, watching me eat. "But if that's not true, I can branch out a bit."

I fully expected eating one-handed at my desk. But I would never miss a moment with Elise. "Make whatever you want to make," I tell her. "Anything is good with me."

She looks me over, staring for a long moment. I resist the urge to move, to say something, letting her work out whatever is in her head. "You're a very interesting client," she says after a minute.

I raise an eyebrow. "That doesn't sound very complimentary."

She shrugs. "Interesting isn't a bad thing."

"It doesn't sound like an entirely good thing, either, though."

"Interesting is a man who gives me nearly unlimited creative control, tells me he likes everything, offers to pay for anything, and registers no opinions whatsoever."

"I've registered opinions," I counter. I've told her when I enjoy her food. And if that just so happens to be every time, well, I can't help that.

She shrugs again. "If you keep eating what I make, then I guess there's no problem."

Then there will never be a problem. I take the last bite of my sandwich. "I should get back to work," I say, reluctantly pushing to my feet. "Dinner will be at five?"

She nods slightly. "Thank you for that. It means a lot to me," she says.

My voice gets caught in my throat for a moment. "Anything for you," I promise her, before beating a hasty retreat to my office.

As promised, I emerge promptly at five. Dinner is ready, a hearty stir-fry that smells delicious and probably tastes like heaven.

But the dinner is almost an afterthought, because my eyes go right to her, with her coat already pulled on and that worn bag over her shoulder.

One part of my brain is making a mental note that she could use a new bag and coat. The rest is consumed by the pang that goes through me at seeing her so ready to leave.

"Breakfast is in the fridge," she tells me. "I'll see you at nine tomorrow?"

It's on the tip of my tongue to tell her not to bother getting here earlier—what difference will it make, really—but I can't make myself say it. I can't make myself give up an hour with her.

"See you in the morning," I confirm. "Get home safe, Elise."

She flashes me a harried smile and then rushes out the door like she needs to be home right this second.

CHAPTER 12

Elise

I'm home a little after six. It's a massive improvement, and surely Ethan hasn't beaten me back by much, if he even managed to beat me back at all.

But when I enter the apartment, the tension in the air practically chokes me, even before I turn to see Ethan sitting stiff as a board on the couch.

My mind races. What could possibly be wrong? Did someone get hurt? Does he have some terrible news to give to me?

Oh god, is it my mom?

I swallow, not knowing what to say, but knowing I need to say something. "Hi." I mechanically take off my coat, not taking my eyes off of him as I set it aside.

"That's all you have to say?" His voice is ice cold and rock solid, an unmovable force that I can't see my way through.

"Hi, baby?" I try, even though I know instinctively that he isn't just looking for an endearment.

"Why'd you lie to me, Elise?" He says it so precisely that I can feel the shiver go down my spine.

"Lie?" I sputter. "I didn't... what did I lie about, Ethan?" But I know. There's only ever been one thing I've been less than truthful with him about.

I don't even know why I did it. There should have been nothing to worry about. Marcus Golde is a rich client. I get paid to cook him food. There's nothing between us whatsoever.

But I knew. I knew Ethan wouldn't like it. That he'd jump to conclusions and freak out.

Case in point.

"You've been acting weird," he tells me, his voice still in that chilly, precise tone. "More distant. Less here when we're together." Those accusations sound unfair to me, but I don't interrupt, knowing it'll just make things worse. Instead, I let the dread pile up inside me, growing and growing, turning into a writhing mess in my stomach as I wait for him to keep talking. "So I followed you today."

He followed me? Like I was some cheating wife he needed to track down? Something sinks in me, heavy and leaden in my gut, and then it feels like I'm free-falling, like that weight just pulls me through the floor.

How'd he follow me without me noticing?

But trains are crowded, and I definitely wasn't looking out for anyone following me.

I feel violated, like he stripped me naked somehow. Even if all I did was go to work and do my job, exactly as I was supposed to,

I feel like he saw something he shouldn't, like he took something he shouldn't.

"I went to work," I tell him when I can find my voice again. I spent all day in that apartment. I didn't even have to do any grocery shopping today. I spent all day at work, exactly like he might expect. I did nothing wrong.

And maybe if I repeat that often enough to myself, my nerves will calm down and I'll believe it.

"It wasn't hard to find out from there," he continues like I didn't speak. "I called the service. Told the girl who picked up that I was supposed to pick you up today and forgot the address. And she was oh so helpful. Told me you were at Mr. Golde's place. That you're there full time now." He stands, the movement stiff and almost mechanical, but that doesn't prevent the air of menace as he takes two steps closer to me. "Are you cheating on me, Elise?"

I can't make my feet move. Why can't I make my damn feet move? "No, I wouldn't do that," I tell him, words spilling out like they're being yanked from me. "I'm cooking for him. That's all. I just go there, and do my job."

"Something's been on your mind," he says, taking another step closer. "Something's been distracting you. What am I supposed to think, hm? You and some millionaire, cooped up all day? You doing a little more than cooking, Elise?"

"I wouldn't do that," I find it in me to snap. "Ethan, this is ridiculous, you know I'd never—"

He takes two more rapid steps towards me, closing the distance and grabbing my arms before I can blink. His grip is a vice on my wrists, squeezing and dragging me into him.

I stumble that last step, running smack into his chest because I don't have my hands to stop me from falling.

"Ethan," I gasp, mind frantically spinning, trying to grasp what's going on, what my next steps should be. His grip tightens on my wrists.

"Don't lie to me." he says, voice low and lethal, like a man absolutely in control. This isn't a man in a wild rage. This is a man entirely aware that he's squeezing my wrists so hard I'm worried he'll break one of them. "Don't play with me, Elise. It's fucking obvious what you're doing."

It's not like that, I want to shout. I want to plead, to beg, to offer any proof that I can. It's Ethan. Ethan's always been my person, my safe place; surely he wouldn't believe this.

Ethan was my first everything. I'd had one boyfriend in high school, but we hadn't been that serious. I'd never slept with him, barely even kissed him. And then I'd met Ethan, and it was like he could be my whole world. I gave him everything. Wanted everything with him.

And here he is, throwing it all away.

"Ethan," I plead, hoping against hope that this isn't it. That he'll come to his senses. That I can somehow show him I'm sincere. That I'd never do anything to hurt us. That he's over-reacting. That this isn't him.

Fuck. I can hear my own thoughts, and I think I'd hate myself if I said any of them out loud.

I jerk on my wrists, but he doesn't let up. His face, previously eerily calm, twists into an ugly sneer that I've never seen before. "No rich boyfriend to sneak around with and save you now, Elise."

The way he says my name feels like cold ice down my spine. I jerk my wrists again, and he just squeezes tighter. "Please," I whisper. "Ethan, you know me. You know—"

"You think I haven't known for years that you're the type who'll eventually stray?" he spits. "Look at you. Desperate for validation. Always looking for the next thing to cling to."

That's not true. I want to shout, but I bite my tongue, terrified to rouse any more of his wrath.

And anyway, isn't it? Not like Ethan's saying, obviously, because I've never been tempted to stray. I've never even thought about anyone else, not the entire time I was with Ethan. No, that's absolute bullshit.

But the idea that I'm desperate for validation, that I was looking for someone to cling to? Well, how else do you explain clinging to the first guy to show me any attention for as long as I have?

It's like an illusion is broken, like I look at Ethan and everything has changed. What I used to see is gone. Now, all I can see is the furious, self-righteous malice in his eyes as I'm forced to look up at him.

"Let me go, Ethan," I say, trying to sound as calm and reasonable as possible. "Let me go."

"You're mine, Elise," he tells me, so spine-chillingly serious. "You're mine. You have been since the day we met. I'm not going to let you go now. You're going to quit that job and—"

"I'm not quitting my job," I interrupt, forgetting the rationality I was trying so desperately to hold on to. "You can't make me."

His grip tightens even more. "Can't I?"

I swallow. I don't know if the squeeze is intentional or not, if he's threatening to break my wrists so I can't cook or if I'm just reading into things.

I'm not sticking around to find out.

He has my wrists pinned, but I took a self-defense class when I first got to the city, and I know my hands aren't my only weapons of attack. I shift my weight to one leg and knee him in the balls as quickly as I can, then bring the raised foot down on his bare instep. When he lets go of me with a surprised yelp, I pick up the bag I'd barely put down before this all started, frantically rip out my pepper spray, and nail him in the face.

Then, bag in one hand and pepper spray in the other, I race out the door, firmly ignoring the howling sounds of rage behind me.

89

It's when I reach the street that I realize that I have nowhere else to go.

I shake my head and force myself to keep moving. That doesn't matter. The thing that matters is getting away.

Away from this apartment. Away from this street. Away from Ethan and everything about him.

At least I have my bag and my pepper spray. I still have my shoes on, too, and work clothes. I'm safe enough out here, as long as I keep moving.

Alright, the first order of business is away. I go to the subway almost on autopilot, ready to put some distance between me and Ethan. My Metro Card is in my bag, ready for me to swipe.

There. First thing done.

I have to wait for the train, and every noise on the platform, every time someone else moves, my body tenses up enough that I'm worried I might break. This is the most dangerous moment, I know instinctively. I'm trapped here, without a good exit, and if Ethan chased after me, this is where he'd catch me.

Once I'm on a train, I could be anywhere. But here, I'm prey.

My cellphone is in my bag, but who would I call? The police? All he did was squeeze my wrists. It'll be his word against mine quickly enough. My mother? What the hell is she going to do for me all the way in Pennsylvania?

I don't talk to anyone else, really. I could call Lacey, I guess. But she's not my friend and I know it. We're not close enough for me to just crash on her couch.

No, of course we aren't. Ethan saw to that, didn't he? Suddenly every night he demanded I stay in, every time he convinced me to give up on something because he wanted more time with me flashes through my mind, painted in a whole new sinister light. Of course I have no friends. Of course I don't have anyone I can call.

The train screeches into the platform, and I release a deep breath as I step inside, waiting for the doors to slide closed. When at last they do, I collapse into my seat.

Okay, that part's done. The hardest part is over.

Only it's not the hardest part, I realize pretty quickly, left with nothing to do but think now that I'm just sitting on the train. Sure, that might have been the most immediately dangerous part. But all the truly hard parts are left to come.

I have no idea what to do next. Dinner, I think absently, aware that I haven't eaten yet despite not feeling particularly hungry. I have my credit card in my wallet. Surely I can afford to sit down somewhere, have a meal and get off the street.

I freeze. No. Ethan and I share the card. Will he be able to see when I use it?

I think I have a twenty in my bag. That pretty much prevents going in somewhere nice to sit down, but I'm sure I can find a fast food place. If I sit in the back and be quiet after I order something, then I should be fine for a little while.

Hands shaking, I reach into my bag to pull out my wallet, confirming the crinkled up twenty in there. Thank god.

The glaringly obvious credit card from Marcus catches my attention, but I ignore it, shoving it to the very back of my wallet. I'm not going to spend his money and risk my job. I can fix this. I have a little bit of cash. I have my debit card too, but the account is a joint account. Will Ethan be able to claim that I stole money from him if I use it?

My mom had a lot of boyfriends over the years when I was growing up. Some of them were fine. Some of them really sucked. The difference between my mom and I, though? She was never stupid enough to tie up all her money with any of those losers. I'd thought I was so much better than her with my stable boyfriend, with my long-term, forever commitment, but look at the trouble I've landed myself in.

It made sense at the time. Ethan and I were forever. We had an apartment together, split living expenses. I trusted him.

I squeeze my eyes shut, holding back the tears. I trusted him.

I don't even know how to begin untangling this. My clothes, my possessions, my money. It's all at our apartment. Is it our apartment? Both of our names are on the lease.

Fuck.

I must let out some sort of sound, because the person sitting two seats away from me scoots a bit to their left. Dammit.

Untangling everything is a tomorrow problem. My today problem is just getting away, getting dinner, and finding a safe place to be for the rest of the night.

I get off the train and blend in with a rush of people on the sidewalk when I emerge from the station, grateful it's still early enough that I can blend in with a crowd.

But then I'm left with a bitter reminder of just how many hours I need to fill, how many hours I need to keep myself safe for, before I can go to work tomorrow.

And after work? I have no idea. I just know that Marcus' apartment will be a safe place to be during work hours. He has a doorman who takes security seriously. That guy isn't going to let Ethan in.

And even if he did, for some reason, something tells me that Marcus wouldn't let anyone treat me the way Ethan treated me tonight. That he'd protect me while I was in his apartment.

Of course, Ethan followed me to work this morning, which means he could very well be waiting there tomorrow. Would he do that? Does he care enough?

I think of the cold, possessive look in his eyes earlier. Yes. He cares enough.

So I need to be careful. I touch my pepper spray, now at the very top of my bag, and hope that it'll be enough.

I wander into a McDonalds, buying myself a meal with cash. Then I find a quiet table in the back and sit, picking at the food.

I should be hungry. The last thing I ate was lunch with Marcus, and that was hours ago. I remember vaguely feeling hungry as I was going home. But it's like my body is disconnected from my mind now, and the signals it should be sending are gone.

They're probably lost in the static noise inside my brain, the loud screaming that's making thinking difficult.

I pull out my phone and check the time. Just after eight. I start work in just over twelve hours.

Then I turn off my phone. Ethan could find me through that, couldn't he? We share a cellphone plan. I doubt he would go to all that trouble, but I can't shake the paranoia.

I look around the McDonalds, trying to keep my motions subtle and probably failing greatly. There's not a ton of people here, but there's enough. And probably none of them are looking at me, but what if they are?

What if Ethan walked in right now, following my cell phone? What if he sat across from me?

What the fuck would I say to him?

I almost knock over my drink, my hands are shaking so hard at just the thought. I can't. Not now.

But I'll have to, eventually. I can't detangle my life from his without talking to him.

The door opens, and I almost jump out of my chair. It's two college kids, laughing and joking with each other, but my heart rate doesn't slow down.

Fuck.

In the end, I can only stand the jumpiness for another two hours. I've managed to make myself pick away at my entire meal by then, and the restaurant isn't busy enough for anyone to actually need my table, but I'm sure no one wants me taking up this table all night.

If I keep moving, then Ethan can't catch up to me. With my phone off and not using my credit or debit card, surely he can't find me.

I swipe my Metro Card again and head into the trains, already mapping a route in my head so I can stay on the trains for the rest of the night.

CHAPTER 13

Marcus

There's a sharp knocking on my door at eight in the morning.

I frown, not sure who that could be. The cleaning service isn't scheduled until the afternoon, and Elise shouldn't be here for another hour. If anyone else comes by, the doorman is supposed to buzz me, not send them to my door.

I finish up the muffin in my hand and go to open the door.

It's Elise standing there, watching me with desperate eyes. I'm so thrown by her appearance that I completely forget my manners, keeping her in the hall as I look her over.

Those are her clothes from yesterday, and she's clutching that worn bag like she's worried I'm going to rip it out of her hands. She's not wearing a coat, despite how cold it is outside. Her lovely dark hair, usually so neatly tied back, is a mess around her face, half out of the twist she keeps it in, the ends all teased and wild.

"Elise," I say. "What happened?"

Her eyes dart around the foyer like she thinks someone is going to jump out at her. "I'm early," she whispers. "I'm sorry."

"Don't be sorry," I say immediately. The last thing I want is for her to be sorry; I need answers, not apologies. "What happened?" I repeat, stepping aside for her to come in.

She moves towards the kitchen as if on autopilot, putting her bag on the hook I put up for her just yesterday. She goes as if to take off her coat, like she doesn't even realize she's not wearing one.

And then that motion pulls her sleeve up just slightly, and the whole world narrows down to that one point.

"Who the fuck put their hands on you?" I say, voice low and deadly. She flinches. Too much dragon in my voice, and I fight to keep my cool even when all I want to do is lose my shit. "Elise. Who grabbed you?"

She looks down at her wrist as if she's just noticing the ugly, fresh bruise. She stares at it for a long minute, then says, "I went home last night, and Ethan—" She trails off, like she can't say any more, but I'm already seeing red.

Ethan is a dead man. There is no way in hell the dragon and I could let him live, no way we ever would. That man put bruises on her skin. He fucking hurt her.

Dragons don't think in words, just feelings, but I can interpret what the dragon is thinking loud and clear, regardless.

Ethan is dead.

"Have you been out all night, Elise?" I ask, consciously working as hard as I can to keep my voice soothing. She doesn't need to know how close I am to the edge. She needs a safe place, and I can be that for her.

She flinches again. I hate myself for it, a little bit. "I didn't know where else to go," she whispers. "I couldn't go home, and—"

"You can always come here," I interrupt her. Later, I will get the whole story out of her. I'm not sure I can handle hearing right this moment where exactly she spent the night, not if I'm trying to keep myself collected and even-keeled for her. For now, all I need her to know is that she can always come here. That my nest is hers, and so is everything in it. "Matter of fact, you should stay here." The dragon rumbles inside me at that, his satisfaction with that plan more than evident. Yes. She'll be here, and I'll know she's safe and cared for.

"I can't stay here," she says, blinking at me like I just suggested breathing underwater.

"Why not?"

"Because that's not fair to you. And the full eight hour days are going to pay me pretty well, but not enough to afford rent in a place like this."

I don't give a shit about rent. "Then I'm clearly not paying you enough," I tell her.

"You don't pay me, technically. The service does." Don't I know it. I'd wanted to change that last week, but I understand why it might make her leery to quit the service and work directly for me. That type of situation might feel unstable, considering how short a time she's worked for me. I don't blame her for not trusting me yet.

But if I paid her, she'd have all the money in the world. I'd make sure she could afford rent on an apartment like this, even if she'll never need to.

"I'm not worried about rent," I tell her instead of revealing all that. That'll just freak her out. "You've seen this place. You know the things I have. Everything that goes on here. You're fully aware I'm not worried about money."

She gets a stubborn set to her face. "That doesn't mean I can just take advantage of you."

Her, take advantage? The idea is ludicrous, especially with the dragon in the back of my mind, giving me oh-so-helpful images of the two of us in bed, me curled around her like she's some sort of treasure we need to protect.

"Elise," I say, as patiently as I can, "Please. The way I see it, you either let me put you up in the spare bedroom, or we use my credit card to get you a hotel room. But a nice hotel, with security and twenty-four hour front desk service, because I don't think you should be truly alone right now." I can't stop thinking about the bruises on her wrist. They go through my mind over and over, a looping slideshow of some dead asshole laying his hands on her, and I need to fix this.

I pushed too far. She collapses slightly, her shoulders caving in, her stubbornness melting off her face. "He never hurt me before last night," she murmurs, like it's a rebuttal to what I'm saying.

It's not, though. I scramble to make a plan while I wait patiently for whatever she's going to say next. First order of business, do whatever it takes to convince her to stay. Figure out what she needs to keep moving on with her life, then get it for her or replace it for her. She has her purse, so she might have things like her cards and ID, but I doubt she has any other documents she might need. Clothes, toiletries. Does she need any medication?

Then I need to figure out exactly how legally entwined her life is with that asshole's, so I can get her a lawyer if she needs it. I have a lawyer, but he's a selkie, and I'd much rather no one in my world knows about my human mate, at least not until I've taken steps to protect her. So I need to find a human lawyer who can handle human problems, and will do everything in their power to get Elise everything she needs for the right price.

But all of that is a problem for later this afternoon or tomorrow. Right now, I have only two priorities. One, getting her to agree to stay here, and provide any immediate things she might need, whether that's a shoulder to cry on or a prescription or a fresh set of clothes. Two, go to beat the shit out of her ex-boyfriend.

"Please tell me you'll stay here," I beg. "Or I will get you that hotel room, if you'd be more comfortable, until we can find you a place of your own. But none of this he never hurt me before nonsense. He did it once. He'll do it again."

She's shaking. Just slightly, a tremor in her hands that I might not notice if I were human. But she's shaking, and I have to squash my first instinct to grab her and hold her until she feels better.

"Want a cup of tea?" I offer, needing to do something, needing to keep my hands busy so I don't reach for her.

She nods, so I move into the kitchen, careful to give her space, and set the kettle on the stove. "You drink tea and you don't have an electric kettle?" she asks.

I pause for a second. I don't drink tea that often, but that's hardly relevant. This is the first time she's expressed wanting something for our space. "I'll get one."

"No, that's not what I meant, I—"

"I can get one," I say gently, turning away from the stove. "And anything else you need. Will you stay here?"

She hesitates a moment, but then nods. "Just until I find somewhere else to stay. Or until I'm an inconvenience. Whatever comes first."

The second one will never happen. And as for her finding somewhere else to stay, the dragon once again sends me the helpful image of me, curled around her in my bed. That can be her new place to stay.

I take a deep breath. Not helpful.

"I'm glad you're staying here," I tell her. I reach for the last of the muffins she made, setting it on a plate and putting it in front of her. "Eat. When was the last time you ate?"

She picks at the muffin paper. "I went to a McDonalds last night," she says listlessly. "I ate."

I purse my lips so I don't say anything about that. "I'll be back in two minutes," I tell her seriously. "Don't move."

She nods, so I retreat to my office and grab a tablet, flipping it open as I walk back to the kitchen. "This is for you," I say, sliding it in front of her. "I need you to do two things for me. One, use the notes app to make a list of anything you need, or want, or anything that needs to be done. Don't worry about missing things; this can be a running list. And two, any store apps that are downloaded already have my credit card. Go nuts."

"I don't need—"

I don't let her finish the thought, not able to hear her say that she's taking advantage or whatever nonsense again. "Check out the guest bedroom too, so you can decide what you need in there."

Her hand shakes as she touches the tablet. "I don't need anything."

"You do, Elise," I tell her firmly. "And it's okay to need it. It's okay to take it from me, too. I want to help." I take a deep breath, debating how I'm going to phrase what I need to say next. "I need to go out for a while."

I see her tense up, then curl forward again. She can say all she wants about her boyfriend never hitting her before yesterday and therefore not needing to be physically protected from him, but her posture says a hell of a lot more.

The kettle whistles, so I turn to busy myself with tea. There's chamomile, because sometimes I can't sleep. Something tells me Elise could use a big mug and then hopefully a long nap.

"I'm going to tell the doorman that absolutely no one can come up here," I continue, setting the tea in front of her to steep. "I'll tell the cleaning service to come later in the week, or next week. Only you and I can come into this apartment, alright?"

She nods.

"And I don't think you have my phone number. I'm going to leave it with you, so you can reach out to me if there's any issues. I swear I'll come back right away if you need me."

"I turned my phone off," she mumbles. "We share a phone plan."

I tap her tablet. "That can place calls. Even easier, because my number is already programmed into it."

I glance at the ugly wall clock. "You should drink your tea, eat your muffin. Rest, make your lists. Do anything you need to—have the run of the place, absolutely no part of it is off-limits. Call me if you need me. I'll be back around lunchtime, but if you're hungry, definitely don't wait for me."

She just nods, which is probably the best I'm going to get for right now. I sigh, and with one last look at her and a glance at her still-exposed bruised wrist to bolster my anger, I turn to leave.

I call the front desk instead of going down, because I'm headed to the roof. On the phone, I let some of the full weight of Mr. Golde loose, making it very clear that jobs and lawsuits are on the line if a single person is allowed up to my floor.

I don't want to violate Elise's privacy, so I don't mention the abuse. What I do say is that, in addition to nobody being allowed up, the police are to be called immediately if anyone matching Ethan's description is on the premises at all.

And then I fly to Brooklyn.

The amount of magic needed to fly in broad daylight is significant, but I'm so fueled by righteous rage that I think I could truly do anything. They should study the effect on a dragon's magic when their mate has been threatened.

I was partially worried the boyfriend would have already gone to work for the day, or perhaps be out in the city trying to find Elise. Then I would have to waste a tedious amount of time hunting him down, and I'd be limited in how I could treat him with so many human witnesses.

But with just him? I can do whatever I want. As long as he doesn't live to tell the tale, there's really nothing to protect a piece-of-shit human abuser from a dragon like me.

There are lights on in the apartment. I turn back to my human form, breaking the lock on the front door of the building with one stiff tug of dragon strength, and make my way inside.

Then I knock on their front door.

I can smell Elise's scent lingering in every inch of this place. But then I slowly realize there's something underlying it. Ethan, surely, but...

Oh, fuck no.

The door swings open, and Ethan eyes me like a wild animal. With a snarl on my face, I push him back into the apartment, closing the door behind us and blocking it with my body.

I look him over. He's a big man, but a big man who has shrunk recently, who has clearly lost some of his bulk. Which makes sense, given what I now know.

"How long have you been feeding off of her?" I ask him. I try to keep my voice calm, to restrain myself, to make it seem like I'm in control right now. I'm not sure how well I succeed.

"I think you know," he says.

I think I do too. Every goddamn day since he met Elise.

Because I'm not looking at her piece of shit human boyfriend. I'm looking at a piece of shit empathic demon.

Commonly called psychic vampires, these fuckers feed off of the devotion of others. They feed off the whole-hearted and entirely focused devotion of their victims, and can't stomach their victims having any devotion to anyone else.

I look over this demon that's been feeding from my Elise, and who looks like he's starting to starve.

Good.

"You had no right to take anything from her," I snarl, unable to even pretend at level-headedness. "But you had even less right to touch her."

"Defending the little human?" he taunts. "That's the way of the world. Surely you're old enough to understand that." He takes a step to the side, but I don't move, remaining resolute. "Unless you're just worried about your new human pet."

"What happened, demon?" I can't help myself from returning the taunt. "She not feeding you as well anymore?"

No, she wouldn't be. Not if he looks like this. Is it because of me? Is that why he got angry with her? I feel a slight thrill that I might be more than just a passing thought in her mind, and then the crushing guilt. I'm thrilled over something he hurt her for.

No. His actions aren't my fault, and they certainly aren't Elise's.

"You're dead," I tell him. "For what you did? You're dead."

He tuts. "You can't kill me. Killing something like me, over a human? People will notice that. Questions will be asked. Investigations, probably. I have friends."

I have friends too, but he's not wrong with the fact that it'll draw attention. And I want no attention drawn to Elise, not until I can ensure her protection.

If I kill him and the wrong people come sniffing around, if I draw attention to my human mate while she's still fragile—if I cause her any more pain—then I'll never forgive myself.

I take a step towards him, letting the fire of the dragon bleed into my eyes. That look has been known to make lesser creatures wet themselves. That look, backed with the full promise of the might and fire of a dragon, has promised certain death for millennia.

I'm gratified when Ethan takes a step back from me. I take another step towards him, closing the distance until he's backed against the wall like cornered prey. "Then leave," I tell him, my voice low and even and full of deadly promise. "Leave the city forever. Don't ever return. Don't come back for Elise. Don't even think about her again. She's not your meal ticket any longer."

"Each creature is entitled to their basic needs," he sputters, raising his chin to project an air of toughness that I can see right through. "You know that, you can't stop me from surviving—"

"I'm not," I say, although I dearly wish I could. He is right about him being entitled to his basic needs. He doesn't need to be an emotionally abusive ass to get his sustenance, though. "I'm telling you this woman is out of bounds." I step closer, until I'm right in his space, and grab his shirt as I lean in. "Because if you think you have an argument for your friends, saying I deprived you of your meal ticket? Consider what will happen when I talk to my friends, and say you put your hands on my mate."

His wide-mouthed, gaping look of horror makes something primal curl in me, self-satisfied and victorious. He needs to know how close he is to death. How much I wish to rip his throat out, and the only thing stopping me is protecting Elise.

I glance quickly at the lone window. It'll be a tight fit, but I'm confident I can make it work.

Before he knows what's happening, I tighten my grip on his shirt and use his body as a battering ram to break the window. I push him out of it, my grip on his shirt iron-tight as I follow him.

I wait for his scream of terror before I take the form of a dragon, still gripping him in my front claw as I wince at the magic needed to cloak both of us.

He's still screaming as I fly for the harbor. I roll my eyes. Like a little splat against the pavement would kill him.

"If I see you in my city again, I'll rip your heart out," I promise him. A dragon's voice comes from deep in our too-large abdomens. It always vibrates low and deadly, and it should shake his bones when I speak.

I don't ask him if he understands. I don't make any additional threats. Instead, I dump him in the water from a few hundred feet up, and turn back towards Brooklyn.

I have movers to call.

CHAPTER 14
Elise

I sip that tea so slowly that it's ice cold by the time I finish, trying to grasp what's happened to my life.

Ethan, and now Marcus. Ethan, who turned on me when I never expected it. Marcus, who's gone above and beyond, who was a steady rock this morning despite owing me nothing.

And he wants me to live in this multi-million dollar penthouse, like that's something I can just do.

I understand he has more money than god, but the casual way he offers his support, the way he insists on me staying here or getting a hotel on his dime, is mind-boggling.

When I admit defeat on the tea, I set the mug in the sink. I'll deal with that later. For now, I might as well find the guest room Marcus talked about.

The first door I open is clearly his bedroom. I close it immediately, but not before I get a good view. I think those sheets are silk, and the green duvet looks heavy and soft, like a cloud. There's thick carpet on the floor, heavy light-blocking curtains on the huge windows, and art on the walls that's no doubt expensive as hell. It's the one place in the entire apartment that doesn't have some minimalist design, and I can't say I hate it.

I shut the door and immediately turn away. He told me nowhere is off-limits, but I doubt that extends to his bedroom.

The guest room, it turns out, is on the other side of the room he's using as an office. It's certainly much simpler, although simple makes it sound basic, and it's not. I have no doubt that a five-star hotel would be jealous of the quality of the bedding. There's a dresser and a desk, a huge window with a view of Central Park, and even an en-suite bath.

I make a beeline for the bath. It'll be nice to get clean after riding the subway all night. I don't have clean clothes to put on, but at this point, I'll take any improvement I can get. And if Marcus is going to let me into his home, the least I can do is not be grubby.

There's soap in the shower, and I can easily find a washcloth and a towel in the little linen chest. There's no shampoo, but I'll make do until I can run to a store.

Marcus told me to make a list. Item number one: shampoo. A razor wouldn't go amiss either. A hair dryer would be nice too.

I should go get the tablet, but I can't quite make myself walk that far, so instead I start the shower. It's hot practically instantaneously. I step in, steam billowing around me, and do my best to scrub clean, wiping the grime off me.

And with the grime goes a fair amount of the fear. It's like I'm taking Ethan's touch away with every pass of the washcloth, watching what happened last night circle the drain. I'm safe now. I'm safe.

Marcus won't let anything happen to me in his house. He'll ensure that I'm safe here. I don't know how I know that so resolutely, but I do.

He saw the bruise, and as soon as he knew what it was, there was not a single second where he hesitated. I can't think of many people in my life who would have even acknowledged that they saw it, never mind stepped up like Marcus did.

He's a good man. And, apparently, my roommate.

It sucks to drag back on my grimy clothes, but the alternatives are just wearing a towel or being brave enough to raid Marcus' closet. And I'm definitely not ready for either of those options.

Covered once more in my grimy clothes, but at least with clean-ish skin and hair, I make my way back to the kitchen and pick up the tablet. I know Marcus pointed out the many apps I could use to order what I need, but there's no way I'm going to rebuild my entire life on his credit card.

I squash the little voice that reminds me I have no money, that I might need to accept his charity and find some way to pay him back. I don't want to think about that right now.

So I use the notes app to make a list. Shampoo, deodorant, toothpaste and a toothbrush, a razor, a hair dryer, a few changes of clothes. I add my own money to the bottom, not even sure what either of us can do about that, but knowing Marcus asked me to write down everything I need.

And then I turn to what I'm good at, what I'm comfortable with. What I'm paid to be here to do, I remind myself.

It's definitely time to think about lunch.

I tense when the door opens, despite the fact that I know it can only be Marcus. Sure enough, he walks in, looking me over and smiling. He might even look a bit relieved to see me still here, although maybe I'm reading into things.

"You didn't have to cook," he says, voice soft as he closes the door behind him.

I shrug. "It's my job."

"I think, given the circumstances, taking a day off would be understandable."

Maybe to him. Maybe to the man who insisted I live in his house and let me change my hours for no damn reason and gave me the credit card that still gives me heart palpitations. Maybe that type of man would excuse a day off.

But it's my job. It's why I'm here in the first place. And I will not intrude in his home and not do my damn job.

"If I don't work, then I'm going to spiral. Besides, It's nothing too impressive," I admit. It's an Italian wedding soup, and it smells good enough, but I took enough shortcuts while making it to get it done in time.

"It smells delicious," he says. He looks at the door over his shoulder. "So, I have your things."

I blink in slow confusion, processing what he's telling me. "All of them?"

"I think we managed to get all of them."

"We?" I squeak, because it's bad enough to think of Marcus going through my things, but also some unknown stranger?

"Ethan isn't going to bother you again," he promises me. "He's decided to leave town."

Decided. I gape at Marcus. I don't see him as someone who resorts to threats. Did he bribe Ethan to keep him away from me?

Did that work? Was that all it took?

"There was some damage to your apartment," he says evasively, not quite making eye-contact, and I have to reconsider if he's someone who would use physical force. But surely that's not what he meant. Surely he meant Ethan freaked out and trashed the place after I left or something. "So you can't move back in. Don't worry; I talked to the landlord, and you're released from your lease."

Good, because I can't afford the rent on my own, but I'm not going to say that to him.

"So I called some movers and we packed everything up," he continues. "I put your furniture in storage. If you want any particular pieces here, of course we can get them."

Most of Ethan's and my furniture is crap, which is also something I don't want to say to Marcus, even if I could manage to find the words.

Oh, who am I kidding? He obviously saw it, and he's just being nice right now by not mentioning how everything he has here blows my stuff out of the water.

"As for everything else—anything I assumed was Ethan's we boxed up and shoved in a different storage unit. You can leave it there or set it on fire if you want. And the movers will be up any minute with everything I assumed was yours."

It's like it takes my brain a moment to catch up to all he's saying. This man, who went above and beyond just by noticing the bruise on my wrists, has now done all of this for me? "Thank you," I whisper. "I appreciate it."

"It's nothing," he says. It's not nothing, though, and I want to argue, but there's a firm knock at the door. "Here they are."

He hired three people to move my things, and they move in and out with stunning efficiency. Each box is carefully labeled—clothes, toiletries, books, cookware. I don't need my old chipped dishes here, but I appreciate him thinking about them all the same.

All the boxes are brought to the guest room, and I peek over the shoulder of one of the movers as they stack them carefully in the corner, feeling exceptionally useless. When I return to the kitchen, he's looking at the tablet, reviewing my list.

He looks up. "You have your own stuff now, but if you need anything else, or replacements, or anything, you should order it."

I won't be doing that. The box labeled toiletries means he probably got my shampoo and razor and favorite moisturizer. It's one thing off my mind—one step closer to self-sufficiency.

"Soup?" I offer in a squeaky voice, and he gracefully lets me redirect the conversation, giving me a moment to pretend that this is somehow a normal day.

CHAPTER 15

Marcus

I keep an eye on her all day, watching for any signs that she needs anything or that she's hurting.

I know the marks on her wrists are just bruises. And I know bruises are part of being human, and I can't help her with them. But that doesn't change how desperately I wish I could do something for her.

If we were mated, if we'd taken that final step, I might actually be able to help her with her bruises. The magic of a dragon means we can protect our human mates, but it's not so simple. It would literally require us to have sex, and that's not something we're ready for.

Besides, I know the bruises are the least of it. Bruises heal. It's what he did to her mind that we both need to watch out for.

After we finish our soup, I try to convince her to take the afternoon off, but she rebuffs my offer multiple times. Well, fine. If she needs to hold onto work to keep her composure, then I won't complain. Instead, I send an email to reschedule my afternoon calls, and sit at the counter watching her cook.

She bustles around with little of her usual grace and poise. She always makes cooking look like some sort of dance, like something you can do with a carefully controlled, precise, artful economy of movement. Not today, though. Not that I blame her.

I let her cook in peace for a while, sensing that she needs it. She makes more muffins, clearly having noticed that I gave her the last one this morning.

But finally I have to interrupt her. I don't want to, and I hoped that there would be some sort of signal that she's ready. But that's a foolish hope, because there will never be a signal like that. She might not ever be ready.

It doesn't mean that this doesn't need to happen, though.

"Elise," I begin, reminding myself to keep my voice gentle. "We need to talk."

She goes still. "About what?"

About a lot of things, truthfully. But there are some things I can prioritize. "I'm going to get you a lawyer," I tell her. I'd decided while waiting for the movers that I'm going to call Ben, my selkie lawyer, after all. If she's really been the prey of a demon, then she needs a supernatural lawyer. I'll just have to rely on the fear a dragon inspires, and heaps of money, to encourage him to protect my vulnerable human mate.

"I don't need a lawyer," she tells me.

I had a feeling she'd say that. "You rented that apartment together and already told me you shared a cell phone plan," I remind her. "Any other assets tied up together?"

I can tell immediately that I struck the nail on the head. "We share a bank account," she mumbles, cheeks burning with shame. "All my money." She winces. "He probably emptied it when he left town."

I don't care if she has her own money or not, but I'm sure she'd feel more secure with her own funds. A dragon will always provide for their mate, but that doesn't mean that both dragons don't usually enter the mating with their own treasure.

She could have three nickels to her name and it wouldn't affect me one bit, but I want her to feel the security of knowing she can take care of herself, and that the jackass demon didn't take that from her.

"A lawyer can help sort that out," I offer. "I know a guy. I can have him here tomorrow morning."

"I can't have you pay for a lawyer for me, Marcus; I'm already taking too much from you."

She's not taking nearly enough, but I refrain from saying it. "I have a lot to give."

"I don't want charity."

"It's not charity, Elise. And you won't owe me anything after, either. We're just getting you back on your feet."

She doesn't move for almost a minute, like her furiously spinning brain has frozen her body. "I'm just your employee," she breathes slowly. Maybe she thinks we both need the reminder.

Maybe she thinks she is, but I know better. Because the part of me that had been insistent that I was just aiming for friendship? Something about the removal of the boyfriend has destroyed any and all illusions I might have forced myself to see.

I'll take friendship if that's what Elise offers, because of course I will. I was never lying about wanting to be her friend. Friendship, in my opinion, is an essential component to being a mate. That's certainly the impression I got from my parents.

But I want more. I want her friendship and her heart and her love and her soul. I want to swim in her, to hold her, to make her my world.

I'd like to blame the dragon in the back of my mind. And I think I can blame him for most of it, or at least for the intensity. But the desire under it is my own.

"Elise," I tell her, trying to keep my voice as level as possible. "You and I both know that's not all. We can be friends. And now, roommates." I slide closer to her, trying to be conscious of the amount of space humans like to feel safe, trying to find the line between being reassuring and a threat. "And I take care of my people. To the ends of the earth."

She scoffs slightly but doesn't respond, and I think she genuinely doesn't know what to say.

Who's taken care of her before, to the ends of the earth? Her mother, maybe. Certainly not the man she dedicated her adult life to.

"We'll meet with the lawyer tomorrow," I tell her instead of dwelling on it. "And you're in charge. Whatever you want to happen will happen. He'll get you your money back, and anything else you want."

She's silent for a long moment. "I just want this to be over," she admits.

My heart continues to ache for her. She asked for the one thing I can't provide.

Ben comes to visit us right after breakfast the next day. I made sure we'd be his first clients of the day. Ben's already someone who commands a hefty fee, and I just pile on more, asking him to prioritize Elise and to forget that he ever met my human mate after he leaves here.

We end up at the bank, and Elise walks out with a new bank account and the promise of a new debit card to be delivered in the mail. Delivered to my home, because that's the address she put on record. I could see the way her face scrunched up when she realized she had nowhere else to list, but she did it.

I vow to make it worth her while. To make sure she never feels like she needs to leave, to ensure she always feels safe here.

I can't pretend anymore that my goal is anything other than to woo her, and if I can woo her by providing a safe place, then that's a start.

The only problem is she won't accept any other courting gifts. She insists she doesn't need new things because I boxed up her possessions from her apartment, and while I'm glad she has the stuff that she likes and that brings her comfort, I can't help but resent it slightly. Would it kill her to let me buy her things?

I'm learning quickly that Elise is not one for big gifts. Maybe I need to think smaller, at least for now. I can't currently think of what a small gift is, but I'm sure they exist. I can hire Valerie to redecorate my home, and I can hire Elise to handle the cooking, and I can hire a cleaning service. Surely you can hire someone who picks out gifts.

But even as I think it, the dragon inside me rebels. The idea of someone else picking out gifts for our mate is physically disgusting to me. I don't want anyone else's hands on something I plan to give her.

Instead, I wait until she's distracted by making breakfast for tomorrow and pull up a search on my phone to type in small gift ideas to show you care.

Embarrassing? Maybe. But she hasn't truly accepted a single one of my gifts yet, so I suppose I need all the help I can get.

The problem, I quickly realize, is that a lot of these gifts are food. There's no way I can make her cookies without burning them horrifically and likely offending her palate. And buying her exotic spices just sounds like I'm asking her to do extra work.

Maybe tea. A basket of nice tea isn't a terrible idea. She asked for the kettle after all, so surely she enjoys tea. Or flowers. Women like flowers, right?

This feels pointless, like I'm flying in circles. She hasn't liked my gifts because they're too extravagant. These smaller gifts don't seem like they'd be any more successful. Therefore, the issue isn't that the gifts are extravagant. The issue is that they're from me. She doesn't want gifts from me.

That sits cold and heavy in my gut, but I have to accept it. Because truthfully, it's not that she doesn't want gifts from me. It's that she doesn't want me.

And that's fair enough. She doesn't know me. I'm her boss. I met her at a party where I was the guest and she was working. I haven't known her that long, and all I've done is employ her and try to throw money and gifts at her.

I've invited her into my home, I think sourly, and provided a safe place and tried to make all her problems go away. Surely I'm not just her boss. But then I squash the thought, because I am not the type of man to demand reciprocation over a nice deed. I took care of her because I wanted to, end of story.

She walks into the living room with ginger steps, like she's not sure of her welcome. I hastily close out the search on my phone but don't put the phone down. She looks skittish, like she's not sure she's allowed to just be in this house, and I don't want to startle her further by staring at her.

"Do you mind if I borrow a book?" she asks quietly.

I swallow my immediate response, the instant need to reassure her that the books are all hers, that everything is hers, that she should take what she wants. That would just scare her.

"Of course, borrow anything you'd like," I say. I force myself not to stare at her as she walks over to the bookshelf, but I'm desperate to know what she chooses so I can know what she likes.

It's a sci-fi. An interesting choice, but she makes it so fast that I don't know how deliberate it is. I refrain from commenting, though, watching her sit on the opposite end of the couch, curling her legs up under her.

A soft contentment fills me, my blood infused with a little golden glow from watching her rest in the nest I've made us. Even if she doesn't know that's what she's doing yet, it's a start.

And for now, it's enough.

CHAPTER 16
Elise

This house feels like a dream.

I wake up in this bed that's practically a cloud every day, then get clean in a shower stall that could comfortably fit four. I get to work, making breakfast for the two of us, then lunch and dinner. Marcus tells me to work less.

I have no idea what I'm supposed to do if I'm not working, but on the fourth day of living with him, I'm forced to figure it out. Valerie is here with a team of painters. The amount of people she hires for the job seems like overkill, but maybe I shouldn't be surprised anymore. And on the plus side, more people means the painting will get done faster, and the disruption will be minimal.

Minimal, but not unavoidable. I tried last night to prepare food that we could eat cold today, but I can't even get through to the fridge with the tarps and paint and people. Plus, apparently they're not going to paint the kitchen until the cabinets that Valerie plans on changing are ripped out, so now there's demolition going on in my kitchen.

Marcus' kitchen. Whatever. The lines are getting a little blurry, and it's only made worse by the easy way Marcus refers to this as *our* apartment.

He doesn't know what he's doing, I tell myself, blurring the boundaries that I need so easily. He makes this seem easy and natural, like I belong here with him. Like I could belong here with him.

But I don't belong here with him. I remind myself every chance I get; I made mistakes with Ethan, jumping right into things as quickly as I did and letting the lines blur. I can't let that happen again.

When the workers come, I retreat to my bedroom, which thankfully doesn't seem to be directly in the line of fire yet. But, glancing at the crisp white walls, I have a feeling paint is coming sooner rather than later.

For now, my bedroom is safe and private, and if I don't think too hard about how the hell I'm expected to serve lunch, I can enjoy one of Marcus' many books. This man was not kidding when he said he collected books when I first started working for him. He has books of every type. Some of them look so expensive that I won't dare breathe on them wrong, but he also has a respectable collection of mass market paperbacks, too, and I practically devour them. Mysteries, thrillers, romances, pulpy-old sci-fi—I'm not sure if I'm learning about Marcus' taste as much as I'm learning that the man will simply buy anything.

Today I'm reading a fantasy book, settling in and trying to get through the pages of complicated names and backstory when there's a knock on my door.

If they're here already to kick me out and try to paint this room, I don't know where I'll go.

The knocking starts again, so I drop the book onto my partially made bed and go to open it, mentally being prepared to get kicked out.

Marcus is standing there, half-leaning against the door frame, smiling softly. He's in a button-down shirt and slacks, but he's undone several of the buttons and his hair is even more chaotic than usual, like he's run his hand through it a lot. I run my eyes over him before forcing myself to pull it together and look him in the eye. The way his beautiful green eyes sparkle doesn't help me form a sentence.

"What do you say we give them some space?" he says. "I gave up on working for today, and it's almost lunch time. Let me treat you to lunch."

It's on the tip of my tongue to say that I've let this man treat me to too much already, but I bite it back. Marcus has made his feelings about money clear, and he obviously doesn't see all he's done as a big deal.

It's a huge deal, but I doubt I can make him see that.

I look down at myself. I started this job with a chef coat every day, but I admit I haven't bothered these last few days since I've been living here. I'm wearing jeans and a t-shirt so soft it's a little see-through where it stretches around my tits. "Should I change?"

"Depends where you want to eat, I suppose," he says. "Tell me where and I'll make the reservation."

Anywhere that requires a reservation is a little more formal than I was thinking. "Nothing too fancy, please," I ask.

He tilts his head, considering. "Grab a jacket and some shoes. No need to change; I have an idea."

He's waiting by the door when I'm ready, his own coat on. It's getting colder outside, but he's wearing just a thin coat, something stylish and surely quite pricey.

"You need a warmer coat," he says gently, looking me over.

"Me? What about you?"

"Don't worry about me. I'm always warm," he says with a little smile, then gestures to the door. "You have everything?"

I pick up my purse and follow him out.

The restaurant he picks is an absolutely tiny Thai restaurant. There's only six tables, but thankfully one is open for us.

It could be because it's only eleven in the morning, but I have a strong feeling that Marcus did something. I don't ask.

"Are you going to go into the office for the rest of the day?" I ask him after he orders enough food to feed four people for the two of us.

"No," he says simply. "I just took the day off."

I frown. "I thought you were relatively new to this role."

He doesn't answer for a minute, and I realize I probably asked more than I should. "I'm sorry, I—"

"No, Elise, it's fine. Ask whatever you want. I guess I am new to this particular role," he says. He has a small smile as he says it. "But I'm good at what I do, and people know it. And to tell the truth, I don't need to work. I work because I like being busy." He turns his head so he's looking away, dragging a hand through his hair. "That probably sounds ridiculous to you."

It sounds like a dream, but not ridiculous. Unobtainable, maybe. What would I do if I had unbelievable amounts of money?

I'd probably work still, like Marcus does. Like he said, I like being busy. But I could be selective about what I make and when I make it and who I make it for. I could make fancy things and take pictures of them for my blog and not care that no one is paying attention and not feel any guilt about how much ingredients cost.

"So," Marcus says when it's clearly been silent a minute too long, "If I have the day off and you have the day off, what would you like to do?"

"What would you like to do?" I push back, because I can't come up with a single idea. What do people even do for fun?

"I was serious about you needing a warmer coat," he muses. "We should find you one. Then we could see a movie—do you like movies? Or go anywhere you want, really. The world is your oyster."

I want to say my coat is fine, but even I know it's really not. And once the snow starts, it'll be next to useless.

I shouldn't spend money frivolously; I have no idea how long any part of my current situation will last. Just because I'm not paying rent and making good money today doesn't mean that will be true tomorrow.

"I'll get a coat," I say slowly, thinking it over. A coat is one of those things you just have to accept needing, I suppose.

"Excellent." The food is placed in front of us, and Marcus leans forward slightly, looking at me instead of the delicious meal. "So, Elise, tell me what you like to do for fun."

"I cook," I manage.

"That's work."

It is work, and sometimes it's fun, but that's too complicated to explain. It's fun when I get to play around with it, when no one is limiting what I can make, and when I have a truly receptive audience to eat my food. That doesn't happen very often, although it hasn't exactly escaped my attention that it happens every day with Marcus.

I'm not going to tell my boss when I cook for you, it doesn't feel like work. That's a stupid thing to say, especially when we've already inadvertently crossed so many lines.

"I like to read," I tell him.

He smiles genuinely, leaning even closer and completely ignoring his lunch. "I do too."

"I know. You own so many books." I can't ignore the food any longer, picking up my fork.

"Those are just the books I moved across the country."

"Do you have a favorite book? Favorite genre?" I ask.

"I'm partial to fairytales," he admits. "But I think you'll find that buying books is a different hobby than reading them, and I'm unfortunately often too busy with work to read."

I feel something heavy in the air as he continues to watch me. He's too busy to read, but he took the whole day off to spend with me. He doesn't even seem bothered about missing a whole day of work.

"Well, I don't know much about that," I admit, because my library card is well-loved. "But I'll reap the benefits and read all your books. If you don't mind."

He finally picks up his fork, only to gesture expansively with it before digging into his meal. "What's mine is yours, Elise. You already know that."

So he keeps telling me. No one else in the entire history of humanity has been quite this generous, but he's so completely sincere when he offers it.

"Your food is getting cold," he says quietly, presumably catching me staring at him.

I flush, because it definitely is getting cold and I definitely have been staring at him longer than is socially acceptable. He doesn't react, though, just keeps eating as I scramble to look like a functional human.

"So, coat, then a movie?" Marcus suggests. "That sounds like an afternoon plan, and there's a shop two blocks away that will probably have what you need."

Of course he already has a plan for shopping. I wonder how weird of an item I would have to suggest for Marcus to not know how to immediately find it and buy it, but I don't want to test that. "That works for me."

"I'm going to run down the street to get something while you're getting the coat. Let me make sure you have my number so you can text me when you're done."

"I don't have a phone," I remind him. "I turned it off after…" I still don't want to say it.

Marcus looks stricken. "I'm so sorry I forgot about that. You should have said something, Elise."

Like it's his problem to dig me out of this hole. Still, he looks devastated, and I want to reassure him. "It's fine, really. I have almost no one I need to call."

"Your mother?" he suggests. "Your work?"

I should tell both about my change of address, but I'm not exactly in a rush to do so. I have no desire to tell my mother that my relationship imploded more catastrophically than any of hers ever have. I've never outright said it, but I doubt I've been subtle when I thought of myself and my one stable, long-term relationship as much more superior than her ever-shifting list of boyfriends in her attempt to find Mr. Right. I don't need to admit my failure on a call with her.

I shrug. "I don't talk to them that often."

He frowns, but doesn't comment. "Let's get you a coat. Then, our next stop is a phone."

CHAPTER 17
Marcus

I buy her a brand new smart phone after helping her set up a new account, swiping my card so fast that she doesn't really process what happened. I'm glad, too, because I was not fast enough to successfully buy the coat for her.

She gets to keep her old number and all the data on her old phone, so she doesn't even have to call anyone to give them a new number, something I imagine is a relief to her. I'm well aware that she's been avoiding calling her mother, but I decide not to push her about why.

"You had an errand you wanted to run," she points out softly as we leave the phone store. I hold the door open for her, and she swings the bag containing her new phone gently as she walks.

"Oh, that's nothing. Don't worry about it." I'd seen a jewelry store down the block, and I'd been tempted to go look through it. Dragons like shiny things practically to the point of compulsion, and that goes doubly so if we have a mate to provide shiny things for. But with a little distance, I can admit that it's too soon, and Elise wouldn't react well to surprise jewelry.

I check my phone, wondering what I missed today. I skip past eleven messages from various company executives—who were told in no uncertain terms to leave me alone today—and find a text message from Valerie.

"Valerie says they're done for today," I tell her. "But the entire place smells strongly of paint and she advises us to sleep somewhere else tonight." I click over to a new search, typing in the name of a hotel I've heard good things about.

A quick call ensures we'll have a place to stay tonight, and then I summon the car service to take us over. Elise just watches me the whole time, eyes getting a little wide when I name-drop the hotel brand.

"I could..." she begins, but I shake my head, already sure what she's going to say.

"Paint fumes can make you sick, so you're not staying at home." I refuse to call it my home, despite the fact that she still insists on referring to it as just mine. "And remember what I told you, a few days ago? You're not going to stay somewhere without security now." Ethan should have left town if he had any smarts, but I won't take risks with the safety of my mate. "I got you your own room, Elise. It's perfectly respectable, if you're worried."

She snorts. "I'm not worried about that, Marcus. I live in your apartment."

"There's a nice restaurant at the hotel," I coax her.

"I am certainly not dressed for that."

I shrug. "We need to stop at the apartment regardless. Business-wear should be fine."

"Marcus," she says firmly, "I don't work in an office. My business-wear is a chef's coat, and I don't think that's quite good enough here."

It's on the tip of my tongue to say no one would ever dare deny her entry anywhere when we're together, but I know she won't appreciate it. "We still need to go home first. But we can do room service tonight."

"Fine," she concedes.

We eat together in my room, and it's only now, in a new space, that I realize how dependent I've become on spending meal times with her. The world would be too empty without her there.

"Not as good as your food," I pronounce. It was good, though; I cleared my plate. But nothing can quite top what Elise cooks.

That sparks something inside me. "Not that I want you to change career paths," I say slowly, "Because I very much like having you around. But why don't you work in a restaurant like this one? You're certainly skilled enough."

She blushes. "It's not about skill. I could make the food, but there's a whole other skill set involved, and I don't have that one."

"Like what?" I sit forward slightly, eyes entirely on her, intrigued to hear her explain her work.

"Speed. Organization. The ability to follow others' directions. And working in someone else's kitchen would require me to follow their plans. You've eaten what I make, Marcus. I could never stick to a rigid menu and be happy."

I admire that, her honest self-assessment and choosing something that makes her happy. "What if you set the menu?"

"Then it'd need to be my restaurant, and that's not a risk I'm prepared to take. Do you know the statistics on new restaurants failing? It's something like eighty percent. Besides, that wouldn't fix the speed and organization thing."

I tilt my head, conceding the point. "Your food is still better," I mutter.

She smiles shyly. "It's because it's room service, and that sits under heat lamps a bit. If we ate in the restaurant, they'd blow me out of the water."

Not a chance in hell, but I don't argue with her. I just watch the sweet blush as she finishes her last few bites of salmon.

When she pushes her plate away, she sighs. "I need to figure out how to set up that phone."

"Stay in here," I suggest, glancing at the door. Her room is right across the hall from mine, but that feels too far. "I can help." Probably, at least. Changing identities has required me to set up new phones before, so I'm sure the two of us can puzzle it out.

She doesn't end up needing much help, so I reluctantly look through my emails while she gets it set up. I grit my teeth and reply to as many as I can, but honestly, none of these need me.

I try to be a good boss, but maybe I'm just getting old. My patience is wearing thin.

Then Elise makes a little hitching noise, and my emails are entirely forgotten as I turn my full attention to her. Her hands shake as she clutches her phone before she drops it. She picks it up again, hand still shaking.

"What happened?" I ask immediately, body on high alert.

She tilts the phone towards me, seemingly at a loss for words. She got it set up finally, and the first thing she received was eighty-seven text messages. The first few say things like *I miss you*, and *I'm sorry, babe*. Then there's the *you know I was always good to you* and *don't throw away what we had* and *can't believe you left me for money*.

Ethan. That fucker.

I gently take the phone from her shaking hands, looking through the text messages with a quick scroll. None of them are direct threats, but they get meaner the further down I scroll, the longer he was ignored.

"That fucker," I force out. She flinches a bit, and I immediately soften. "Sorry. I just can't believe he has the nerve."

"We were together for a long time." She mumbles the explanation, not looking at me. "I'm sure he just—"

"He gave up any right to that when he hurt you," I interrupt her, fighting to keep my voice gentle. "And you haven't told me more yet, but I'd bet my fortune that there's more."

"You'd lose," she tells me. "He'd never hurt me before."

"And he always treated you well? Supported you, respected you, talked about you nicely?" I doubt it. I can see from these text messages alone that Ethan is slick; he knows exactly where the lines are and how to push at them. He's a cold-hearted manipulative bastard. None of his acts on their own would be enough to get someone to say that's abusive, but he broke Elise down for years.

"It wasn't that bad."

I shake the phone slightly. "This man is a fucking nightmare. You don't need that kind of thing, Elise. Can I block his number?"

She takes a long second, but she nods at last, and, grateful, I immediately block Ethan's number.

It's not a permanent solution. He didn't leave New York and forget Elise ever existed like I told him, and I need a moment to think about what to do next.

But not yet. I can't think when she's right here, when my only instinct is to be here, be protective and give her whatever comfort she needs. Later, though, once she goes to bed—that's when I can let the dragon's instincts run wild, and make a plan.

CHAPTER 18
Elise

I wake up in a hotel room bed almost as nice as my bed at the penthouse, entirely alone and a little sad about it.

It's ridiculous, and it's not like I expected anything different, but Marcus was so kind and calming after Ethan's barrage of text messages last night that I almost asked if I could stay in his room.

I am fully aware that I would be crossing too many lines. I've already blurred the boundaries of our professional relationship, and I can't ask him for anything else.

Besides, it's not like Ethan can get to me here. We're on the type of floor that you need to use a keycard to even get the elevator to let you off here. I've only seen this type of place in movies. No one is getting up here to bother me.

When I finish showering and getting dressed for the day, there's a text on my new phone. I hold my breath for a moment, but it's Marcus. Breakfast downstairs?

I let out a deep breath. It's just Marcus. Not Ethan, and I don't have to worry about Ethan here.

My fingers are still shaking a bit when I text him back. Be right down.

After breakfast, Marcus comes with me to the grocery store to do our shopping for the next few days. He says it's because he wants to give the paint fumes a little longer to air out, but I doubt that's the reason.

Yesterday's texts freaked him out, even if he's good at presenting a calm facade.

I should probably muster up the energy to tell him he doesn't need to follow me around a grocery store, but I don't even attempt it. I do feel safer with him around, even if he almost certainly has better things to do. Besides, if I told him not to follow me, he'd probably insist on something stupid, like personal security.

"How do you feel about donuts?" I ask him as we enter the store.

"What kind?"

"Whatever kind you want. I was thinking glazed, though."

"Can you make donuts at home?"

"Yup." I smile, ducking my head back to my phone so he doesn't see it. He sounds so surprised, and some part of it is charming.

142

This man clearly never cooked a day in his life. He's probably never even thought about his kitchen as a place he should get to know. On most people, the helplessness would be irritating. But Marcus so genuinely wants to know whatever I tell him that it's endearing.

"I like donuts."

I nod, adding ingredients to the bottom of the list. They'll make a good breakfast for the next few days, and they're a little finicky to make, so it'll take a fair bit of concentration this afternoon. Plus, donuts will be a good recipe to add to my blog.

Marcus gets out of the car as soon as we park, and, while I'm still busy with my bag, moves around to open my door, too. I step out and smile at him. "You don't need to open doors for me, Marcus."

"My father wouldn't speak to me again if he heard I didn't."

Marcus' mother collected pretty china plates so delicate I'm worried about breathing on them. His father insisted on old-school manners. I'm suddenly getting a picture of a very upright, proper young kid. "Is your father...?"

"Still alive. He lives abroad," he says, walking into the store. I notice he slows his pace to match mine, ensuring my shorter legs can keep up with his long strides. He grabs the cart and starts pushing it.

It looks slightly ridiculous because just like I know he has no idea what to do with his kitchen, I also doubt that he's ever shopped for himself before. Even so, he walks along among everyday people like he's not wearing clothes that cost more than most people's rent.

Then again, we're in a very particular part of Manhattan. Maybe this grocery store is filled with people just as rich as Marcus, or at least their staff, shopping for them. They certainly charge like everyone here is a multi-millionaire. I'd already known that, but it hadn't bothered me when I'd just been shopping for Marcus. Rich clients get expensive food, and that was just a fact of life, no more surprising than water being wet. But it's different now that I live there and eat all the same food he does.

I tally up everything I put in the cart as Marcus keeps pushing it, serenely following my lead and never urging me to move faster, even when I spend longer than I should checking avocados. The mental tally in my mind keeps getting bigger.

When we finally go to check out, I try to pull out my debit card, but belatedly realize it hasn't come in the mail yet. While I'm working through that, Marcus brings out his own card and runs it through the machine.

"You don't buy the groceries," he says firmly when he sees what I've been searching for.

"Do I buy anything?" I challenge, waiting for our food to finish being bagged. "Because you've told me not to pay rent, and that hotel last night probably cost a fortune, and I feel like I should buy something."

He sighs heavily. "Elise, I'm trying not to be an asshole, but I need you to understand that I clear what your rent used to be in an afternoon. So, please. Let me buy the groceries."

My brain short circuits at that. "Seriously?" I manage to make myself ask, voice squeaky.

He shrugs. "Or there about. It's a rough estimation." He grabs the bagged groceries, making the six bags look light as a feather, and starts walking for the door.

"You know, I'm realizing I don't know what you actually do," I say, lengthening my stride to keep up with him.

"I run an import/export business."

"Is that code for the mafia? I feel like I heard somewhere that that's usually code for the mafia." I say it before I really think about it, eyes widening when I realize what I just said.

He turns to look over his shoulder, raising an eyebrow. He has to get those done professionally, right? They're so sculpted, like someone took measurements to craft what would perfectly convey a message of striking power. "I'm not in the mafia, Elise."

"And that's exactly what someone in the mafia would say," I point out, forcing myself to stop thinking about his eyebrows.

That doesn't help, because his lips quirk up into a little smirk, and all I can think about is that smirk and the smile lines around his mouth. I almost miss a step.

"I promise you I'm not in the mafia, Elise. I inherited a role in the business, that's all. And I've worked my way up."

145

The car pulls up then, and Marcus shifts all the grocery bags to one arm to open the door for me, still grinning at me the entire time.

CHAPTER 19

Marcus

Having her in our nest is absolutely maddening. She's here, and she smiles sweetly at me all the time. She hums to herself when she gets invested in her recipe and reads voraciously. She takes ludicrously long showers and wears tiny little pajamas.

As Valerie finishes her work on making this apartment an actual place worthy of being called home, my brain calls it our home more and more every day. She unpacked some of her boxes into her room, but most of her stuff she simply put in storage. Still, the entire place feels more like her every single day. Valerie provided a big crocheted throw blanket, and Elise loves it, so it's hers in my brain now. The kitchen is hers. That bedroom is—temporarily, perhaps—hers.

She fights every gift just as much now as she did when we first met, but that's okay. I can provide her a home, a place that's safe for her with everything she could ever need, and the dragon is satisfied with that.

I think our lives could be considered just about perfect, if it weren't for the phone calls.

Ethan is texting and calling just about as fast as Elise can block him. I want to kill him for it, but unfortunately I've come to the conclusion that I can't go and find the fucker without leaving Elise undefended, and I'm hesitant to call in anyone else to help. Not when my mate is still so fragilely human, and I haven't even thought about how to tell her what I am.

We're both reading after dinner, drinking an absolutely decadent hot chocolate she's had in the works for an hour or so, when I feel her go stiff from across the couch.

"Did he text you again?" I say, mindful to keep the growl out of my voice. I'm fucking pissed at him, of course, but that's no excuse for scaring her.

"Either that or some other unknown number is calling me a whore," she says, trying to make her voice light and failing miserably.

I squeeze my book tightly enough that I hear pages ripping before I get a hold of myself. That's a new escalation for him, and I hate it. I hate it for what he's doing to her and how he's making her feel, of course, but also because any man who feels comfortable saying that is a risk who might go further.

"I think you need a new number, Elise. I know it's a pain to change everything, but I'm sure there's a way to let all your contacts know what happened."

She's quiet for a moment, then murmurs, "It wouldn't be that hard. I don't—part of the problem is Ethan kept me from knowing too many people."

I can imagine. If he'd been feeding off her devotion, and he'd been an unscrupulous, greedy asshole, then he'd have wanted to keep her entirely focused on him and his needs. Keeping her from building friendships would only make sense.

She ticks people off on her fingers. "It'd be my mom, Lacey, the doctor I barely ever visit, and the service. Everything else is just noise."

Elise needs friends. Not that I'm in a position to speak, considering I can count the number of people I speak to regularly on one hand. And most of those people perform a service, really, so they maybe don't count.

I'd introduce her to my limited group of friends, but they're all creatures like me, and it's too soon for that. Maybe someday, but not yet.

Elise needs human friends. "Well, we can get you a new number, and then you can pass it onto those people. Or maybe you should have Lacey or your mother visit you here. Tell them in person."

She raises an eyebrow. "You want those people here? In your space?"

"Yes." I refuse to let her hear any hesitation. I want absolutely anyone she wants in our space, even if the dragon in me might be a bit territorial.

She pauses for a bit, staring at me, but then shrugs. "Lacey, maybe. My mom isn't close by."

"Thanksgiving is very soon," I point out. "Maybe she'd want to come to dinner here?"

"Maybe. I'll ask," she says, in a way that tells me she's not going to ask.

"Did you want to do something special for Thanksgiving?" she asks, and it's only then that I realize the faux pas of me telling her to invite her mother to Thanksgiving dinner at our house.

"You don't have to cook," I tell her immediately. I very much wish she would, of course, because I always want her food. More than anything else, I think her cooking has made this place feel like a home. I've spent centuries hoarding priceless artifacts, but her food is something else, a category above everything else I've ever collected. I want to keep every morsel to myself and revel in the fact that she makes it for me. But Thanksgiving is a holiday, and I should make sure she gets the day off.

"I'll cook," she dismisses with a flip of her hand.

"You don't have to," I insist. "You deserve days off. I didn't invite you to stay to force you to cook for me all the time." With a start, I realize she's been cooking on weekends, too. It's just become routine for us, our own little ritual, but that doesn't make it fair for her.

"Were you planning to eat somewhere else?" Elise asks.

"No, Elise," I say patiently. "But where I'm going doesn't matter." Except for the fact that I don't want to be anywhere but at her side. "Were you going to see your mother?"

"No," she dismisses quickly. "Do you want to have Thanksgiving dinner with me, Marcus?"

I consider it for a moment, wondering if there's a tactful way to remind her once again that she isn't expected to cook for me, but I'm worried I'll just confuse things further. "I'd love to."

"Excellent. I'll start thinking about it. Do you have any guests who might be coming?"

"No guests," I say just as quickly as she said she wasn't traveling back home. "Just us, if you're alright with that."

Surprisingly, she smiles. "That sounds nice, Marcus."

I bask in exactly how nice it feels for a moment, and then her phone buzzes again. She tenses even before she reads it.

"New number?" I ask, already standing.

"Can someone even do that tonight?"

There's no price I wouldn't pay for her safety and peace of mind. Someone will certainly open the doors for us tonight.

CHAPTER 20
Elise

I go downstairs to pick Lacey up from the doorman. Technically, with Marcus' or my permission, they'll let her go up on her own, but I need the time in the elevator to warn Lacey of what she's getting into.

She blinks at me from beside the doorman's desk. "This is where you live?"

"It's a long story." I nod my thanks at the doorman, then go to turn back to the elevator, but Lacey catches my arm.

"Start talking," she insists. "I don't hear from you for like a month, and now you're living in a place like this? No chance this is actually your apartment."

I squirm slightly under her grip, because she's hit the nail on the head. It's not my apartment, and I'm essentially a free-loader roommate. Worse than that, I'm a free-loader roommate who's actually getting paid to be here.

Marcus insisted I take today off when Lacey agreed to come by, so I made a big pot of stew last night, hoping leftovers would get us through today. But not actually needing to cook while

Lacey is here doesn't change that I'm essentially a hired worker who's taking advantage of Marcus' hospitality.

I sigh, moving the two of us closer to the elevator before I explain. No point spilling my sorry story for the doorman, even if I'm sure he has some thoughts on what I'm doing here already.

"Ethan and I split," I tell her evasively. "It got ugly."

"And you won the lottery?"

"And a client of mine offered me a place to stay," I correct.

"Some client." It's said with so much judgment that it makes my skin bristle a bit.

"Look, it's weird. But he's a nice guy and he's done something super nice for me. Way above and beyond what anyone would ever expect. And he just sees it as what anyone would do, because he's such a nice guy. He's home, too, even if he's probably in his office. So please, don't make it weird?"

The elevator dings, and she stares at me as she follows me inside. "This is real, right? It's not a hostage situation or some sort of thing I should rescue you from?"

"I don't need rescuing from Marcus," I tell her. The idea of ever needing saving from Marcus is ridiculous.

Then again, I once thought that the idea of needing saving from Ethan to be ridiculous. Maybe I'm not the best judge.

Lacey shrugs, shaking her head in disbelief. "Alright, then. Looks like you scored, really. No normal person lives somewhere like this."

The elevator dings again, letting us know we're at the penthouse level, and I lead the way through the front door, showing Lacey inside the apartment.

I never had Lacey over to my apartment in Brooklyn. She came to the apartment Ethan and I rented when I was still in school a few times, but Ethan had found her annoying, so I'd stopped asking her to come around. Looking back, it had clearly been just one more attempt to cut me off entirely.

Marcus is thankfully in his office when I push open the front door, so I don't have to deal with introductions right away. We've already had lunch, too, so we shouldn't see him for a while.

Not that I don't enjoy seeing him. It's like a little spot of sunlight in my day when he turns the corner to the kitchen and smiles at me. And when we spend the evening together, he's a comforting warmth next to me.

Maybe it's too much like the warmth of a safety blanket, though. That's why I've called Lacey after Marcus urged me to. If I'm moving from latching onto Ethan to latching onto Marcus, am I getting any better?

No. I'm just getting worse, really, because everything Marcus is giving me is something I could never hope to duplicate on my own. I might be able to dig my way out of the damage Ethan did to me, eventually. I would never be able to dig myself out of fully relying on Marcus.

It doesn't matter that Marcus doesn't seem like someone who would ever hurt me. Ethan didn't either, and I'm not making the same mistakes twice.

"God damn," Lacey says, interrupting my thoughts about Marcus. "This is something, girl."

Valerie has done a lot of work. The already-impressive apartment with its huge windows and million-dollar view now looks like it's positively dripping in luxury and comfort. It's an eclectic mix, but Valerie made it all work together.

I thought millionaire businessmen liked the minimalist aesthetic that the apartment was decorated with when I first started working here, with the sharp angles and crisp lines and lack of comfort. But Marcus' taste is much more homey.

"Yeah," I say. "Want to sit down?"

Lacey takes off her shoes before walking any further inside, then follows me to the couch.

"So, Ethan," she prompts, pulling her legs up under her and clearly settling in for what she knows will be a long conversation.

I eye her speculatively, wondering how much she actually wants to know. It's not like she was close to Ethan, after all. I'm not even sure if she's close to me, really. "We split," I tell her. "Turns out, he was a little too controlling for me."

"He was an asshole," she mutters.

"He was sneaky," I say. "I didn't see it for a long time, but then he got bad. He didn't like that I worked for Marcus," I explain.

"Asshole," she says again, like that's that. She leans forward a bit, then says, "Marcus treats you right?"

"It's not like that," I protest quickly.

"I didn't say it was. But I can check if he's good to you anyway."

"He's fine," I tell her, not really wanting to discuss it. How do I explain how good Marcus is to me? No one else in the world is like Marcus. No one else cares for people like he does without expecting anything in return. No one else has ever been so caring, so generous. If I tell her what he's like, she's not going to believe me. Or worse: she's going to point out that I thought great things about Ethan, too.

"Do you want something to drink?" I ask, remembering my manners too late, but it makes the perfect excuse for changing the topic of conversation.

"Sure. Water's fine." She follows me into the kitchen when I go to pour her water out of the pitcher in the fridge, and she whistles low. "This is nice. You cook here every day?"

"Every day," I agree, looking around at the kitchen I've grown used to, the one that in my mind I keep calling mine.

"And is that as a resident or as staff?"

What a particularly thorny question. Staff, I suppose, because I certainly still get paid. As far as I know, Marcus hasn't said a single word to the service about me living here now and eating his food that he still won't let me pay for. I still get paid.

To tell the truth, now that I have practically no expenses, my salary is going a long way. My bank account—my bank account, now, completely mine and mine alone—looks healthy, and I might actually see myself out of debt in a year or two.

But I can't think like that, because this isn't a long-term solution. I'm not Marcus' kept woman, and he's not going to care for me forever. There's a limit on his generosity, surely. I'd be concerned if there wasn't.

"That stove costs twelve grand," Lacey says before I answer her question.

"Yup."

"I think that blender costs my rent payment."

"It probably does."

"This man is rich-rich, huh?"

"You have no idea." *I* have no idea. I know he works in an import/export business and makes a shit ton of money, even if I can't define what he does day-to-day. I know that at least some of the money has to be serious generational wealth, given everything he's said about his parents and his childhood.

"Nice." She drains most of the water in one gulp, so I take the cup back and refill it.

"How's the catering business?"

She shrugs. "Busy time right now, with holiday parties booking up. So I can't complain. I don't sleep, either, but money is money." She looks me over, then eyes the kitchen. "Any chance you're looking for work?"

Even when I move out, I think Marcus will still want me to cook for him, and that should be enough to keep me going. "I'm all set," I say, smiling. "But I'll keep you updated if I am." I pour myself a glass of water too, and we make our way back to the couch.

She sighs. "For as out-there as you can be, you're good help, El. I wouldn't mind having you as a permanent partner."

A warm brush of pride surges through me. "You'll find someone."

"Maybe," she says, then brings her legs back up under her once more. "Well. Now that you're free of Ethan and cooking on a twelve-thousand dollar stove, how's the blog? Bet you can make great things."

I've posted a few new recipes, but not as many as she clearly thinks I have. "I've always had a policy about using a client's ingredients for my blog," I say.

"But you live here."

"But he buys the food. And when I'm cooking, I'm on the clock."

She chucks a pillow that probably costs several hundred dollars at me. "Girl, please. As if a guy who casually moves you in here would care if you take pictures before he eats."

She's probably right, but I haven't had the courage to ask yet. "Maybe," I deflect. "Tell me about the parties you have coming up."

We chat for an hour or so, and thankfully we avoid the topic of Marcus or my living situation or Ethan. Lacey tells me about her last job, and the venue's horrifically poor facilities. She's in stitches now, but I'm sure it was grueling at the time.

I hear the click of the office door opening almost on instinct now, like my body is trained for it. I've already noticed that Marcus coming to see me is the best part of my day, and apparently my body has started to respond like Pavlov's dogs.

Lacey's voice trails off when she hears his footsteps. When he turns the corner into the kitchen area, he stops and smiles, and my brain blanks out for a moment.

It's not even a big smile. I've seen bigger from him, more inviting. Smiles I could drown in. This one is just an everyday smile, and I still can't think for a moment.

Fuck. I need to scramble to remind myself that this is just a friend doing me a favor. That someone like Marcus is not my knight-in-shining-armor, happily-ever-after.

He's a millionaire that I work for. His generous heart doesn't change that fact, even if it makes my own heart confused.

"Hi. I'm Marcus," he says, turning his attention to Lacey.

She frowns. "I know you from somewhere."

"We've actually met," he acknowledges. "A charity dinner. Elise was cooking there."

"That was you?" she chuckles. "You really liked her food."

"You have no idea." His voice is deep and full of promises. Promises he doesn't intend to make, which I have to remind my heart of.

He turns away to get his own drink, and Lacey turns to me, mouth partially open and waggling her eyebrows at me, a gesture so ridiculous that I have to suppress a laugh, or else Marcus will know something is up.

Is this what Lacey and I could have been, if Ethan wasn't already in my life? If I wasn't willingly cutting off any and all connections at his slightest hint that he didn't like them?

Marcus turns around with a glass of water in his hand. "Don't mind me," he says. "I'm headed back to work."

I watch him as he goes. I know full well that he has a mini-fridge with a pitcher of filtered water and a few sodas next to his desk in his office, and he has no need to come out here.

He's checking on me, which I think is kind of sweet.

It's also just one more sign that my mind is misreading. Marcus is the type of guy who's concerned about people. It seems to be just a part of who he is. It doesn't mean anything else.

When he disappears back to his office, I turn back to Lacey, who's just smiling smugly at me.

CHAPTER 21

Marcus

T hanksgiving isn't a holiday I'm particularly prone to celebrating.

I wasn't born in this country. I'm older than the United States. There's nothing particularly compelling about the holiday to me, so I typically ignore it. But that isn't an option this year.

Elise deserves a moment to celebrate. And really, if we're truly celebrating what we're thankful for, then I have a list as long as Elise is tall.

The trouble becomes making this an actual holiday for her. I don't want to give the impression that I'm looking for her to serve me. The solution I arrive at while I'm supposed to be in an acquisitions meeting one afternoon is relatively ingenious, even if Elise seems gob smacked by it.

"You want to cook... for me?" she checks, like she's convinced she suddenly has a hearing problem.

I nod. "Yes. I told you, Elise, you're not expected to work on holidays."

She opens her mouth, then shuts it, seemingly holding something back before it comes spilling out, anyway. "Can you cook, Marcus?" Her words are laced with judgment, a clear condemnation of what she thinks of my abilities.

A not inaccurate one, either, I'm afraid to say. It's not exactly my skill set.

Make a business deal? I can do that. Find a rare, one of a kind artifact? Well within my skill set. Strike fear into the hearts of many? Easy. But cook a Thanksgiving meal?

I'll figure it out, and it won't be as good as what she makes us every single day, but I'll do my best.

I could hire someone to do it, I suppose, or order food from a restaurant, but that would defeat the point. I'm not doing this to pass off the job. That would send a shitty message; the point of this is to show her that I'm just as capable of providing for her as she is for me.

So I don't let her judgmental looks or my distinct lack of knowledge change anything. I'm going to do this. It's going to be impressive.

I use the internet to help me compile a grocery list, and go shopping alone a few days before Thanksgiving. The store is an overcrowded elbow-to-elbow nightmare, but I get through it.

There's a strange feeling as I get out of my car at the store. I've felt it every time I've escorted Elise to the store recently, and it doesn't take a genius to figure out that it's Ethan, spying on his meal that got away.

When Elise is with me, I have to ignore him, just stepping between her and where I assume his prying eyes are, trying to use my body to block her. Now that I'm alone, the crowd of humans keeps me in check while I try to formulate how I can root him out and potentially end him.

Before I figure out a strategy, the feeling disappears. Clearly, without Elise here, he's lost interest.

I can't move for a long moment, my anger holding me in place as the fury surges through my body. Ethan really should have known better than to disobey a dragon.

I force myself to take a deep breath. He's gone for now, and today is not about him. It's about Elise.

I want to give her this. She doesn't like gifts, and has barely accepted the simple things I've provided to make her life easier. So I want to be able to give her this, something she understands, something she gives to me. Something practical and straightforward and hopefully meaningful.

In a reversal of roles, she sits at the counter while I cook. Only I'm sure I look much more frazzled than she ever does.

I like to think I'm usually calm, cool, collected, and hopefully not too painfully lovesick while I sit at the counter watching her. Elise, in contrast, seems slightly frazzled, making little aborted hemming and hawing sounds that only raise the tension.

I know I'm not good at this, but I didn't think I'd be so bad that I'd give her anxiety. Finally, it seems to be the last straw, and she pushes to her feet. "What if we cooked it together?"

I pause, whisk in my hand, and consider for a moment. That could work. In fact, it might be the perfect solution.

"Alright," I say, making a little bow to indicate that I'm handing the space over to her. "I'll be your sous chef."

She moves like a shot, like she's been desperate to get into the kitchen and fix every one of my mistakes. I stay out of her way, watching with amusement as she moves around, getting her hands on everything I have going.

Her eyes are intent on her work, like the whole world is gone except for the kitchen in front of her. And I can't take my eyes off of her when she moves, leaning up to pull spices from the rack in the cabinet by the stove, her cozy green sweater pulling up slightly.

She's always beautiful. But here, she's happy, and that makes her practically glow.

I touch her hip, just lightly, just for a moment, my fingers briefly pressing over the fabric of her leggings. "I'm here to help," I remind her softly, trying to get her valuable attention back on me, just for a second. "So, give me a job."

She turns away from the food to me, looking me up and down, making my breath catch. I'm still standing too close to her, but she doesn't seem afraid like almost every other human does when they're this close to me.

Instead, she smiles. "Think you can handle chopping some herbs for me?"

Chapter 22
Elise

Working as a private chef, the only time I have to work with others in my kitchen is when I used to moonlight for Lacey's catering business. I'm not used to sharing space, and I wouldn't guess I'd like it very much.

But there's actually something comforting about it, something soft and gentle. The herbs he's cutting are an uneven mess, and it's taking him forever, but the soft clicks of the knife hitting the cutting board behind me are a reassurance.

I can't believe that he tried to cook me dinner. And not just any dinner, but an entire Thanksgiving meal.

This man hires a full-time personal chef, a housekeeping service, and an interior decorator to entirely re-do his already expensively furnished million-dollar apartment. This man doesn't spend his time on the menial, everyday things that the rest of us worry about. But he's been determined to cook me a meal.

When was the last time someone cooked a meal for me? Other than going to a restaurant—which is a truly rare event—I can't think of the last time. Maybe my mother, but I'd done most of the cooking in our house since I was thirteen or so.

It doesn't matter that his meal would have been a disaster and little better than inedible. It really is the thought that counts.

But that sums this man up in a nutshell. He's thoughtful. He invites me into his home, and then he makes sure I have everything I need and that I'm comfortable. And he wants to make sure I don't feel like I have to cook for him on the holiday.

I turn, looking for the zester, but Marcus is right there, his warm heat and large body boxing me in. I freeze, and he does the same, standing stock still, watching me with eyes that remind me of a banked fire.

He holds perfectly still, the only thing moving being his chest as he seems to take in big gulps of air, like I've asked him to run a marathon and not chop herbs. "Are you okay?"

"I," he says slowly, like the words are coming from somewhere deep inside him, as his eyes rake over me, "am great."

He certainly is. I look him over now, unable to help it, seemingly liberated by him looking at me like he is.

For a businessman who sits in his home office most of the day, he keeps himself in great shape. I've never even seen him go to the gym, but Marcus is made of lean muscle, powerful and self-assured without being too flashy.

Flashy or not, he always carries himself with an air of confidence, a self-assuredness that I doubt anything could shake.

And usually that wouldn't be attractive—self-assured men are usually hiding a mean-streak a mile long—except for his eyes. I've never, not once, seen his eyes be anything less than kind.

Is it my imagination, or is he bending his head closer to me? I tilt my head up, captivated by those eyes, and then, before I know what I'm doing, I'm kissing him.

It's a sweet kiss, a tentative brush of lips, and it's over before it really begins. The real world comes rushing back to me, my brain finally escaping his sweet eyes and intoxicating presence and letting me just think.

This incredibly rich and powerful man that I'm basically assaulting in his own kitchen doesn't want me. This man has been kind and generous by letting me stay here, and now I'm going to ruin everything with my greed.

I rip away from him, squeak out, "I'm so sorry," and run away.

CHAPTER 23

Marcus

I stare, watching the spot she disappeared from, trying to force my brain to catch up to what just happened.

Her lips were so soft and achingly sweet under mine, and just when I was half a second from turning the kiss into something more—something no doubt hungry and desperate—she apologized and fled.

What the fuck could she feel the need to apologize for? Surely she knows I'm obsessed with her. I couldn't have been more obvious, only resisting saying anything out loud in deference to the abusive piece of shit she just left and her recovery from that relationship. She can't not know.

Maybe that's why she's apologizing. Maybe she didn't feel anything when we kissed, and she's apologizing instead of flat-out rejecting me.

The dragon inside me flinches from the thought. Our mate rejecting us would be devastating. Well within her rights, of course; her choice is hers. But I can't pretend it wouldn't destroy me.

There's a crashing sound of something being knocked over from her bedroom. I need to move. I need to make myself face this.

I'm a damn dragon, and I'm not known for retreating when things get tough. Trying to convince my mate that I'm worth her time is a different type of conflict than I usually confront, but I can handle it like any other.

I check the stove, turning off the burners. The turkey still has two hours to go, so I leave it, forcing myself to take a deep breath before I go to her room.

The door is partially open, but I knock anyway, not wanting to start this surely awkward conversation on the wrong foot. "Can I come in?"

There's silence for a few seconds that seem to stretch on forever, then, finally, "Yes."

I push the door the rest of the way open, standing in the door frame to look over the space. It's immediately obvious the crashing sound came from her knocking over a lamp, and that she'd knocked it over trying to get to the duffle bag that's currently on her bed.

"Where're you going?" I ask her, and I can't quite make my voice come out evenly, immediately choked up to see her packing to leave me.

She doesn't look away from the bag. As far as I can tell, there's nothing in it yet; it's just spread open on her bed, with her sitting next to it, staring at it forlornly. "I'm so sorry, Marcus. I crossed a line."

I don't know how to respond. It feels like the ground has been pulled out from under me, and until I have a better idea of my footing, I can't keep moving forward. How do I convince her to stay?

Where will she even go? Dammit, I don't think she has a place to move to. Maybe Lacey will take her in. I don't like the idea of Elise couch surfing, but it's infinitely better than the alternative.

It pales in comparison to what I can provide for her here, though. I've tried so hard not to make her uncomfortable, to give her everything she needs without crossing any lines. I wanted her to warm up to me in her own time, and I didn't push.

But that's all for nothing, because she's packing to leave me.

She continues talking, unaware of my racing thoughts. "What I did, that was unacceptable. You've been so nice to me, and you've given me so much, and I took advantage of you. I'll get out of your hair. Give you some space. Get my head on straight before I come back to work on Monday. Unless..." She darts a quick glance at me, there and away again, "Unless I don't have a job anymore. Which I would understand."

She speaks so fast that it takes my racing thoughts a second to catch up. Take advantage of me? I'd like to see her try.

"Elise..." I begin, then stop, unsure where to even start about how wrong she is.

171

But she must read my hesitation as rejection, because her face crumbles. "I understand. I'm sorry. I'll—"

I don't give her a chance to finish the thought. I cross the room, stop in front of her, and drag her up into another kiss. I try to be careful about pulling her around, knowing I'm stronger than her, but I'm desperate, needing to feel her, needing to reassure her that whatever is going through her head is wrong.

She takes a moment, but then she kisses me back so sweetly, leaning up against me to get closer. When I try to taste her mouth, she opens her lips for me immediately.

I pull back reluctantly. "You're not fired," I murmur, wanting to ensure that there's not even the slightest bit of confusion.

"I got that," she asks, tilting her head up for another kiss, her dark eyes sweet and soft between half-lowered lids. There's so much promise in them, like I can see the entire perfect future in her eyes.

I kiss her again, but the idea of that future stops me from pushing it any further. The dragon is practically roaring his frustration with my hesitation when our mate is standing before us hungry for more, but he doesn't know shit about existing in the real world. He can wait patiently.

I peck her on the lips, then kiss her nose, then her forehead. She pulls back before I do, and I can see the emotions warring on her face, the confusion, the frustration, all mixed with her uncertainty about saying anything.

Elise, I realize suddenly, is too used to being on shaky ground. Ethan ensured that, yes, but her thinking I'd fire her over a kiss tells me that Ethan isn't the sole culprit, and I've inadvertently played into the same issues. And I need to do better for her.

That means making my thoughts crystal clear to her. "Elise, I have been interested in you since we met. I tried not to be, I tried to be satisfied with your friendship, but I can't deny how badly I want you. And I'm honored that you're interested in me too."

"Honored," she repeats, a half smile crossing her face, making her somehow more beautiful. Her arms reach up to wind around my neck, trying to pull me back down to her. "Sometimes, you know, you sound so old-fashioned."

I'm sure I do. Frankly, it's a miracle that I don't always sound old-fashioned. I try to keep up with the times, but it's a big ask.

I resist letting her pull me back down. "I wanted to make that perfectly clear so you understand where I'm coming from for what I say next."

She raises her eyebrow, clearly not impressed with my delay. "Alright, Marcus. I'm listening."

"You, Elise Wilson, deserve romance. You deserve to be dated and seduced. You deserve every nice thing I can give you. And that includes a proper first date."

"A first date?" she repeats, incredulous. "Does that Thanksgiving dinner you were cooking for me count? Or any of the times we've had dinner and lunch together?"

A part of me aches to say yes. To call it a date, to say it's good enough, and to go back to kissing her stupid. But I know better. I know she deserves better.

"Nothing we would just do anyway counts as a date," I decide. "Trust me: when it's a date, you'll know it. There won't be any confusion, Elise. I'll be the guy there seducing you."

"You could seduce me right now," she complains, her hands dropping from my shoulders down to the front of my shirt, trailing down my chest.

I risk leaning down to kiss her forehead, trusting myself to not get carried away. "Elise. You are worth all the stops being pulled out. Don't sell yourself short."

When I pull back to look at her, she's staring back at me, an odd look on her face. I'll show her how to appreciate herself properly. I'll make sure she learns what it means to be truly cherished.

I need to separate from her before I give in, and I need to do it without letting her know how close I am to falling over that precipice. "We should check on dinner."

She nods, almost absently, still watching me. "Am I going to have to wait long for this date, Marcus?"

"Saturday?" I ask. That will give me just enough time to plan something worthwhile. Surely I can wait until Saturday.

She narrows her eyes, assessing me. I don't breathe until she nods. "Saturday," she agrees.

Saturday. I just have to think of how to impress her before Saturday.

CHAPTER 24
Elise

Thanksgiving dinner is a delicious if awkward occasion, and we rush through it to escape the tension.

Damn him for insisting on a date.

Should I be grateful that he doesn't want to just fuck me and call that good enough? Absolutely. Do I remember that right now at this moment? Barely.

I'm burning up for him. I enjoy being touched, crave it, and I don't think I realized how badly I've been missing it until now. And Marcus' touch is electric, leaving me desperate for more.

Resisting crawling into his lap during dinner is a heroic effort.

And it's only when I'm lying in bed that I pause and think about the fact that Marcus has more money than I could even comprehend, and I can't imagine what someone like that considers a date.

I don't even own clothes nice enough for a date more in my income bracket. When was the last time I went out on a date? I can't even guess. Ethan and I didn't really go out much.

Well, we made enough food today that I won't need to cook tomorrow. I'll have a few hours to slip out and buy a dress. I'll have to brave the crowds of shoppers on Black Friday, but there's really no other option.

And shoes. I definitely don't own heels anymore, either. I own two pairs of clogs and a pair of beaten up Converse, and none of those are date shoes.

Nerves spark in my gut, thinking about what exactly I'm getting myself into. New shoes, new dress, a type of date that I probably can't even comprehend. But there's excitement there too.

That was a hell of a kiss.

I roll onto my side, drawing my knees up slightly. One kiss shouldn't realign my worldview, but here I am, realizing just how much I missed with Ethan.

Ethan never would have insisted on taking me on a proper date first. He never would have said that I was someone worthy of being seduced.

No, Ethan had just expected me to be there, no seduction necessary.

All thoughts of the dress and the shoes and being made to wait fall aside. It's nice to be wanted, really wanted. Wanted enough to wait and to do it right.

When I broach the idea of going shopping with Marcus, his brow furrows. I expected him to be working, which would allow me to slip away mostly unnoticed for a while, but he evidently took the day off to give himself a long holiday weekend.

A part of me wants to know if he'd always planned to do that, or if last night changed things. Most of me is too scared to find out.

"I'll take you," he says.

"It's Black Friday," I remind him, trying to deter him. "It's going to be crazy out there."

"Black Friday isn't much of a thing where we're going," he dismisses.

I raise an eyebrow. "It's very much a thing at every single department store around here, Marcus."

"We're not going to a department store."

"Marcus, a department store is where my budget is," I hedge. Money feels like a thorny topic, and I don't want to imply that he doesn't pay well, or that I'm asking for more. I'm not, and a department store dress is just fine with me. Besides, I definitely don't want to ask this man for money.

"Where your budget was before, maybe, but not now," he brushes it off.

"My budget hasn't changed."

He reaches out to take my hand across the counter, and all I can notice is how warm his skin and gaze are. "Elise, part of being seduced is letting me spoil you. Showing you what you mean to me."

"I don't need fancy things, Marcus. And I'm not dating you to get them." I nearly stumble over *dating you*, not even sure that's the right words for what we're doing.

"I'm well aware," he grumbles, and when I just stare at him, completely thrown where that might be coming from, he clarifies. "Do you have any idea how many gifts I've tried to offer you, Elise? Gifts you've turned down. It's maddening."

I can't help but smile again. "I'd take another one of those kisses. If you're in a giving mood."

He slides closer to me and kisses me, a gentle, sweet thing that's over far too soon. I should be grateful he's so gentle, I remind myself, thinking of how I felt last night. I should be grateful that he cares enough to take things slow.

Instead, I'm just hungry for him. And, judging by the way he watches me when he pulls back, he is too.

"Kiss delivered," he says, his voice lower than I thought possible, a rumble that makes me shiver. "But you're still getting the shopping trip, Elise. When do you think you'll be ready to go?"

Marcus has a car service take us to a shop that's so exclusive it doesn't even need to advertise that it's a store. I can see what he meant about Black Friday not mattering at a place like this.

Once we get past the bland exterior, the interior is a classy show of opulent money. It's clear why Marcus likes this place; if I didn't know better, I would assume he'd chosen the decorating scheme.

A young woman with her red hair pulled back in a severe-looking bun hurries over to us. "Mr. Golde. So good to see you."

He nods his head, then steps aside slightly, gesturing me forward. "This is Elise. She's looking for a few dresses, and a few pairs of shoes."

The woman gives me a perusing look, and I get the feeling she knows every single one of my measurements, my preferred type of underwear, and the appendicitis scar on my stomach just from that one look. She nods. "I'll be back shortly," she promises.

When she darts off, I turn to Marcus. "You shop here a lot?"

"Never," he says as someone else hurries over with flutes of champagne. "I called them after we spoke, though. This place requires appointments."

"They act like you're here all the time," I say, accepting it because it would feel rude not to, despite it being eleven in the morning on a Friday.

"Places like this thrive on two things: relationships and word of mouth. So they'll do whatever it takes to make you feel like you're building rapport with them," he explains as he sips his champagne, clearly not worried about the time.

I take a sip too, and damn, this is good. Champagne is always a very special occasion thing, but I shudder to think just how special occasion this bottle they pop open for strangers on a random Friday is. Just how much money am I drinking, exactly?

I assume someone will direct us to sit down, but almost immediately the woman with the severe bun is back, pushing a rack of clothes in front of her. "Thoughts?" she asks, stopping the rack in front of us, looking back and forth between the two of us like she's not sure who she should be asking.

Because she's not, I realize. While Marcus made clear that the dresses are for me, it's equally obvious that he's paying.

But Marcus just turns his attention to me, letting me make the decision, so I look them over. Each dress looks impeccably made, with clear, bright colors and relatively simple cuts. They also look far too nice for someone like me.

"This is a little more formal than I was anticipating," I say, stumbling over my words, not wanting to seem ungrateful or like an uncultured idiot.

Marcus isn't deterred, though. "Try them on anyway?" he asks. "Indulge me."

He watches me with those gentle, earnest eyes, and I don't want to say no, not after what he said about gifts earlier. It's obvious giving is important to him. I don't really think I can say yes either, though, so I just nod, grabbing one of the hangers at random.

"Oh, take the whole rack in," the woman says, and pushes it over without waiting to hear from me.

When she pushes it into a changing room four times bigger than I expected, she doesn't leave, and it becomes apparent to me that she intends to help. "I got this on my own," I say, hoping it comes out firm.

She just blinks. "If any alterations are needed, or additional sizes, it's best that I'm here to help."

I turn to Marcus for some support on this, but he's being shown to a seating area and not paying me much attention.

Fine. I can either raise a stink about this, or accept it. I don't honestly care that much if this woman, who clearly does this for a living, sees me in my underwear, so I just accept her presence and close the curtain.

"I'm Elise," I tell her, hoping to break the ice.

"Amanda. Try the blue one?" she says, offering a dress to me.

Just touching it tells me it's expensive in a way I could never hope to afford, but I force myself not to think about it. Marcus wants to give me gifts, he said. So I'm going to accept this one.

One dress. One date. Then, we can negotiate from there.

Love languages are mostly a pseudoscience, but they're a pseudoscience that my mom was obsessed with when I was growing up. Real or not, I vividly remember her talking about them every time one of her relationships fell apart. It's obvious that if you had to classify Marcus, his love language would be giving gifts. Judging by the way his eyes get all soft and his voice all low and grateful when I cook, I'd guess acts of service would be his favorite way to receive affection.

I remember thinking when I first got together with Ethan that physical touch was my love language, and that worked out really well in that relationship for a long time. I guess it's time to see if it still does it for me.

But after this date. If that's Marcus' rule, then I'll follow it. Something about his proclaimed desire to seduce me is undeniably nice.

Amanda straightens the seams of the dress, getting right into my space. Then she steps back, running a critical eye over me. "Passable, although I think we can do better. Do you want to see what Mr. Golde thinks?"

I almost say I don't need Mr. Golde's permission to choose clothes, but, well, if he's paying, then I suppose he does get the final say. So I nod and push open the curtain, stepping out and hoping to get his attention.

I have it immediately, his eyes turning to me as soon as the curtain pulls back. "What do you think?" I ask.

He stands from his chair, the mostly empty flute of champagne still in one hand. "What do you think?" he returns, stepping closer.

I shrug. "I've never been on a date that requires a dress this fancy." I suppose for some people, this type of dress might be normal. It's not like Amanda gave me a ball gown to try on. The dress hits just above my knees, and the fabric is simple, with clean lines and no extraneous decoration, but everything about it screams money, nonetheless.

"I'm all for casual dates, too," Marcus promises me. "But for this first date, let me pull out all the stops. Let me make a big deal out of it. Out of you—you deserve it."

I duck to hide my flush. If he's not careful, all this is going to go to my head.

"You didn't really answer the question," he prompts. "Do you like the dress?"

I stop to consider for a moment before answering. "It's stiff," I admit. "And fancy dress or not, I'd prefer something with a little more movement, I guess? If that makes sense."

He nods seriously, like my complaint is the most important thing he's heard all day. "Go tell her that," he says, nodding his chin towards the changing room. "She'll understand."

I'm halfway back to the changing room before I realize he didn't offer his own opinion on the dress.

It takes the better part of two hours, but I eventually leave with a dress carefully packed in a garment bag. It's a deep green, because Amanda advised me that "jewel tones really suit you," and, as Marcus promised, more unstructured and flowy. Despite that, it still manages to do amazing things with my bust.

Much to my consternation, Marcus talks me into buying three other dresses. "I thought you said one formal date," I say quietly.

"You never know what the future holds," he says. "While we're here and they have your measurements, we might as well get them."

I deliberately chose not to look at the price as Marcus handed over a black credit card that matches the one in my wallet that I refuse to touch.

I'm carrying the garment bag, but Marcus is carrying the shopping bag that has the strappy silver heels in it. They have a thick wedge, so I won't have to pretend I'm comfortable balancing on knife points. Amanda had offered to pull lingerie and jewelry too, but I'd declined, and Marcus had, thankfully, not pushed it.

Maybe I should have taken her up on the lingerie, if tomorrow's date goes how I want it to. But I have at least one nice set in my drawers at home.

Marcus puts his free hand at the small of my back as soon as we emerge from the store, and I feel his warmth like a brand through my shirt. It sends tingles through me, and they're distracting enough that it takes me a long moment to realize that he's looking around suspiciously, like he's sensing danger.

"You okay?" I check in.

His hand presses more firmly at my back for a split second. "I'm great," he says, turning to give me a small smile before looking away again. "I finally got you to accept a gift."

"You know, I live in your house rent-free," I point out. "That's a gift that I've been accepting."

He ignores that and goes back to scanning the street. "Are you looking for someone?"

"I hope not," he mutters, and it's only then that it clicks in my mind.

"Ethan."

"I don't think he'd show up here."

But we've both been slightly paranoid since the texts. He hasn't found my new number, thankfully, but I suppose it's not out of the realm of possibility that he could find us.

I doubt Ethan would go to all that effort. He never liked working hard for things, and I want to tell Marcus he doesn't have to worry so much.

But his worrying feels kind of nice, so I keep my thoughts to myself.

"Car's up here," he says, and, hand still on my back, he leads me to the car.

CHAPTER 25

Marcus

I pace my bedroom, desperate to burn off some of the nervous energy while waiting for Elise to be ready.

I've pulled out all the stops I can for tonight. I was serious yesterday when I promised her that I like casual dates. Being curled up on the couch to watch a movie sounds just as appealing as a fancy dinner or a Broadway show. But for tonight, I want to impress her.

And not just to show off my wealth and my power, although I admit there's a small part of me that wants her to see what I can give her. But mostly, I just want her to understand that she's worth someone pulling out all the stops. That she deserves someone who puts that type of effort in for her.

I want her to see that I'll treasure every damn moment with her, and that I can be the exact opposite of what she had before. I want her to know what it's like to receive care and effort instead of always giving it. I'm hoping that she'll understand what I'm trying to say.

So it starts with a nice dress, not because I care one bit what she chooses to wear, but because I want to make sure she feels special tonight. I saw her in the dress briefly at the store, but I'm eager to see her tonight, all dolled up and ready to go.

I can hear her moving around in her room. She's been in there for a while, and a quick glance at my watch tells me she should be ready to go soon. I force myself to take a deep breath and leave my room.

Dragons don't get nervous, especially over something like a date. Then again, I've never dated my mate before, and you only get one chance to make a first impression. This has to go well, well enough to convince her to stay with me.

I'm only pacing in the living room for a few minutes before I hear her door open. When I turn, she's walking into the room, looking resplendent in her new dress and those strappy silver shoes. Her hair is loose for once, and she's curled it, making me hungry to play with her hair, to bury my face in it.

Maybe if the date goes well. But for now, I take a step forward, stopping just shy of touching her. "You look beautiful, Elise." She looks like an angel.

She blushes, making her skin glow pink even through the makeup she's wearing. "Thank you," she murmurs. "This dress is clearly something special."

"You make it beautiful," I tell her firmly, and she just blushes more, but she doesn't argue with me at the very least. I offer her my arm. "Shall we go?"

She looks at my arm for a moment, but then her red-painted lips twitch into a smile. "Old-fashioned," she murmurs, but takes my arm without protest, so I escort her out of the apartment.

I've chosen an exclusive, small restaurant on the Lower East Side. If I was aiming to dazzle her with trendy restaurants, there are several others that I'd think of first, but I brought her here because I think she'll genuinely like the food.

Elise looks over the restaurant with a keen eye. "Japanese-Mexican fusion?" she asks.

"You've heard of this place?"

She shrugs. The slightly off-the shoulder look of the dress shows off her beautiful cleavage, made more evident by the gesture. I want to add some hickeys there. I fight to draw my eyes back to her face. "I keep up on things people are trying. It interests me."

"Have you eaten here?"

"It can take weeks to get a table and it's out of my typical price point," she says, then, after hesitating a second, admits, "And Ethan wouldn't have liked it. So, no."

I steel myself against Ethan's name, not wanting to be angry going into the restaurant. Not tonight; tonight should be about Elise, and Ethan can stay away, both physically and emotionally.

"Then I'm glad I get to take you," I tell her, offering her my arm once more.

She looks at me sidelong as she accepts my arm. "Do I want to know how you just got a reservation?"

I shrug. "Same way I do a lot of things, I suppose. Money opens a lot of doors."

She doesn't say anything for a moment, but when the hostess finishes escorting us to our table, immediately ready and waiting for us upon arrival, she says, "That must be interesting. To just live like that. To have access to that kind of money."

I drop her arm so I can pull her chair out for her, then push it back in before taking my own seat. I like that she doesn't shy away from the conversation, that she isn't keeping her curiosity back. If she wants to know something, then I want to tell her.

"It's interesting," I say. "I've never known much different, though."

She touches her fork, turning it over, then back again, not looking up the entire time. "You saw my apartment from before, so you know. I'm very much not used to it."

I know. I have known, too, since the day I did the background check on her. What I don't know is how to tell her to get used to it, that yesterday's shopping trip and tonight's dinner and the gifts and everything else aren't one-offs, or just short-term courting gifts. That this is forever, and, as a dragon's mate, she's now the proud co-owner of a giant hoard of wealth.

We'll get there. First, we have to get through tonight.

The waiter is immediately at our side, offering wine and cocktails. "We're here for the chef's tasting," I tell him, and he nods, disappearing to return with the wine that will match our first course.

"I know you like trying new things and experimenting," I tell her. "So I hope the chef's tasting is okay. It's a prix fixe menu with four courses."

"Sounds great." She touches her fork again. "You didn't have to do all this, you know."

"I want to do all this. It's not an imposition—I'm happy to be out on a date with you."

She smiles shyly. "I'm just saying, I was—you know I've had the worst crush on you."

I didn't know that, actually. Did I catch her looking at me sometimes? Sure, but lots of humans do that. It didn't mean she wanted to do any more than look. "Why was it the worst?"

"Because it felt like a trap," she admits. "Ethan, the night he went off, he'd found out I was working for you. Was convinced I was cheating on him with you, and he lost it." There we go, the specter of Ethan coming up between us again. I want to exorcise that man from our lives entirely. But if Elise needs to talk about him—if that will help her recover after what he did to her—then I'll listen.

"And obviously I didn't cheat on him, but then you were so kind, letting me stay, and generous, and, well, you look like that, and every single day it just got harder to pretend I wasn't looking at you like that, and turns out maybe Ethan was right after all, just a little early in his prediction."

I turn that over in my head for a moment, forcing myself not to dwell on the fact that she was attracted to me, despite how much I liked hearing that. "You didn't cheat on Ethan," I point out. "He was a piece of shit who lost any right to your time or attention. What you do after him is entirely none of his business."

She smiles, wide and relieved. "Am I supposed to read that as an invitation to do you after him?"

That's not how I intended it, but I can absolutely accept that as a plan. "If you'd like. You know where my bedroom is."

Our waiter takes that moment to swoop in with wine, taking a moment to explain the selection, which we pay attention to with varying degrees of enthusiasm. Elise, at least, seems interested in the conversation, but I can't seem to take my eyes off of her.

That fucking dress. I remind myself to send some sort of bonus to the boutique.

But it's not the dress, not really. As nice as it is, her smile, the flush on her cheeks, the curve of her neck, it puts the dress to shame. When the waiter finally leaves us alone, I'm staring at her with a soft, unfocused gaze, simply basking in her glory.

She shifts in her seat, moving enough to get my attention. "That's not true, though, is it?" she asks.

I blink stupidly. "The wine?" I'm usually more coherent than this, right? Surely I must be. I run a company worth billions of dollars. Surely I must be able to string together a coherent sentence, a skill that has seemingly escaped me tonight.

"No. What you said about your room," she clarifies. "Or else we would have ended up there two days ago."

Fuck, now I'm an incoherent idiot who is also half hard underneath the tablecloth. "I was worried," I admit, because she deserves the truth.

"Worried?"

"That if I didn't get you to agree to a date first, you'd give me one night and then be done with me. And I'll do everything in my power to avoid that. I'm after more than that."

Neither of us has taken a drink yet, but Elise raises her glass to her mouth, then sets it down before even taking a sip. Her fingers are shaking ever so slightly. "How much more?"

Everything. I'm after an eternity, a bright future together. I'm after all her hours, I'm after gifts and movie nights and dates and long, lingering dinners and every single moment we can have together.

That seems a bit much to say on a first date, so I swallow it back and admit, "A lot more, Elise. Whatever you're willing to give me. You captivate me."

193

I see her mouth captivate, but she doesn't say anything for a long moment. Then she says, "You realize that I'm just me, right?"

I take it she doesn't mean anything positive by that, and I bristle at the insinuation. "I'm aware of who you are, Elise. You captivate me. You."

The waiter comes back with our first course, and it's a testament to the tension between us that Elise barely seems to notice.

"I'm not proposing," I tell her. Yet. I'm going to need a truly extraordinary ring sometime in the future, but humans are touchy about the timing of that type of thing. "I'm just telling you that what I'm looking for, it's serious."

She laughs softly, but it's an uncomfortable sound. "Well, I think you know me; I apparently only do serious relationships."

"This isn't like that," I promise, although I'm hard-pressed to explain why. I need her, I'm desperate for her, and while Ethan was a parasite and I want to give her the world, I know there are some uncomfortable similarities.

"Did you hire me because you were interested in me?"

"I hired you because I like your food," I promise her. Maybe the dragon had known the moment we tasted it, but I hadn't understood yet. I'd just been interested in the food. "Everything else came later."

She gives me a smile, and this one looks sincere. "There's truth behind the whole, the way to a man's heart is through his stomach, I guess."

The way to a man's heart—or at least mine—is by being Elise, but I know better than to say that out loud. "If you don't want to cook for me—"

She waves it away. "Ethical questions of dating my boss aside, I like what I do. I just wanted to make sure. You feel genuine, Marcus. I didn't want to tarnish that."

The guilt of the secrets I'm keeping from her goes down sour and heavy. I try to keep a straight face.

Soon. But not yet.

"What are you looking for, Elise?" I ask her instead.

She opens her mouth, then closes it, tilting her head slightly. "I want normal dates too," she says after a moment.

I look around. This isn't even the most over-the-top place I could take her. As a matter of fact, this is relatively tame. "This is normal."

"I don't need you to try to impress me, Marcus."

"I like impressing you."

She sighs. "I'm impressed. I was impressed the moment we met, you know that, right? You are an impressive person."

"That's not what I met by impressing you," I murmur, leaning a little closer. "Elise, I want to impress upon you how special you are. How you deserved to be cherished."

Her cheeks are bright pink, and that makes something low in my gut heat up. "Thank you," she whispers. "But I need both, Marcus. I can be cherished in ways that don't have this kind of price tag."

"I'll always cherish you," I promise. "So, prepare for greasy street-corner pizza and walks in the park too. What else?"

"I feel slightly uncomfortable that you're my boss, but I like my job," she admits.

I smile, because this thorny little problem has a neat enough temporary solution. "I'm not your boss. I don't pay you. Your company takes care of that." Semantics, maybe. But I'm not about to suggest that she quit. I don't think I'm secure enough to tolerate the idea of her giving the gift of her cooking to someone else yet, and I know she's not ready to believe that I'd happily support her for the rest of our hopefully very long lives.

She takes the Band-Aid to the problem easily, showing me she wants the convenient excuse as much as I do. "What else?"

She raises an eyebrow this time, her eyes brightening and her lip quirking. "Do I get to kiss you goodnight?"

The dragon inside me purrs at just the thought. "Angel, you can do whatever you want to me. If this is serious for you too." Would I let her have me if all she wanted was a few hours? Probably. I'm not a strong man, not when it comes to her. But I'm smart enough to know that I'll probably regret it later.

"I'm serious," she promises me, leaning closer so I can see the intensity in her eyes.

I feel like I could fly without my wings. "If you're serious," I tell her, "Then eat. Enjoy your dinner, so we can go home."

CHAPTER 26
Elise

It should be a crime to rush a dinner at a restaurant like this one. And if it is, then I am absolutely guilty.

I barely resist shoveling the food into my mouth to get it down faster. That would probably make Marcus change his mind about me, and anyway, I know he's paying through the nose for me to have the privilege of being here.

Do I know what I did to trick this man into thinking that I'm something special? No idea, unless I really did lure him in with food. But I think I'll stop looking the gift horse in the mouth and just accept it for as long as I can.

Finally, our four course meal is over, and while I can objectively say that it was delicious, I'm unable to put the level of thought into it I usually would. I should think about the menu, the careful work that goes into crafting such clever fusion food. I should maybe snap a few pictures for my blog. But I can't stop staring at Marcus, who's staring right back.

He pays, tipping generously, and we leave together. He keeps an arm around me while we wait for the car to pull up, eyes darting around, but for once, not even the thought of my ex can get to me. His hand on my lower back feels electric, even through the thick fabric of this dress.

I'm practically dancing out of my skin by the time we get back to the penthouse, rudely hurrying past the doorman with barely an acknowledgement. The elevator ride seems endless, and it's obvious that Marcus feels the same way, because the hand on my back slips lower, a tease of what's coming next.

He stops before he gets to my ass, though, which is really a shame. I want those hands on me. I want to feel him.

After Marcus fumbles the apartment door open, he slams it behind us and turns to me with eyes that are wild.

"Tell me exactly what you want," he says, stepping directly into my space, one arm wrapping around my waist again to pull me closer to him. "Be specific, Elise."

Be specific? The only thought in my brain is more, and now. I try to string a thought together. "Marcus—"

"Yes, Angel. What can I do for you?" he says, voice practically a croon, his grip on me tightening, his hands creeping down to squeeze my ass. He might be trying to play the gentleman, but he's as desperate as I am.

"I want you to fuck me," I tell him firmly. Then, unable to wait for him to act, I grab the front of his no doubt very nice suit jacket and go up on my tip-toes to kiss him. He groans into my mouth, biting gently at my lower lip like he needs to entice me to open up for him.

I knew he was tall, but I never realized how tall until my neck cricks from standing like this. Like he can read my mind, he lifts me and encourages me to wrap my legs around his waist.

"This okay?" he asks, voice a rasp against my neck. He presses a sucking kiss there, temporarily distracting me from responding.

"Okay," I agree. It's better than okay. The skirt of my dress is rucked up on my hips now, and my lacy panties, the nicest set I own, are pressed directly against him.

He's wearing too many clothes. I need to feel him, skin to skin, not allowing a single inch of air between us. I grind helplessly against him, wishing his clothes would simply disappear.

He breaks the kiss to mutter a low, drawn-out fuck, then groans and turns, walking with me in his arms, and puts my ass right on the kitchen counter.

I should tell him this isn't sanitary, but that is the very last thing on my mind. I pull him back towards me, using my legs to trap him right where I want him.

Marcus drops to his knees right on the kitchen floor. It's hard as shit, I know from experience, but he doesn't so much as wince, just running his hands up my bare calves, eyes hungry as he looks up at me. "Is this okay, Elise?"

My knees spread apart without any conscious input from me. "Please," I whisper.

He spreads my knees even wider with reverent hands, then slides them up my thighs to push my skirt up until it's bunched

199

around my hips. I want the dress gone, out of my way, but that would require moving, and I'm afraid if I move an inch, this will somehow all go away.

His fingers trace the blue lace of my panties with the lightest tease of a touch. I can barely feel it through the fabric, but it makes wetness pool between my thighs, nonetheless. "Lift your hips for me, Angel," he rasps, and I use my hands to support my weight so he can remove my panties.

Bare and exposed before his hungry eyes, I fight not to close my thighs, doing my best to let him look his fill. "Fucking beautiful," he rasps, and that's all the warning I get before he buries his face in my pussy.

Fuck, this man knows what he's doing with his tongue. He's so gentle with me, a delicate tease, like he has to warm me up to it. He flicks my clit with barely any pressure, like he wants to see how I'll react.

My legs subconsciously tighten around his head. I force them to relax, but he pulls back enough to say, "Put me where you want me, Angel. You can't hurt me."

He sounds so sure when he says it that I let my body respond as he drives me higher and higher, a slow, nearly tortuous ascent that has me moaning his name, letting the sound echo through the kitchen.

Marcus steers me towards my orgasm deftly, easily, like he already knows exactly how my body works. Maybe he does; maybe he knows it better than I do, I think half-deliriously, and then I fall over the edge, all thoughts completely wiped from my mind.

Marcus moves languidly, licking his lips as he looks up at me, a self-satisfied smile firmly in place. He looks like a cat, all contented smile and soft, watching eyes.

"You're very good at that," I tell him, my voice rough.

"No need to sound so surprised," he teases, not actually sounding the slightest bit affronted.

He nuzzles at my knee, pressing a kiss there with a sort of soft reverence that makes my breath catch.

I dare to reach down to touch his hair, letting the silky soft strands slide from my fingers. What kind of shampoo does he use? Or is it genetic?

Either way, he must like me touching his hair, because he kisses my knee again, then trails a few light kisses up my thigh. "What can I do for you?" I ask him softly, not wanting to break the moment that feels so precious between us.

He looks up at me with those soft eyes again, and then, like a switch is flipped, surges to his feet between my legs, startling me into wrapping my legs around him.

He puts his hands on my hips and lifts me like I weigh nothing. "Fuck this," he says, his voice so low that it might be called a growl. "The first time I fuck you is not going to be anywhere but a bed, no matter how fun the kitchen counter sounds." He squeezes my ass. "But we'll keep that idea in mind for later. I'm sure it'll come in handy."

"Not when I'm actually cooking, do you have any idea how unsanitary—" I start to say, but he cuts me off with a kiss.

CHAPTER 27

Marcus

The taste of her lingers on my tongue, sweet and addicting. She moans so adorably when she comes, too, and I'll never forget that sound.

In short, Elise is perfect. I always knew she would be, but now it's confirmed.

I walk us directly to my bedroom, needing her in my bed with a desperate sort of urgency that I've never felt before. Our bed. Is it too early to think that? Maybe, but I'm thinking it, regardless.

I lay her down gently on the bed, putting her in the center, and watch her smile and reach for me. I crawl over her, leaning in for a kiss and trying to touch every inch of her I can possibly reach. She's so fucking soft beneath me, lush curves that seem to fit my hands perfectly, and I want this dress out of the way.

It looked beautiful when she tried it at the store. It looked stunning on her tonight, but all I want is it gone. I need to see her, to hold her, to taste her skin underneath it.

She breaks our kiss, putting a hand on my jaw to stop me from chasing her mouth. "Marcus," she groans.

I kiss the palm of her hand. "Angel?"

She shivers when I call her that, and I kiss her palm again. Noted, and filed away for later.

"Marcus," she practically whines, squirming a bit under me, which forces a groan out of me. Fuck, is that sexy. I want to see what else I can do to make her squirm. "You're not going to damage this incredibly expensive dress." She smiles up at me. "Someone really sweet gave it to me as a gift."

Well, I definitely can't rip it now, not if she considers it a gift. I force my hand to be more gentle. "Then we need to take it off," I tell her, reaching down to find the hem and push it up, stroking the delicate, soft skin of her thighs.

She plucks at the shirt I'm still wearing. "You're overdressed too."

I reluctantly get off the bed, tugging her to a sitting position before going to my knees again. As close as I am to her sweet cunt, I'm more than tempted, but I refrain, instead reaching for the straps on her shoes, carefully unthreading them so I can remove them.

I set them aside carefully. They're a gifts she accepted from me just like the dress is, which makes them infinitely precious now. Plus, they're incredibly hot on her, and I want her to wear them again for me, maybe while wearing nothing else.

But that's not going to happen if I don't impress her tonight, so I re-focus on the task at hand. Namely, getting my clothes off like she asked.

My shirt is already gone, my shoes kicked off, and I'm reaching for my belt when she stops watching and stands to pull down her dress. I forget my own clothes, my hands still half grabbing my belt, and watch as her perfect skin is revealed.

Apparently, this is the type of dress that doesn't require a bra underneath, and I am the luckiest dragon to ever live.

Her skin looks so damn soft. I want to stroke every curve, want to kiss every inch. I want to consume her, pleasure her, turn her into the idol I worship. My fucking mate.

The dress hits the floor entirely, leaving her naked and bare before my eyes, and I drink the sight in like a starving man.

"You're still overdressed," she says quietly, shifting her weight to one leg. All that does is make the delectable curve of her hip pop out more, but her words cut through my thoughts.

Right. Overdressed. My hands scramble to unfasten my belt, then drop my trousers and underwear in one swift movement, kicking them off so they're out of my way. I'm usually nicer to my things, but in a competition between my clothes and Elise? It's no contest.

She's staring. "You're pierced."

I look down, which is stupid, because it's not like I need to confirm that I'm pierced. I know very well that I am, and it's been decades, but I very much remember the pain of doing it. "Yeah."

"Is that…" she raises a finger partway, pointing towards my dick for a moment before lowering her hand, "going to hurt when it's inside me?"

"I'll never hurt you, Elise," I tell her, suddenly solemn, because I need her to know this. "If anything, you'll like it. Trust me."

She looks down for a moment, her eyes darting to my cock, then back to my face. I can see the skeptical look, but it fades, and she's clearly decided to trust me. "Is that why you got it?"

"I don't need piercings to make you feel good, Angel," I tease, watching her flush even more. "I got it because I like pretty things, jewelry included."

It had seemed like the thing to do at the time, just one more opportunity to display beautiful little things, even if only to a very select audience. Besides, if humans could do it, I'd assumed it was well within my capabilities.

Her eyes dart downward for another look, like she feels that she needs to sneak a peek, when in actuality, I'll let her look all damned day if that's what she wants.

I'll let her feel it, too. With her hands, her tongue, her soft wet cunt—whatever she wants.

"Can I…?"

"Yes." It's out of my mouth before she can find the words, but I hardly need to hear them. Whatever she wants, the answer is yes.

She steps closer, and I watch the way she moves, eyes rapt as her breasts bounce slightly with the movement, as her hips swing. Then her hand is on me, too gentle and hesitant. "You're big," she blurts out.

"It'll feel good," I promise her. I guarantee it will. I won't allow it to go any other way.

I got her wet and dripping with my mouth, and I have every intention of having her soft and open for me before I even think of pushing inside of her. I plan to make her come all night long. And somewhere in there, she can learn that I was serious when I told her the piercing will feel good.

She strokes me, still too gentle. I bite my lip, wanting to let her explore, but she laughs slightly. "Tell me what you like, Marcus."

Fuck. I like her saying my name a hell of a lot, apparently, and my cock twitches in her hand. I look at her face to see her smirking slightly. She noticed, then, and I trust she'll take full advantage of it.

"I like you," I tell her. "Grip a little tighter, Angel."

She tightens her grip and moves her fist over my cock. I widen my legs, steadying myself so I can hold on as long as she'd like to play with me.

"I don't know if you can tell," she murmurs, looking at my cock instead of my face, "But I'm not the most experienced person. Ethan was..."

I get the picture without her needing to explain, and I can certainly get it without hearing his name. Ethan was the first and only before me. That dumbass really had the world and squandered it with his petty jealousy. I won't make the same mistakes. "That's fine, Angel," I tell her. It's more than fine. I'll blow her mind tonight, make sure I show her how it should be.

I've kept my hands to myself, letting her explore, but I think I've shown an incredible amount of restraint and frankly, I can't maintain it much longer. I trail one hand over her hip. Her skin is soft here like silk, and a few gentle brushes of my fingertips have her shivering, then have gooseflesh rising to her skin.

"Pretty Angel," I croon at her. "You need to tell me what you like." She doesn't answer me quickly enough, seemingly too focused on stroking my cock, now getting slightly more adventurous when playing with the piercing. It feels like every nerve in my body is on fire, begging for more of her touch. But I won't be deterred, not even when her hands are driving me mad. I want to know exactly what she likes, so I can ensure that tonight is perfect for her.

"You liked my mouth on you," I muse, moving my hand from her hip to her cunt, cupping her gently. "Came so sweet all over my tongue, didn't you?" She shivers, and I don't think it's from that gentle little touch I'm giving her. No, Elise likes listening to me talk to her. "What else do you like?"

"I like the idea of you inside me," she tells me.

"Lie down for me." She sits on the edge of the bed, then scoots back until she's once more in the center of it, spreading her thighs seemingly unconsciously for my eyes. Fuck, she's beautiful.

"Going to open you up," I tell her, crawling up the bed until I'm hovering over her. She doesn't lie down when I get in her space like I expected, though; she grabs my face and kisses me, deep and desperate, sucking on my lip and biting down. She doesn't release me until she gasps when I cup her cunt once more, sliding a finger inside her in a smooth, easy motion.

Her head falls back. She uses her arms to support her weight, so I'm left to stare at my absolute goddess of a mate, head tilted back, tits pushed up in the air and thighs spread as if she's welcoming me inside.

Because she's so beautiful and so fucking wet for me, I give her another finger, and then another. She groans, no longer even attempting to hold back. Good. I need her wild for me, hungry and chasing her pleasure. I need her to know that I'll always give it to her, too. "That's it," I encourage her, circling her clit with my thumb, needing to hear that desperate little groan again. I get my wish, which just makes me even hungrier for her. "Are you ready for more?"

She picks up her head to look at me, eyes glazed with lust, her lips parted slightly, looking the perfect picture of a debauched angel. I can feel that she's getting close. To tell the truth, so am I, desperate and starving for her. I need to know if we're going to finish with me inside her, or if I'm getting the both of us off with my hands.

"More," she agrees, eyes still hazy but locked onto mine. Her cunt squeezes around my fingers. "Marcus—"

Hearing my name on her lips could practically make me come. It's not even the name I was born with, and I've used dozens of names over the years. But I never want to be called anything else again. The way she says that name pulls at something directly inside me, making it more my name than anything else anyone has ever called me.

"I got you, Angel," I promise her. I slide my fingers out of her, listening to her whine as she's suddenly empty again. "I know," I sympathize. "Lie back for me." She does as I ask, looking even more like an angel with her hair spread around her as she reclines against the pillows, blinking up at me.

I spread her thighs so I fit between them, hitching one leg around my hip. "I'll go slow," I promise.

"Don't want you to," she murmurs. "Marcus—fuck me, please."

I abandon slowness in favor of something like measured and in control, or at least as much as I can be. I don't want to risk hurting her, but I'm also not planning on ignoring what she asks for.

She squirms on my cock when I bottom out, like she's somehow trying to get me even deeper. There's nowhere else for me to go, but when she gets my piercing at just the right angle, her eyes go wide and she whines.

I smirk, rolling my hips just slightly to try to duplicate that. There. Right there. She clenches around me, her leg tightening against my hip like she needs to hold me in place.

I told her it'd feel good.

I move my hips in earnest, driving into her in steady, deep strokes. I'm too close. She's too pretty, has been invading my mind every second since I met her, and I can still taste her on my tongue and can see her beautiful body move beneath me. No man could resist.

But I'm not coming without her. I find that spot with my piercing again, and at the same time I tease over her clit with my thumb. She shouts my name, her whole body tightening around me like a vice as she comes, and I give up on any last ounce of resistance I had, spilling inside her.

I'm mindless with it, thrusting inside of her through both our orgasms, desperate to fill her as white-hot pleasure bursts behind my eyes. When my senses return, I slow my thrusts, breathing like I just ran a marathon.

Her contented, fucked-out expression beneath me is beyond tempting. I can't resist kissing it right off her face, basking in her lazy, overwhelmed kisses. I kiss over her jaw, her cheeks, her nose, touching every inch of flushed skin I can reach. "Let me clean you up," I murmur, reluctantly pulling away from her so I can go to the en-suite to get a cloth for her.

I only buy nice things, yet somehow, my washcloths all feel scratchy in my hand, like I'm planning on cleaning my mate up with a burlap sack. It's unacceptable. I make a mental note to buy better, softer, more gentle washcloths for Elise before wetting one and returning to our bedroom, only to find her completely asleep, curled up in the center of the bed.

My heart might genuinely explode from how enamored I am with her. I gently pull her leg to the side so I can clean her up, but I can't resist pushing the come dripping down her thigh straight back inside her.

I watch the bead of white drip out of her again, rapt in a way that come probably doesn't deserve, except for when it's dripping out of my mate.

Because me coming inside her will change her. It's what makes our story not a guaranteed tragedy. It's why a dragon can have a human mate.

Elise will always be human, and I'm grateful for that, because I could never imagine her being any other way other than exactly what she is. But my come, my claim, is its own form of magic, as sure as the magic that lets me change from dragon to man, or hide amongst the shadows of the sky. And it's the form of magic that means she can stay with me, and that we can have forever.

I'm hit with a pang of guilt, which is the last thing I want to feel when I have my sleeping mate's warm skin under my hands. I try to push it away, but I can't quite do it, not yet.

I've functionally made her immortal—or as immortal as I am, at any rate—without telling her. She doesn't know a single thing about the truth of who I am, and I've changed her body.

It's not permanent, I remind myself. It's only permanent with, shall we say, repeated doses. I'll need to fuck her regularly for as long as we both want the immortality to last, or, that is to say, for the rest of our hopefully very long lives.

I'll tell her, I promise us both, stroking over her hip and abandoning the washcloth on the bedside table. I will. Just not yet.

Chapter 28
Elise

When I wake up, I take a long moment to process where I am and why I'm so warm.

Marcus keeps this place warm, but this amount of warmth is ridiculous. I'm sweating in bed.

I'm also naked. Why on earth did I fall asleep naked?

And I'm a little sore, too. It's this last realization that makes the pieces click into place, that makes me realize what I should have seen right away; this isn't my bed.

I'm in Marcus' bed, held by Marcus and under an impressive array of blankets and pillows. I'm naked and sore because we fucked last night, the memories of it sending a delicious jolt of warmth between my thighs. Unconsciously, I roll my hips, trying to get some friction. Judging by the warm skin I can feel when I move, he's naked, too.

He's also asleep, breathing softly against my neck in a way that makes something inside me go soft and gooey.

The man made my cunt go soft and gooey last night, but this isn't that. This is somewhere further north, and Marcus was right yesterday, at the restaurant—this is the type of thing you only do with someone you're looking for something long-term with.

This man wouldn't have anything as plebeian as a regular alarm clock by his bed, and I couldn't even begin to guess where my phone got to. But we were a little too distracted to fully close his blackout curtains, so I can see that the sun is fully up in a way that tells me it's likely far past time for me to get up.

Working my way out of Marcus' grip and the restraining pile of blankets and pillows is a Herculean task, but I manage it mostly by giving him some of the pillows to hold in replacement. When I'm at last free, I look around the room, debating.

No way am I squeezing back into that dress, all grubby and sleepy. And I suppose nothing is stopping me from walking naked to my bedroom to change, but...

But Marcus' shirt is right there, light blue and wrinkled from being tossed aside, which is weirdly endearing for a man who usually seems so careful with his things. I bet he polishes his shoes with some special ritual, but for me, last night? He tossed this shirt aside like it meant nothing.

So I grab up the shirt and slip it on, buttoning it partway. Even needing to fit over my breasts, it's still long enough to hit just below my ass. Soft, too. I thought dress clothes were meant to be stiff, but I've owned sweatpants less soft than this shirt.

I go back to my room as quietly as I can, where I use the bathroom and clean up a bit, washing the last remnants of makeup off my face and brushing out my hair.

I should jump in the shower. I should also change. It's the professional thing to do.

His shirt is so soft, though. And I think we both have to admit that we left *professional* somewhere in the rearview.

So I walk to the kitchen, barefoot and only wearing Marcus' shirt, and start the coffee before I cut up fruit to serve alongside the remaining muffins.

Should I do something more special for breakfast today? Or is that too much, too weird?

"What a sight to wake up to," Marcus rumbles, his voice deep and rough from sleep in a way that rasps down my spine. It's a delicious sort of roughness, like that light touch of stubble on my thighs last night, and a strong counterpoint to the man usually so put together and polished.

"You didn't have to get up, Angel," he continues, stepping closer to me. He's only wearing sweatpants, and I watch the flex of lean muscle as he walks closer.

I look at the muffins and not at him. "It's still my job, Marcus."

He keeps moving closer until he's leaning against the counter near me but not touching. "Do you regret last night?"

"No." I can say that instantly, at least. I don't regret this.

Do I regret that it's complicated? Maybe. But I don't regret us.

"I wish we could separate it out," he muses. "I would take care of you, Elise. No strings attached. But I don't think you're ready for that."

"No," I agree, again not looking at him. I don't know if I'll ever be ready for that. I don't want to become his unemployed dependent, but I'm also not stupid enough to think we can make this a real relationship while I also work for him. Still, we are a day into this relationship, and it's too early for this. If I can kick this problem down the road for a bit, then I'm going to.

"Besides," I say, trying to find something lighter, "if I didn't cook for you, you'd starve to death. Don't lie to me."

He smiles, wide and carefree. "I would," he immediately confirms. Then he gets serious again. "But that doesn't mean I expect you to be my chef forever. There are other options."

And we might need those one day, but not yet. I offer him a plate. "Breakfast?"

He steps closer, a slow, slinky prowl that backs me against the counter. "I forgot to tell you something last night."

My ass hits the edge of the counter, one of the knobs on a cabinet digging into my thigh. "Oh yeah? What?"

"I made a decision. About breakfast."

"What kind of decision?" I ask, already half breathless as he leans in closer. He still smells good, even though I didn't hear the shower. What kind of man still smells this good after a night of sweaty sex?

I worry for half a second that I don't smell nearly as good—I shouldn't have skipped that shower—but then he's burying his face in my neck, inhaling deeply and obviously, and he clearly likes it well enough.

"You don't need to make me breakfast, Angel," he murmurs against my neck. "All I want to eat is you." Then, to prove his point, he tries to lift me onto the counter.

I squirm. "It's one thing that we did this here last night," I tell him, already annoyingly breathless. "But today, when I'm getting ready to cook for the day... no."

Marcus chuckles, the reverberations making his chest rumble as I lean against it. "Alright. Whatever you want." Then he carries me over to the couch, deposits me on the plush, over-stuffed cushion, and goes to his knees.

"I like my shirt on you," he says, staring intently between my thighs where his shirt has already ridden up. His hands gently spread my thighs, stroking over the skin of my inner thighs like he just can't help himself, and then his mouth is on me again.

I groan a little bit. He sucks my clit and my legs spontaneously tighten around his head. I immediately force them open again, worried I hurt him until he drags my thigh in closer again.

"Show me how good it feels," he murmurs, the vibrations making me nearly thrash in pleasure.

"I could have hurt you," I protest.

"No, you couldn't have." Then, seemingly done with discussing it—just like Marcus, to assume he said his piece and now everyone will do it exactly how he wants—he dives back into my pussy.

Fuck, this man knows what he's doing, and I can't help when my thighs tighten around him again. I also can't help the sounds that escape me, and I have to wonder how thick the floors are, or if Marcus' downstairs neighbors are listening to me moan and whine.

When I come, he licks me clean, taking his sweet time like he wants to taste every drop. He doesn't stop until I can't take another second of it, and then he backs off, licking his lips while looking up at me with dark, heated eyes. "Delicious," he proclaims, voice sending shivers through me.

I'm a little too stunned to move for a moment, and when I do, Marcus is already up, going over to the kitchen. I hear a cabinet opening, then a drawer. "What are you doing?"

He returns and puts a bowl of the fruit I just cut and a fork in my hand. "You need breakfast," he says, watching with a look I'd describe as almost nurturing.

"I think I should get the same breakfast you do," I counter. I've been wondering since last night what a pierced dick would feel like in my mouth.

He chuckles. "Call that a mid morning snack, then. But you should eat."

I spear a chunk of pineapple and eat it, then pick up a strawberry with my fingers and hold it out to him.

He looks at me for a long second, eyes a little wide. Just when I think he's not going to take it, he swoops in and sucks my fingers into his mouth, swallowing the strawberry and licking at my fingertips.

I try to remind my pussy that I just came, thank you very much. And that it's greedy to want more already. But with the way Marcus looks at me as he sucks my fingers, I can barely keep that thought in my head.

"Thank you," he murmurs, releasing my fingers. His eyes are intense as he continues to stare at me, and I have to swallow to keep from saying something stupid, like begging to suck his cock.

"Can I take you out again tonight?" He reaches over to tuck my hair behind my ear as he says it, a gesture that sends a small shiver down my spine.

"Not that fancy again, right?" I ask when my brain comes back online.

He smiles softly. "We could see a movie?" His thumb traces over my cheek, making me shiver.

Something tells me that, despite what he says to me, Marcus isn't a man used to going to the movies. He isn't a man used to nights out that don't require the price tag he put into last night.

I lean in to kiss him impulsively. I mean it to be a quick peck, but Marcus clearly has other ideas, one hand holding the back of my head and the other slipping around my waist, mussing his stolen shirt even further.

I chase his mouth when he finally pulls away, and he chuckles and presses one more kiss to my lips, then to my forehead, moving the hand cradling the back of my head to hold my chin. "Pick a movie, Angel. Whatever you want to see."

CHAPTER 29

Marcus

I've taken her to the movies, to three more restaurants, and to a Broadway show. I've taken midafternoon walks with her through the park on days where it's warm enough to go out. I've held her on the couch and in bed, and I've fucked her six ways from Sunday, reveling in the desperate little moans I can work out of her when I get her right to that point where she lets go.

We're moving fast by human standards. If I was a better man, I'd back off, but she's my mate. I'm desperate for her. I revel in her presence, and I want her to be just as desperate for me.

Elise doesn't know any better. I imagine Ethan pushed her to move quickly in their relationship, and that's simply what she's used to. I can at least console myself with the fact that she knew me before we began our relationship, and she could judge me on what kind of man I was first.

But there are a lot of loose ends. Ethan is one of them. Her status as my employee is another. And the fact that I haven't told her the truth of what I am yet is the biggest of them all.

Ben's office is fifteen minutes from the penthouse. I encourage Elise to have Lacey over again and set my appointment with Ben when she's supposed to visit. This is partially to give them space—another way I'll never be like Ethan, because I will never take her friends from her—but also hopefully a way that she won't ask too many questions about Ben.

I'm going to tell Elise the truth, but I'm not going to blow my secret over one meeting with a selkie.

Ben has set aside time for me, and I bring by lunch as a thank you for seeing me at the last minute.

"I need to set aside some money for Elise," I tell him.

"You don't need me to do that. Any banker can."

I'm already shaking my head. "I've already given her a credit card, I'm not worried about that." Not that she'll use the damn card. She won't even use it to buy groceries anymore, saying that she isn't paying rent, so she should buy food. It's not usually a problem, because I'm shopping with her and am faster than her, but still. It's the principle of the thing. "I want an account that's just hers. Legally untouchable."

"Why? I get wanting to provide for your mate, but are dragons too mistrustful to go for a joint account?"

I growl, and only all the years I've known Ben stop me from reacting any stronger to the insult. How dare he imply I won't provide for my mate? Half of my entire hoard has been hers since the very moment we met. Not only do I trust her with it, but I ache to see her using it, whether she chooses to spend our money or hoard it like a dragon.

Ben doesn't even have the manners to look alarmed by my growl. "I pay the company that employs her for her services," I say through gritted teeth. "It's ethically questionable and she's rightly worried about her livelihood should something go wrong." Not that I could ever walk away from her, but, as much as I hate to think about it, she's entitled to change her mind about me. "And I want her to have a safety net."

Ben shrugs. "Seems pointless when I'm sure you already added her name to your accounts, but it won't be too hard." He's not wrong about the accounts, but I think Elise will freak out if I tell her, so I'm holding off on that.

Do I tell her about the bank accounts before or after I show her the physical hoards of priceless objects? Which one will be less shocking to her?

"What else?" Ben asks, picking up his sandwich. "You can take your time, but I am billing you for every minute you're in here."

"That asshole is still bothering Elise. We got her a new phone number, but I know he's there. I can feel him watching us sometimes. I want to know what I can do about it."

He raises an eyebrow. "She's your mate, Marcus. You're entitled to do whatever you think she'll accept from you, up to and including killing him. No one will punish you when they find out what she is to you. An investigation will be nothing more than a formality, and a short one at that."

When I was young, the idea of rules to govern creatures like us was laughable. Perhaps a strong leader would rise in one faction or another, but no one could ever lead us all.

But then some sorcerer had to mess with the laws of nature, and some upstart little shifter had to push right back.

Lucius Lawson doesn't scare me. I follow his rules by virtue of there not being any of them I'd particularly like to break. What he asks for—demands, really—isn't exceptionally unreasonable. For a man who's made himself king in all but name, he takes no tribute, demands no honors. He just insists we keep ourselves in line and out of the human eye, and keep the infighting to an absolute minimum.

Before this year, I had no desire to draw the attention of humans, and no need to fight with creatures weaker than me.

But now, everything has changed. Because I have a human I very much want to spill the truth to, and I have creatures I'd like to kill for her.

Mates will trump just about anything in our world. Any rule, law, or assumption will be completely overturned when faced with a mate. Who could argue with fate? Or, more concretely, who wants to argue with a crazed dragon capable of focusing on only one person?

"I haven't broached the mate conversation yet," I admit. "And I'd prefer not to have to explain murder to her as the first step. Or, worse, have someone else barge in and tell her before I can. So, alternatives?"

He blinks at me. "Marcus," he says slowly, "I know I'm not as old as you, but even I know how dragons work. You've essentially changed her, haven't you? You've made her immortal without telling her?" He looks at me shrewdly. "Unless you're holding off. But I saw how you looked at her, so I doubt it."

No, holding off definitely was not something I even considered for a moment. She responds to me so beautifully, soaks up pleasure and attention. Like I'd ever deny her an ounce of that.

And yes, doing so has changed her. But it's not permanent, and I tell Ben that. He doesn't seem impressed. "You need to tell her, Marcus."

I have been dating Elise for a week, and I'm supposed to tell her that she's eternally tied to me? That I've effectively made her immortal, as long as she keeps fucking me, and that I've invited her into a world with a lot of violence? That I will never truly let her go, even if she rejects me?

That will go over well, right after Ethan and his possessive abuse. I do think I'm different, but I'd like a chance to prove it before I ask Elise to see the differences between us.

"Not yet," I tell him.

Ben looks like he thinks I'm an idiot. He's entitled to do so; it doesn't mean it will change my mind. "Then I think your options are limited, Marcus. Keep an eye on her. And think about what you'll do if push comes to shove."

When I get back to the apartment, it smells amazing. If Elise's routine hasn't been thrown off by Lacey's visit, we're about fifteen minutes from eating dinner. It certainly smells done, but she's swearing to herself in the kitchen.

When I walk in, Elise is using a flashlight with a piece of paper taped over the end held in one hand and her cellphone in the other. She seems to be trying to take pictures of the plated dish in front of her.

I raise an eyebrow. "Can I hold the light for you?"

She drops the flashlight in surprise, whirling on me. Clearly, she was so distracted she didn't hear the door. "Marcus! I, uh—"

"This seems like a lot of effort for a picture," I observe. "I'm sure we can come up with a more efficient way."

She shakes her head quickly. "No, no. It's not important. Let's eat."

I frown. No one puts that amount of effort into something not important. "I have a ring light behind my computer," I tell her. "It's for video calls, because apparently people care about that sort of thing. Do you want me to go get it?"

She shakes her head again, too fast. "No, I don't need—"

"Then let me hold the flashlight, if that works better for you," I interrupt, pressing onward. I don't know why I'm push-

227

ing so much when she clearly wants to move on, but something tells me that this moment is important. That this is the moment where I show her that I'm safe and that I can provide for her.

She might like the dress I bought her, and she might like the apartment that she knows is safe, but I know that's not enough. She appreciates it, surely, but it isn't that final touch that shows her what I'm worth as her mate.

If she wants a better picture, then I'll do anything in my power to get her one. It doesn't matter why she wants it; she wants it and I want her to have it.

"Can we just eat?" she asks softly.

I tilt my head. "We can," I acknowledge. "But that doesn't seem to give you what you need. Besides, what's a picture going to hurt?"

She freezes for a moment. "Nothing," she admits. "I would appreciate it if you held the light, thank you."

I take the flashlight and do my best to hold it at an angle that works, and somehow feel like what she's asked me to do is more significant to her than all the times I've touched her body, kissed her, and fucked her. I'd felt irrationally proud that she trusted me with her body, but with this? It's a whole new level of pride.

"So, what do you do with the pictures?" I ask as soon as she's done. I wait until she's done, not wanting to spook her, and speak with a deliberately neutral voice. I don't want her to think my curiosity is judgment.

It's hunger, a desperation to know her and every last detail I can learn about her. Does she like photography? Is she sending pictures to Lacey? Is this particular meal just something she is incredibly proud of?

She doesn't answer for a moment, then admits in the quietest voice, "I run a food blog."

"A food blog?" I repeat. "For recipes and pictures of what you cook?"

She nods. "And I used to try not to take pictures at client's houses, because that was their food and their time, but honestly it was always hard because I would buy way better ingredients for clients and I didn't make anything that nice at my home, never had the time. And now I live here, so..." She says it all in a rush, and then stops talking, like the train of thought has simply ran out.

"You can take pictures of anything you want," I reassure her slowly. "And if you want to cook specific things just because that's what you want pictures of, you know I won't complain. And buy any ingredients you need to make whatever would make you happiest."

Is this what I could give her? Because I will give her every resource and tool possible to have the best food blog in the world. What does she need? Cameras. Better lighting, obviously. Probably backdrops and editing software. Does she need a new computer?

She pauses my thoughts when she bites that full lower lip. "It's a side hobby," she justifies. "I've never been able to give it as much time or attention as it would actually require. I had other things." She's quiet for a moment, then says, "Ethan couldn't object to me working, even though I wasn't always where he wanted me to be. We needed money. But the blog doesn't make money, and I wasn't giving him enough attention, so..."

So I get one more reason to want to kill Ethan. Not that I'll let her see that; she doesn't need me angry on her behalf. She needs me to be soft, and reassuring, and a place to land. I can be that for her. I will be that for her.

"You can be as serious or not about any hobby you want," I tell her, daring to reach for her hand so I can run my thumb across the back, trying to reassure her. "If you want to take up a dozen hobbies just to see what you like, do it. If you want to spend a few thousand dollars on a photography set-up, then you absolutely should."

She flushes. "I know my expenses have been down since I'm not paying rent, but I don't have that kind of disposable income, Marcus."

She truly doesn't get it. I take a deep breath, because she's not misunderstanding on purpose. She's a human who's had to fight for every single thing in her life.

"Angel, I didn't give you that credit card to make your wallet more cluttered."

"You gave it to me to buy food," she counters.

I shrug. "So buy food. Buy everything you need related to food, if this is the hobby that interests you. If you want another hobby, then buy that."

"I can't just take your money."

It's her money, by rights and by every instinct deep inside me. My hoard became equally hers the second I recognized what she is to me. I'm not stupid enough to say that to a human, though. "You can," I assure her, debating how to put this. "Trust me, Elise. I've met you. I highly doubt you could find a hobby that would damage my bank account." I worry that'll come off patronizing, or even belittling to her, but she just swallows.

"What kind of hobby could damage your bank account?"

"Collecting private jets, maybe," I concede. But even then, she'd have to be a really avid collector for it to truly financially impact us. "Or mega-yachts, I suppose. Space travel would be another one."

Her eyes widen. "That is not a hobby."

"Then you haven't met some of the people I have. It's not a hobby I see either of us engaging in anytime soon, though. What I'm saying is, if you want to take up pretty much any hobby you can imagine, then you should."

She's flushed and not quite looking at me, shy now, but she nods, slowly. "I'll keep taking my pictures," she murmurs. "And maybe spend a little more time on the blog."

"And buy better lighting," I press, because I think I might actually get her to agree.

"Maybe."

Definitely. If she doesn't, then I will. But I don't need to tell her that. It can be a gift that just shows up tomorrow, as a nice little surprise.

"So, what did you make, anyways?" I ask her, content that I've managed to win this round, that I'll get to give her the things she deserves. I turn my attention to the food under her rudimentary lighting set up.

"We're starting with a cheese soufflé. Lacey and I dug through those recipe books of yours earlier, and I found these. And I don't know if you know this, but those are considered kind of finicky, slightly impressive, so I was somewhat motivated to take some pictures again." She glances behind her at the oven timer. "The quail is almost ready, too. So, sit down, let me get you your starter."

I glance around. The table is mostly set, but there are no drinks yet. "Wine?" I offer her.

She gives me a full smile at that. "I'd like that."

And I like her, with that smile and the flush still tinging her cheeks. I should convince her to take more pictures tonight—the soufflé, the quail, the fully set table, anything and everything she could turn into a few blog posts. Anything to show her that this hobby is something she can and should have.

And, maybe after a glass of wine, she'll tell me the name of her blog.

CHAPTER 30
Elise

I 've slept in Marcus' bed every night since our first official date.

His guest room was a luxurious cloud, but this room is something else entirely. The sheets are certainly made of satin, and the mattress might literally be a marshmallow.

Marcus is what makes it perfect, though. He's always warm, smells heavenly no matter what time of day it is, and touches me in a way that's beyond comprehension. I've never felt anything like this before.

Maybe Ethan was just really selfish in bed, and I was too inexperienced to know the difference. I'm starting to suspect that must be the truth, or else Marcus has some incredible skill that puts him above normal men.

I usually wake up first between us, but ever since that first morning I can't so much as push the blankets down without Marcus waking up, like he's developed a sixth sense to my presence.

"Good morning, Angel," he murmurs, pressing kisses into my neck while he rolls me underneath him.

"Morning," I say softly, caged beneath him and finding that I don't have any desire to be anywhere else. I close my eyes as he continues to kiss my neck, my hands finding his shoulder blades, digging in to keep him close.

"Did you sleep well?"

Like the dead. I somehow only ever sleep well in this bed. "Mhm," I groan, all I can manage when his lips trail down to my breasts.

He sucks my nipple in between his lips, nipping lightly at it to draw another moan from me. My toes curl, my fingers unconsciously clawing at his shoulders. More, always more with him.

We're still naked from last night, so there's nothing preventing him from touching me, stroking me, exploring every inch of me. He takes full advantage, pressing our naked bodies together while he sucks at my nipple. I arch against him, wanting more, needing more, but he cages me in, pinning me in place.

"Marcus," I groan.

He licks up to my neck. "Yes, Angel?" He sounds so sincere as he says it, too, like he really doesn't know what I'm ready to beg for. Asshole.

But he's an asshole who drags that perfect cock right across my pussy, like he needs to remind me just a little bit more that he can make me see stars.

"Elise?" he prompts, like he really doesn't know why I'm unable to string together a coherent sentence. His piercing drags over my clit, and I spread my legs wider, mewling and trying to show him exactly where I want him.

I sound half feral. But, judging by the dark, hungry desperation in his eyes, he doesn't mind. He grins, and I've never felt so fucking wanted.

"You want me inside you?" he asks. "Want me to make you nice and full, Elise?"

"Please."

And then he does the last thing I expect. He rolls off of me, making me whine when his heat disappears. But before I know what's happening, he pulls me on top of him, making me straddle his hips.

"What are you doing?" I demand.

He grins. "I'm going to watch you take your pleasure from me, Elise." He bucks his hips slightly, as if he's trying to get me to notice the cock that I could never hope to ignore. "I want you to take what you want."

His eyes don't leave mine as he speaks, so deep and adoring. His hand strokes my hip, touching me with such reverence I stop moving for a second. It's not the first time I've thought of the word reverence when thinking about Marcus and I. It feels conceited to even think it, considering we haven't been together that long and he's him and I'm me, but that doesn't change that the word keeps coming to mind. Marcus adores me.

Marcus reveres me. And I feel like a queen straddling him right this moment.

"I think you'll like the piercing in this position," he murmurs. "It's meant to make you see stars."

Fuck. "I'll let you know if it works, then."

"Trust me, Angel. You won't have to let me know. We'll both be able to tell."

I lower myself slowly onto his cock, taking my time because even with all the sex we've been having, he's still big. He watches me hungrily, holding still and letting me control the pace. When I stop halfway down for a moment, letting myself adapt to him inside me, he reaches up to tweak my nipple, smiling when it makes me moan.

"Beautiful," he murmurs, still looking me directly in the eye as he continues to toy with my nipple.

The tease of his touch makes me so wet that I can slide the rest of the way down his cock with ease. I'm so full, and I just rock my hips from side to side for a moment, feeling the stretch.

"You feel so good around me," he says, voice practically a rasp now. "So soft and warm, fuck, Elise—"

I move up on my knees, giving myself the leverage to almost pull off his cock before I slide back down. He was one hundred percent right—that piercing makes me see stars as I lower myself back onto him.

I rock my hips up again, wanting to see if I can duplicate that feeling. My moan when I find out that I can probably shakes those over-large windows, but Marcus just grips my hips lightly, murmurs, "That's it, Elise," and helps me replicate what I just did.

His aim is perfect, his hands big and steady, and his eyes warm and smoldering as he watches me, so I don't think it's a surprise that it doesn't take me long to come. Marcus always seems to know my body, knows exactly what I need, knows how to push me that much higher, and can do it with an unerring accuracy that boggles my mind. No one should know me that well.

I come, squeezing around him and gripping at his chest to stay upright while his hands hold me steady.

When I look at him after, he's watching me with desperate eyes. "I don't want to hurt you, but can I keep going?"

Yes, I almost say, but think better of it at the last moment. "I have a better idea."

I'm so wet that the noise when I pull off of him is obscene, and I pretend not to see the string of wetness connecting his cock to my pussy. I move to kneel between his legs, spreading them to make room for myself.

All I can taste at first is me, but then I get the salty taste of his pre-come. My tongue instinctively finds that little metal bar, playing with the studs on either end, exploring. Judging by the low, filthy swear Marcus lets out, my exploration is paying off for him.

"What you do to me," he growls.

Good, I want to say, because it's more than mutual. I don't drop his dick from my mouth, though. I have better things to do than talk.

I can't get much of him into my mouth, so I use one hand to keep myself from face-planting into his crotch and the other to stroke the base, taking a moment to tease his balls, which leaves him groaning my name. I trace my tongue around the head, paying special attention to his piercing.

It's an intense kind of guy who gets his dick pierced because he likes jewelry, but I think I can safely say it's paid off for both of us.

"I'm not going to fucking last, Elise," he groans.

I'm surprised he's lasted this long. I dip my tongue into his slit and gently squeeze his balls, and then he's arching off the bed, uncontrolled and beautiful with it, moaning my name while he comes down my throat.

I can't swallow it all, so I pull back, letting his come land on my tits, stroking his cock through the orgasm.

"Fuck. Me," he groans, his body at last at rest once more. He picks his head up, something that seems to take a great deal of energy, and watches me with heavy eyes. "You look..."

"Like a mess?"

"Like a goddess, Elise. Beautiful."

I look like a mess and I know it. I'm sweaty and probably flushed. I have come on my tits and my thighs are wet, and I don't want to think about my hair. But Marcus watches me with reverence, nonetheless.

"I need a shower," I say instead of acknowledging all that.

He gives me a lascivious grin. "I'm happy to wash your back."

After he washes my back—and just about every other part of me, including a slow, luxurious scrub of my hair—Marcus and I dry off with the softest towels known to man, then get dressed for the day.

My clothes are still in the other room, half because we haven't talked about me moving them yet and half because Marcus' closet is just absolutely filled to the brim with all his stuff, so we meet in the kitchen after we're both dressed. Marcus sits on the barstool at the counter, waiting for the coffee to finish percolating so he can fix us each a cup while I prepare our meal.

"Picture?" he asks me when I slide a bowl of fruit and yogurt in front of him.

"Not for this," I snort. Fruit and yogurt would be a boring recipe.

Marcus, of course, managed to worm my blog title out of me, and seems to check it religiously. I wonder if he has an alert set for it, or if he just logs in compulsively.

I am posting to it more lately, now that I have a fancy lighting setup, and permission to photograph and make whatever I want. And I swear Marcus is checking it three, four times a day. He mentions it every meal, like he's determined to remind me to enjoy my hobby.

I think I am enjoying it. For the first time, it doesn't feel like a guilty waste of time, and if I'm still shouting into the void without anyone caring much to read it, well, that's okay. This is for me, Marcus has reminded me. And if I like it, then I should have it.

I'm building an eclectic pile of recipes, something for every occasion. I used to focus on posting the most technically impressive recipes, but I'm also building out a section on my blog for more sustainable, simple, everyday meals.

I'm briefly blinded by a flash and blink to find Marcus studying his phone intently. "I said I didn't need a picture."

He grins. "This one's for me. Cute, too."

I highly doubt I'm cute right now, with wet hair and lazy clothes and staring unfocused at a bowl of yogurt. But he looks at his phone again before sliding it away.

"Then I want pictures of you."

"Then take them." His voice has a slight challenge, but his lips quirk into another smile.

I dig my phone out and take a picture of him, just as impromptu and unflattering as the one he took of me. Somehow, it turns out incredibly attractive.

This man is not fair. No one should be this perfect.

"Eat your breakfast," I tell him, putting my phone away.

"Don't tempt me," he says, his voice low and dark and full of promise.

My pussy clenches. What the fuck has this man done to me?

Made my pussy needy, my life fuller, my standard of living so much higher. Hell, just made my standards higher. That's what Marcus has done to me.

"You might not think you need food, but I do," I manage to say.

He just smirks at me again, with no regard to what it does to me, and eats a spoonful of yogurt.

"I actually did have something I wanted to talk to you about this morning," he says when I'm about halfway done.

"Oh?" he says it so calmly, so he's probably not mad. It can't be anything too serious, certainly. I take a deep breath, trying to remind myself that Marcus isn't Ethan, and I can calm down.

"The company Christmas party is this upcoming Thursday," he says, completely unaware of where my mind has gone.

It takes me a moment to register what he's said and calm down enough to respond. "Oh? Are you actually going in person?"

"After the first of the year, my duties at my old position will have wound down, and I'll be working at the office here in person at least three days a week," he says.

Oh. I didn't know that, hadn't asked, although I should have realized that this little bubble we're in would have to pop, eventually.

"So you should show your face at the party, huh? Get to know people?"

"That's the idea. Do you want to go out today or tomorrow to get whatever you need for the party?"

"I'm coming?" I ask, surprised. I hadn't even considered the possibility.

"If you want. I'd like you to be there."

When was the last time I went to a party not as the help? I can't even make an educated guess.

Not that I'm complaining about working at fancy events, but the idea that Marcus wants me there with him blows my mind. He wants me there when he's trying to form relationships at this company, meeting the people he needs to in order to get them to listen to him and follow his commands.

"You bought me plenty of dresses," I say slowly, thinking through the logistics. "Unless the party is fancy dress or I need a black-tie gown or something." Please don't let it be that.

"You don't want something new?"

"Do you want me to wear something in particular?" I check.

"I want you to have everything you want, Elise. Whatever that might be." The thing is, he means it, too. He'd buy me literally anything I asked for.

But I don't want anything much. "I'm all set, then," I tell him. "I'll wear one of the dresses I have."

He tilts his head, and I worry for a second that he's going to insist. But all he says is, "One of the green ones?"

"Green's probably good for Christmas," I concede.

And if I'd already planned to wear a green one because no one looking around this apartment could fail to conclude that it's Marcus' favorite color? Well, he doesn't need to know that.

CHAPTER 31
Marcus

I spend half a day bothering different employees of mine to learn who's catering this party, because I won't have whatever food is being served embarrass me in front of Elise.

I rarely attend these types of events. It's a bad look for the boss not to attend, maybe, but most employees will admit to having a better time when their boss isn't there, so I don't worry too much about it. If I go, I make an appearance, shake some hands, then slip out quietly as soon as it's possible to do so.

Not this year. This year, I have a beautiful, perfect mate, and I'm ready to burst with how much I need to brag that she's mine and I'm hers. Pretty much everyone at this party will be human, so it's a safe enough place to bring her and brag for now.

So I find a suit appropriate for the evening, put on the snowflake tie I bought just for tonight, and wait for Elise in the living room. She doesn't leave me waiting too long, emerging in a deep green dress that makes me salivate. It fits her every curve, dipping low to show off her cleavage. I want to bury my face there, but I restrain myself for now.

"This is for you," I tell her, holding out the blue velvet box. She takes it, opening it slowly. The diamond snowflake necklace catches the light just right, even sitting in the box, and I feel a rush of pride that I chose so well.

"This is too much," she says, voice slightly shaky.

"It's not," I assure her, taking the box back from her so I can pull the necklace loose. I step behind her and fasten it around her neck, leaning down to press a kiss to the knob of her spine when it's secure. "I saw it and thought it would be perfect for tonight." I spent two hours looking at various jewelry stores first, sure, but when I finally saw it I did know it was the perfect choice, so I'm not lying.

"Thank you," she says, reaching up to tremulously touch the pendant.

"You're more than welcome." It looks good, sitting just beneath her collarbones, shining perfectly. "Shall we go?" I reach over to her coat, which I'd left on the arm of the couch, and help her into it before taking her arm and leading her outside.

"How much money does your company have?" she mutters to me as we enter the ballroom selected for the evening.

It's a fair enough question, I suppose; this building has gravitas, and for tonight, it's all ours. "Enough," I say, turning to the coat check so I can hand off our coats. I help Elise out of hers, watching her smooth her dress back into place subconsciously before turning to the attendant.

I offer her my arm again, leading her into the event space.

We're overdressed, I realize immediately. I'd spent so long worrying about the food that I'd apparently not focused enough on the dress code, and as a result there's a sea of holiday themed sweaters around us. Thankfully, they're not any of the especially tacky ones; the first time I see a blinking reindeer nose on a sweater, I'm leaving.

Well, I'm the boss. Being overdressed is probably expected.

I snag each of us a glass of champagne, then scan the room for who I'd want to introduce her to first. There. Jackie Strong, head of finance. I don't know if she and Elise have much in common, but I at least know something about Jackie, having spent so long on video calls with her. She's nice enough, and it's a good place to start.

Introducing Elise to Jackie becomes a whirlwind of Jackie calling others over. None of those people have met me in person yet, but I think Elise is more of a draw than I am. Well, I can't blame them. I think Elise is more interesting than I am too. I don't present the most gentle face when I'm online with these people, so seeing Elise's smiling face, with her still holding my arm, must be a bit of a shock to them all.

"You hungry, Angel?" I ask quietly, but apparently not quietly enough, judging by Kara's nearly violent head turn in my direction. I ignore her—she can think what she likes, and the only person who matters is Elise, anyway—and wait for Elise to make a decision.

She smiles. "I could eat."

"Excuse us, please," I say politely to the gathered crowd, then make my way over to where food is being served. I wanted a sit-down meal, but was told that this wasn't that type of party, so I compromised. It might be buffet style, but it's an incredibly high-end buffet.

From the small smile on Elise's face, I think I did a good job.

As several of my employees crowd back around us, interested in speaking to Elise, I'm reminded of how much I've inadvertently isolated her. She didn't have many people after Ethan was done with her. The single person she's seen besides me has been Lacey.

I've done her a disservice. She's so likable that people are literally crowding around us right now, wanting to get to know her. And she deserves that. She deserves the world.

The dragon inside me registers a brief complaint, still jealously hoarding her attention, but I squash him down and tell him to shut up. Elise is what matters. His jealousy is worthless.

Besides, she holds onto my hand the whole time we're talking. Even if she makes a thousand friends, she's not going to forget about me.

She's absorbed in a conversation with a woman named Mercy, who I've never met before, talking with the hand not holding mine. That means she's completely abandoned her meal, which might bother me if I couldn't see how her face lights up with joy while she's talking.

"You're quite the center of attention," a voice to my left says.

I turn reluctantly away from Elise's conversation to John, the only other non-human here. John is a vampire and almost as old as I am, which is what makes it interesting that he is so excellent with technology. I like to consider myself as someone fairly proficient with the modern world; after all, I've run my business successfully online for the last several months. Despite that, I have nothing on John. He makes it a point of pride to keep up with the most modern technology, which makes him an excellent chief of technology. He uses his skills to help my company, and in turn, I pay him obscene amounts of money that he uses to fund his personal technological collection.

I don't consider us friends. Dragons are not particularly known for being friendly, even more so than the rest of the mythical creatures in the world. Despite this, I have known John for many years, and I've been happy to employ him on and off as he goes about his life.

He is the only person here who knows what I am, and as a result, he is the only person here who poses an active danger to Elise. I can't threaten him, not with her holding my hand right next to me, but I harden my eyes and let the dragon peek through.

He holds up one hand to indicate he gets the message, looking down and breaking eye contact with me, a universal sign of avoiding conflict. "No harm will come to her," he whispers, so quietly that I doubt any of the humans could hear it. "I swear it."

We all know that I'm in charge around here. Even though dragons are loners and it's not in our nature to build packs or communities or anything bigger than an immediate family unit, we all know that I could rule the roost here, and every supernatural creature bows to my command. It's a power I don't feel the need to take advantage of often. But for Elise? I'll exert every inch of influence I have. I'll push and pull and make every creature bow at our feet, if that's what it takes to keep her safe.

"I'm glad you found her," he says, just as quietly. "It's about time."

I would wait millennia longer, I want to say, but don't. His eyes look almost hungry, but not for Elise. It's for the promise of what she might mean. I finally found my mate; maybe he will find his soon too.

It doesn't work like that. There are no timelines with mates, and there are no promises. I don't tell him that, of course. Hope is a powerful drug.

Elise squeezes my hand. "I'm going to the restroom. Be right back."

I almost stand to follow her, but the plethora of human eyes stops me. That would look strange. It would look like I'm trying to control her, or give everyone the impression that I want to fuck her in the restroom.

I do want to fuck her in the restroom, but I can have some self control.

I squeeze her hand right back. "I'll be here," I tell her. "Then, I think you owe me a dance."

Her eyes drift nervously to the dance floor. I'm sure she has no idea how to dance, but I can be a great leader when properly motivated. She'll be safe in my arms.

I want to show her that I can be a safe person. I can be her guide, and I can give her new experiences. I daydream about it for a moment too long. Then John's eyes snap up, smelling her blood just a second before I do, and we both take off running.

CHAPTER 32
Elise

T he bathroom looks like some sort of modern art piece. Like it's meant to be a showpiece, something to wow people instead of a place to pee.

Honestly, if there weren't two women in here fixing their lipstick in the mirror and one pair of stiletto-clad feet under one of the stalls, I'd worry that I accidentally walked into an art exhibit. But their casual use of the space tells me that it's safe to be here.

Surely some of these people must be normal, right? Some of them are executives like Marcus, but this is a company-wide party. Some of them must earn an ordinary wage and live ordinary lives.

Maybe, but I can't pretend that this isn't the type of party I'm more suited to working at than attending. Not that I'm having a bad time. Everyone has been so nice, and, despite Marcus warning me that he's going to be in this office full-time soon and needs to make the connections that I'm sure are necessary to do his job, he's been attentive all night. The most he did was talk quietly with some guy while I chatted with two women from payroll, but even then, he didn't let go of my hand the entire time.

And he wants to dance with me after this. I'm sure he's smart enough to piece together that I have no idea how to dance, but he said it with such confidence that I bet he's found a way to work around that.

I have no basis for this claim whatsoever, but I bet a guy who can fuck as confidently as Marcus can lead someone around a dancefloor with ease.

After I wash my hands, I check my lipstick in the mirror, applying a fresh coat. I side-eye the woman next to me, and, okay, that tube of lipstick looks like a luxury purchase. I have my drugstore lipstick, a tried-and-true red I only bring out on special occasions. Maybe it's time to upgrade.

Does Marcus know the difference? Probably not, I realize, because he would have already taken me to some luxury beauty store I'm too average to even know the name of. Not because he'd be embarrassed to see me with crappy lipstick or anything, but because he genuinely just wants me to have the nicest of everything possible.

The woman finishes her lipstick, then makes eye contact with me in the mirror and smiles. "That dress is gorgeous."

"Thanks." What am I supposed to say; Marcus bought it for me? That doesn't seem like a good opener.

"I'm Marsha."

"Elise."

"I work in logistics."

I have no earthly idea what that job would entail, but I'm not going to let on. "Nice."

"So, the bossman..."

"Mhm." I don't say more, wondering where she's going with this.

"Those of us not high enough up to meet with him on the daily are all wondering... is he going to be a good boss?"

Well, I can hardly tell her that he's been a good boss to me; coming here and being introduced as his girlfriend and admitting I'm simultaneously his employee sounds like a terrible look for both of us. And surely she can't expect an unbiased answer from me, anyway. But regardless, I say, "He's going to be great."

She smiles again. "Good, I'm glad." She fixes her hair. "Scoot back out there. If I had a guy like that staring after me, I wouldn't leave him waiting."

She's not wrong. I give myself one last quick look, then walk out of the bathroom and straight into someone waiting.

The air leaves my lungs in a great heave, the pressure around my throat forcing my body back against the wall. I squirm and kick out, but I don't hit anything. I just lose my balance in these stupid heels, and then for a brief, terrifying second, the hand around my throat is the only thing keeping me upright. I lash out, trying to grab onto anything I can, but the face in front of me is getting blurrier. The squeezing gets even tighter, and my vision goes blurry as I fight to get enough oxygen.

"He keeps you practically a prisoner in that golden cage, huh?" A voice snarls right next to my ear. The hand on my throat loosens just slightly, just enough for me to gulp air, and I realize as I desperately try to fill my lungs that it's Ethan holding me by the throat.

The idea is so ludicrous that it almost doesn't compute. Ethan, my below-average manipulative ex, is holding me by the throat in a grip stronger than I thought possible. When I try to hit him, he kicks out at my leg, knocking my shin hard enough to bruise and pushing me off balance again, leaving me at the mercy of his squeezing fingers to keep me from falling to the floor.

"Now that I have your attention," Ethan mutters darkly, squeezing and then releasing just slightly, "We can talk."

Did Ethan seriously sneak past security to a party like this, with hundreds of people on the other side of a door, just to talk to me? I know the calls and texts were aggressive, but I never thought he'd be stupid enough to stoop to this.

And for what? Why is it so damn important to get me back? I'm nothing, not really; he doesn't need me, and how hard can it be to just move the fuck on?

"It's been fucking impossible to get a moment alone," Ethan continues like we're having this discussion somewhere completely casual, like we're both mutually participating. "But now, the boy-toy you cheated on me with is distracted."

"I didn't cheat on you," I grind out, forcing air into my lungs to protest. Somehow, that seems important to say. Not for him, though. I don't give a damn if he thinks I cheated. At this point, he deserves to think that. It's for me, and a bit for Marcus. We deserve better than for people to think that of us.

He completely ignores me. "You like being kept like some pretty pet so much? I'll take care of it. You'll come with me and I'll keep you just like a dog, waiting at my beck and call, begging for scratches behind the ears."

I squirm again. "I'm not going fucking anywhere with you. I—"

His eyes flash, something so bright and horrendous it can't be natural. The fight leaves me as I stare into his eyes. "You're coming with me," he repeats.

His words are a gentle counterpoint to his hands, soft, nearly persuasive. I can't remember for a split second what's going on. Going with him sounds like a good idea suddenly, and I can't remember why I didn't want to.

But then I do. Ethan's hand is around my neck. Ethan pushed me around and isolated me. Ethan sucks and I deserve so much better. I found it, too.

I shake my head, both to clear it from whatever I saw and to make it obvious that I'm not going.

He growls, sounding more like an animal than a human. "Fucking mystical bullshit," he grunts, and then I feel pain in the side of my neck.

I try to move back in shock, but there's a wall there. Did he drug me? It didn't feel like a syringe, although I really don't know what a syringe feels like. But that felt like multiple punctures, and wider than a needle.

There's a ripping growl like a wild animal on the loose, and then Ethan backs away from me quickly. Someone is in front of me in a flash, and it takes my dazed mind a second to place them as Marcus.

Marcus. Somehow, he knew. He came for me.

The world is spinning. Maybe Ethan did drug me.

Fuck, he's dangerous. Marcus needs to know, needs to be warned—

"Marcus," I whimper, trying to warn him about the needle. Maybe that was all Ethan had, but if he has more, Marcus needs to know.

Marcus freezes, then barks, "John," before turning to me.

A blur pushes past Marcus, running at a speed that looks practically impossible, but then Ethan is running too, and my body is sliding down the wall.

Marcus catches me before I fall. "Go back to the party," he barks, and I can't figure out how he expects me to do that before I follow his gaze to see Marsha from the bathroom poking her terrified head out of the bathroom door.

Fuck, how much did she see? I flush in humiliation. It was one thing having Marcus and his lawyer know I'd gotten myself into this type of relationship, but now Marsha saw Ethan's delusional little attempt to get me back.

She's pale as a ghost, and just nods before hurrying away down the hallway, back towards the party and away from the direction Ethan and whoever was chasing him ran.

"Angel, can you look at me?" Marcus breathes. He's clearly trying to be gentle, but there's a violent, barely contained raspiness to his voice and his hands grip me a little too tight. I turn to look at him. Everything is a little blurry, but I latch onto his eyes.

Fuck, Ethan's eyes. What the hell had that been?

I must be getting worked up, because Marcus' hands stroke my arms. "Easy, Elise," he murmurs. "You'll be alright. Deep breath, alright?" It's easier said than done, but he slides one hand to my chest, miming moving up and down with even breaths while he keeps soothingly saying the same message, and eventually I feel like I can breathe. "That's it. Good. Thank you."

"Is he... is he..." I can't quite force the full question out.

"Don't worry about him right now," Marcus says. "He won't touch you again. I'll fucking kill him before he gets close."

"He was... I've never seen him like that," I mumble, my mind still spinning with what just happened. "He was deranged. And his eyes... something weird happened with his eyes."

"I know," he says, and I suppose I'm just relieved that he sounds sincere, and not like he's trying to placate a crazy person. "Can you tilt your head for me? I want to check the wounds on your neck."

"How did you know..." I ask, but I turn my head like he asked.

His fingers are feather-light when he touches me. "Bastard," he growls, an intensity I didn't know Marcus could have. "Put his fucking claws in you."

"Claws?" I ask, sure I must be delirious now. Maybe I was drugged, and this is a hallucination.

Marcus freezes. "Elise, I..."

Someone comes running up the hallway. Marcus' arm on me tenses, and he slides slightly more in front of me, but otherwise doesn't move us. "Is he dead?" Marcus asks, voice cold.

"He got away. Bastard is fast."

"He's some young pathetic little psychic vampire. They're not exactly known for being powerhouses," Marcus seethes. "How did he lose you?"

None of what he's saying makes any sense. My eyes slip closed. Maybe if I let myself sleep, the drug will wear off and everything will start making sense again.

"First off, they're demons. Don't call them vampires, it makes the rest of us look bad. Second of all, he did, okay? Bastard went out a literal window, and by the time I caught up he was gone. Third, are you going to heal that, or am I going to keep having to smell her blood?"

"Go away, John," Marcus says, his voice still cold and firm. This isn't the Marcus who tells the cleaner or the interior decorator or his employees how he expects things to be done. That Marcus is firm but kind, used to being obeyed because people believe in him. That Marcus doesn't need force.

This Marcus is a little terrifying.

Maybe I should be terrified. His hand is still on my chest, though, ensuring my breathing stays relatively level. He strokes my sternum gently with his thumb, almost like he doesn't know he's doing it.

I force my eyes open to look at him. He's probably as freaked out as I am, and I need to let him know I'm okay. Or going to be okay, at least.

I don't look away from Marcus, but I hear John leave, going down the hallway away from us. Marcus doesn't move until the door back to the party shuts, and I somehow know that no one else will come through it. John will ensure it.

"Angel, I'll explain everything in a moment," he murmurs. "But I don't know where his filthy hands have been and I need to deal with these, alright?"

Sure. Some Neosporin sounds like a great idea right now. Only instead of somehow producing a first aid kit, Marcus bends down so he can lick at my neck, which seems absolutely counter-intuitive for sanitary concerns.

But when he pulls his mouth away, pressing a gentle kiss to my neck before he does, the pain of the puncture wounds is gone. "All better," he rasps, his voice gentle again.

"Marcus," I manage to say as I take stock of my body. I'm still shaken, and my throat hurts from the force of Ethan's grab even if the puncture pain is somehow gone. I force another deep breath. "Marcus, what is going on?"

He looks pale, but he nods. "I owe you some explanations, Elise."

CHAPTER 33

Marcus

I should have told her before.

Maybe the first night before I accidentally altered her body. Maybe even before, so she'd know everything before getting involved with me. Certainly in any of the time we've spent together since.

I don't know what I was waiting for. Some perfect moment? Can't get less perfect than this, but now I'm backed into the corner.

Knowing that Elise needs me here more than she needs me to chase down and murder Ethan is the only thing keeping me from flying apart. My dragon is roaring for blood in my mind, and if I wasn't holding our precious mate, I know the dragon would force a transformation and go on his way.

But I need to be here with her. I need to make sure she's okay and make sure she can process all of this.

I need to tell her the truth.

I regret every night sitting on the couch in our penthouse that I didn't say anything. All the mornings holding her in bed and refusing to let her get up. Meals at our kitchen table I could have said something but didn't. A hallway outside a restroom is no place for this conversation.

"Look at my eyes, Angel," I murmur, accepting my fate.

When she does, I let them change, showing her a glimpse of what's inside me. The dragon's eyes terrify humans, and I just have to hope she can see me past them afterward. I know I can't just tell her what I am; I'll sound like I've lost my mind. I need proof, and this is the best proof I have without turning fully, which really won't work in the confined space of this hallway.

She flinches, her own eyes going wide and her mouth opening slightly. "Ethan's eyes did the same thing," she murmurs. "What the fuck does that mean, Marcus?"

It means Ethan tried to exert influence over her, use whatever type of magic scummy bottom-feeders like him have to compel her to do his bidding. It means the dragon inside me is even more pissed off.

"It's magic, Angel," I say heavily. Fuck, I sound crazy. "I am a little more than I pretend to be." I don't want to talk about him, but she needs to know. "And so is Ethan."

"What does that mean?" she demands, voice slightly raised now. "Magic? More than you pretend to be? What does that mean, Marcus?"

"It means I'm a dragon, Elise. I was born a long, long time ago," I tell her softly, trying to bring some calm back into the conversation. "And when I was born, there were a lot of creatures like me. We're not as common anymore, but we still exist."

"A dragon." Her voice sounds empty and robotic, like she's just repeating it without believing it. She starts to push out of my arms, and I have a moment of panic. If I let her go, I might lose her forever, but if I hold her to me, I might ruin what's between us and scare her away.

"Elise," I say firmly, speaking quickly before she can muster up too much energy to get away. "I can prove it to you."

"How?" she asks, her voice taking on a half-hysterical tone now.

"I healed your neck with my saliva," I point out, but I already know that won't be convincing enough. "And Ethan used talons to puncture your neck. I have them too, although mine won't drug you," I say, and show her a half-shifted hand.

Except for the eyes, I've always found a half-shift incredibly hard to hold. It's a shame, because having claws or just wings at will would be useful, but the concentration it takes makes it an unrealistic option. I focus all my energy into the claws, letting Elise look her fill.

"Dragon?" she mumbles, like she needs to hear herself say it out loud to believe it. I let my claws disappear. She doesn't stop staring at my hand. "And Ethan is..."

I shift her in my arms, wanting to make sure she's comfortable while I explain a whole hidden world to her. "Most of us call creatures like him psychic vampires, but John—he was here a moment ago—objects to that. Empathic demon is the more official term, because they are demons, but they're basically bloodsucking creatures. They suck the emotions right out of you and feed on unadulterated devotion."

"Fuck," she whispers, clearly having already caught on to what Ethan wants from her. "Marcus, what the fuck, how is this even possible, I—"

"I know," I interrupt before she tries to get up and storm off again. "I know it's a lot and it's unfair to expect you to handle this, but I really am asking you to just hear me out, alright?"

She goes still. "Did you know Ethan was... that?"

"Only after I went to kill him, after what he did to you," I admit. "I had no idea before that."

"You didn't kill him." Her voice is still mostly empty, but I hear it as an accusation, nonetheless.

I still, my brain tripping over itself to figure out how to explain this in a way that doesn't sound like I don't value her life. "If he'd been human, I absolutely would have, no questions asked. But he's not human, and there are certain rules that govern how I can respond to my own kind."

"You can't kill each other?"

"There are rules," I say again. "And breaking them over a human would be frowned upon."

"Oh," she says, voice dull again, like I just sucked all the energy right out of her. I'm desperate to put some life back into her.

"You're the exception, of course," I hasten to say.

"Sure." She doesn't sound very invigorated.

"Elise," I tell her firmly. "You are the exception because whatever rules govern my kind, there is one rule above all else: never get between a creature and their mate. We can and will do anything for our mates, and trying to hold us accountable for that is like trying to hold back the tide. You are my mate, Elise, and I could have killed him for you in a heartbeat, if I wasn't worried about exposing my human mate to the types of people who would come sniffing around to investigate it."

She blinks at me. I can feel her heart beating faster, an unsteady thump-thump that worries me slightly. "What does that mean?"

"It means you are mine, and I'm yours, and I've always been and always will be. It means you complete me, that the dragon inside me has waited for you. That half of everything I have is yours, and I want to spend the rest of my life with you." I wanted this declaration to be more meaningful; now, I'm just glad she's listening at all.

She's silent for a long moment. "Fuck, Marcus. What am I supposed to do with this?" I don't really have an answer for that, and before I can formulate one, she demands, "What does it mean? And I mean for real. Not spiritually, or whatever. Literally."

"It means the dragon inside me thinks we're perfect for each other," I explain. "In whatever form."

"Is that why you hired me? Took me in?"

"I didn't know when I first hired you," I tell her slowly, knowing that the weight of each of my words matters. That if I don't answer this correctly, she will walk away.

As she should. She has money now. She has a lot of money now, actually, even if she doesn't quite know about the bank account I made just for her. She can walk away from me if she doesn't feel safe with me and still make a good life for herself.

"I knew something," I admit. "I wanted you in my life. It took me some time to figure out why."

"And when you let me stay with you?" she presses.

"If it had been anyone else, the dragon inside me would have been far less willing to let someone into our nest. For any other woman knocked around by her boyfriend, I would have been sympathetic. I would have brought in lawyers and probably threatened the boyfriend. I would have paid for a hotel room for as long as you needed. But I wouldn't have opened my home, no."

"So it was, what, because you wanted to sleep with me?"

"Elise, if you never slept with me, I would still be your mate," I say firmly. "That penthouse was your home the minute you stepped foot in it. You are entitled to it." I fight the frustration down, because she doesn't deserve it. It's not her fault that our instincts don't mesh. "I can't explain how the dragon in me works, Elise. It works the way it works and that's always been my experience, just like your experience is being human. But inviting you into our home wasn't a manipulation or a bargain. It's what you're entitled to from me." I wait a moment, feeling out how she takes that. She doesn't seem angry at least, just contemplative, so I risk it and nudge her side lightly. "That's also the reason you should start using the credit card I gave you. All my money is half yours."

She sputters. "What, like a marriage?"

"No," I tell her firmly. "Marriages can end, Elise."

"We've barely started dating, Marcus!"

"You can leave me. It won't change how I feel about you."

She goes very quiet, and I fight every instinct to push to know what's in her head. "I don't want to be here anymore."

Fair enough. I'm also not enjoying the floor of a hallway to the bathrooms for our major, life-changing conversation. "Do you want to go home?" I ask, hoping she still wants to be there.

She shakes her head. "Show me," she says. "Take me somewhere you can show me the dragon."

CHAPTER 34
Elise

E than drugged me and this is the weirdest hallucination I could ever dream up. That's the only explanation.

My boyfriend is claiming he's a dragon, and also my mate, which apparently means our new relationship is permanent, and also that I'm entitled to half his money. Also, as far as I can tell, he healed me with his spit, and said he'd planned to murder my ex if only it wasn't a complicated political decision, but that murdering him still isn't off the table.

Whatever was in those drugs, I don't want it again.

Marcus takes me out a back door, which is good because he refuses to put me down, and I refuse to be carried in front of his co-workers and employees. We avoid the coat check by the front entirely, but Marcus is radiating enough body heat to keep me warm, which I don't let myself think about too hard.

The man I got just a glimpse of earlier is there. "John," Marcus says, nodding his head.

John holds out his keys. "Bring it back, please."

"Find Elise's purse for me," is all he says, and then he walks around to put me in the passenger's seat of a too-nice car.

He drives without talking. I see him open his mouth a few times, then close it again. Which is both a blessing and a curse; I think any more information would make my head explode, but not talking also leaves me too much time to think.

Because the thing is, I'm coming to the realization that this might not be a hallucination. It's crazy, but the scary part is that it makes sense. Aren't hallucinations supposed to fall apart when you examine the logic too closely?

Okay, so I apparently have a habit of dating supernatural creatures. I've now lived with two of them without being any the wiser.

I force myself to take deep breaths.

When we leave the city, I have to say something. "Is this where you bring me to a deserted place to hide my body?"

He grips the wheel so tight the car jerks slightly. "Don't even joke about that," he says, his voice hitting that deeper resonance I've noticed before, that now I know comes from the dragon inside him. "I would literally die before hurting you, Elise."

I don't get the feeling that he's being dramatic. "So, you're taking me to the middle of nowhere to…" I prompt, instead of unpacking what he said.

"To show you, like you asked," he says. "The magic takes a lot of space, so I'm finding us somewhere quiet."

"Oh," I say, and my voice sounds far away. "You have magic now, too." Of course he does. This just keeps getting better.

Ethan has magic. That thing with his eyes, and his claws—is this the first time he used those on me? My breathing picks up again, and I try to force deep breaths, but I'm barely successful.

"Did you think turning into a dragon at will isn't magic?" he challenges. "I have magic. I'm not a sorcerer, but I was born with an innate sense of magic. It's not limitless, and it's very much related to who I am. I can hide and summon the dragon. I can, with great exertion, use magic to cloak the dragon's presence so humans don't see a giant winged beast flying in the night sky."

"You healed me," I remember hazily.

His hands tense on the wheel again. "I did," he agrees hesitantly. "That's more because it's you, though."

I take a deep breath before I demand, *what the fuck does that mean?* I can tell he's trying, and he's right; it's not his fault he's like this and I'm me. "Why because I'm me?"

He shrugs, then flips on his directional to turn left. "You're my mate. You'll find that my fluids are kind of potent."

Okay, this time I can't resist. "What the fuck does that mean?" That's not the type of line you just drop on someone. His fluids are potent? That sounds like an STI or something.

He winces. "Continuously taking in my fluids will have effects on you," he says evasively.

That is the opposite of helpful. "Say what you mean, Marcus."

271

He sighs. "My semen, Elise. My spunk. Whatever. Taking in my seed will functionally change you temporarily." Before I can wind up to ask what the fuck that means, he's already explaining. "I've lived a very long life, and I have many years yet to go. Having a human mate would be a miserable existence if I couldn't give you a life as long as mine."

I'm left speechless for a moment too long. "So you altered me?"

"It's temporary. Keep sleeping with me and it keeps happening. Stop, and you'll go back to what you think of as normal."

He's talking about immortality. He's talking about me being functionally immortal because of his dick. I don't know what to do with that. "You didn't tell me."

He grimaces. "It's automatic. I can't stop it. And I should have told you, but that would involve spilling this whole mess, and I wanted to do that more delicately. When we were both ready."

"When you knew it wouldn't send me screaming," I correct.

"Ideally, yes. But if you want to run screaming, I won't stop you. I promise, nothing I did ties me to you."

"You wouldn't stop me?" I press, because from everything he's saying, I doubt he'd truly just let me go.

"Your choice," he says, with a forced levelness to his voice. "Always, Elise." His hand tightens on the wheel again, and I wonder if he thinks I'm about to run from a moving car.

Am I? I probably should be, because this man is telling me he's an ancient mythical being and, what's worse, I'm becoming more and more convinced we're both in our right minds and that I believe him. That should be the sign to get away before I get myself in too deep to yet another something I can't escape.

But it's still Marcus next to me. Marcus, and everything that comes with him. Marcus, the man who I dove in head first with, even with all the lessons I learned from the past. Even when I should have known better.

"You didn't explain the spit thing," I mumble instead of sorting through all of that.

He shrugs. "Wouldn't be a very worthwhile immortality if a little injury could take you out, would it? Dragons have magic; this is just a practical application of it."

If he thinks that's a clear explanation, then he has another thing coming. But I don't ask. I don't think I can really take anymore.

But there is one thing I have to know. "Your eyes changed."

"Yeah," he agrees hesitantly.

"Ethan's did too. When they did, I felt..."

"Like you truly wanted to do whatever he wanted?" he suggests when it's clear that I can't find the words. I nod, and he continues. "If you're wondering if I can do that, I can't. My claws don't drug people either. Ethan feeds off of emotions; he can manipulate his victims in that slimy way of us. I just am a dragon. All my magic is related to that."

273

The giant knot in my belly eases slightly. I don't know if I should believe anything right now, but I somehow still trust Marcus.

"Ethan was trying to... what, exactly?"

"My guess is convince you to leave with him, come back to him. He wanted to force you to feel the dependence you used to have on him." He darts a quick look at me. "I don't know for sure, but I doubt it's the first time. I'm sorry, Elise."

"He needs me to feed?" When Marcus just nods, I huff. "Surely he has to have realized I'm not going to do that anymore."

Marcus is quiet for a long moment. "Elise, I hate thinking about this, but he's been manipulating you since the beginning, both in normal human ways and mystical ways. I'm sure of it. If he put all that work into you, I doubt he'd want to give you up."

My stomach twists at the thought, and I curl my arm around it, suddenly convinced I'm going to puke. I force myself to breathe through it. I'm not going to puke in this car that isn't even Marcus', and I'm not going to get so bent out of shape over Ethan. He's not worth it.

Marcus makes a noise low in his throat. "I'm sorry. He'll never touch you again."

"You going to protect me?" I ask. I know Marcus is bigger than Ethan, and I know he's telling me all these crazy things about what he is. But I just can't picture Marcus, my Marcus, hurting anyone.

"You'll see." He turns onto a quiet road. He parks, then turns to me. "If this freaks you out, you can come back to the car," he says. He sounds calm, but I know it's a front; his whole body is practically vibrating with tension. "Just know that, no matter what form I'm in, I'd never hurt you. Never."

Deep down, I think I know that's true. It doesn't mean I'll remember it when confronted with an actual dragon, though.

And here I am, just accepting that my boyfriend is about to turn into an actual dragon.

"Okay," is all I can manage to say.

He opens his mouth to say more, then closes it and nods definitively, unbuckling his seatbelt and opening his door. I follow suit.

What's the minimum safe distance from a dragon? Should I be worried about being stepped on, or burned to a crisp? Or eaten? I know he said that I'm safe with him, but surely there's only so much control one can have over a mythical creature like that.

Marcus steps smartly away from me, and I wait for the inevitable moment: either this insanity is all real, or the hallucination will fall apart now.

The change is so quick that I'm honestly not sure if my brain fully processes it until afterwards. One minute there's a man I know, and the next there's a dragon. Tall as the house I grew up in, a deep forest green, and looking like he could kill a human without a second thought, Marcus the dragon turns to me.

"Don't be afraid." That voice could knock over the trees near us, it's so powerful. "Angel, you don't need to be afraid of me."

I don't know how he knows I'm freaking the fuck out when he won't look directly at me. Can he hear my pounding heartbeat? Or maybe he can smell it. Reptiles have good senses of smell, don't they?

He doesn't move, holding still like he can somehow blend into the background. It's somewhat ridiculous, and the silliness of Marcus, tall as a tree and with an arm—or front leg, because I'm unclear on the appropriate terminology—bigger than my whole body trying to hold still like that won't scare me, breaks my fear for a moment.

I take a step closer.

Like he forgot that he's been trying not to scare me, Marcus spins towards me. His eyes are still green in this form, but somehow deeper, like there's a flame crackling behind them.

It's mesmerizing, and I find myself unable to look away.

Marcus holds still again, and I think he might actually be holding his breath. I take another step closer.

"Are there any rules?" I ask him.

"Rules?" he repeats like the word is entirely foreign.

"Forgive me, I don't know the etiquette of interacting with dragons."

"Angel, you could do literally anything right now. Nothing's off limits for you."

That sounds like a lot of bullshit, and something I don't truly want to test out, considering the size of him. When he speaks, I get a good glimpse of those teeth, and no, thank you. I'll do whatever I need to in order to stay on the right side of those.

Not that I think Marcus would ever hurt me. I've been stupidly trusting towards that man from the start. But here he is, menacing and huge, and I'd be an idiot not to think about that. Even if it was an accident, there's no question that he could literally step on me in this form.

Even so, I take him at his word. With a depth of courage I didn't know I had, I step all the way up to him.

"You'll have to bend down," I whisper, confident he can hear me, regardless. "You're too tall for me to reach, Marcus."

"Do you want me closer to you?" he asks. From this close, the rumble of his voice literally shakes my bones. I hold steady, trying to make myself see the sound as soothing rather than intimidating.

"Yes, Marcus. I do. That's why I asked."

Slowly, looking at me the entire time like he expects me to change my mind, he bends his head down to my level. When I can reach, I lay a hand over his snout, sure that's some-how rude—is it the equivalent of putting my hand over his nose?—but he did say I could do whatever I wanted.

The scales are rough under my hands. They're hot, too, which I didn't expect, but maybe I should have. Marcus heats the bed like a space heater when we're sleeping together, and I've taken to wearing practically nothing to bed. Of course, a dragon would be hot.

"Can you blow fire?" I ask.

"If I wanted." I wait for a beat, expecting some sort of demonstration that doesn't happen. "This isn't a safe place to do that," he points out. "I could burn all these trees down. And you're too close for it to be safe."

"Alright. Any other dragon abilities?" I wonder, oddly touched that even as a giant creature, Marcus is being careful and safety-conscious.

He shakes his wings out behind him. They make enough of a breeze to rustle my hair. "How do humans not know you're here, if you can fly? Do you just not?"

"On the contrary, that's some of the magic I was talking about. It takes concentration, but I can prevent them from noticing me."

I lean my head forward, resting my forehead where my hand was a moment before. The scales abrade my skin lightly, but I don't move, just breathing him in. He even smells like fire, like bonfires and crackling wood.

He's holding perfectly still, like he thinks I'm going to panic any second. "You're not scared of me?"

"Should I be?"

"I'd hoped you'd never be," he says. "But I worried…"

"This is going to take…so much getting used to," I tell him as honestly as I can. "But I know you're the same person who took a risk to give me this job, who let me live in your penthouse when I needed a place, who sat with me when Ethan was sending all those messages, and everything else. You're the person who took me dress shopping because you wanted me to feel special on our first date, and who got pizza on our second because that's what I wanted. You just have this too."

CHAPTER 35
Marcus

I'm in absolute awe of Elise. My pretty human mate, so stunning, always so brilliant, and handling this world-altering information better than I could ever have imagined.

I shouldn't have had to break the news to her this way, but I appreciate that she's handling the changes so well. And I'm sure there will be rough patches; at some point, the adjustment will no doubt catch up to her. But for now, my mate is looking at me with a calm in her eyes that I can't quite believe.

It's not just calm. It's confidence, a quiet sort of knowledge. She knows I'm hers. She's confident that this new revelation won't change that fact, and she's holding my gaze, letting me see all of her, letting me know she's not backing down from us.

Most people can hardly stand to look into the eyes of my human form, never mind the dragon. Even humans who don't believe in dragons can't quite forget the instinctive fear. But not Elise. No, she stares me right in the eye, calm as can be, and tells me she isn't scared.

"Do you want to fly?" I ask impulsively, wanting to give her the sky I like so much.

She raises an eyebrow, twitching slightly in her surprise. "Is that allowed?"

"I told you: everything is allowed if you want it."

"Just wasn't sure if it'd be rude," she mumbles.

"Rude?"

"You know. Riding you. Like a horse or something."

I huff a laugh, which in this form sounds unnaturally deep. "Angel, anytime you want to ride me, in any form—you're always more than invited."

She flushes. "Maybe later." I'm already imagining it.

"I've never done this type of riding before," I freely admit, needing her to know that she's the first and only. That she's special, and that this part of me is for her and her alone. "So bare with me while we figure out logistics. If it's something you want," I add, realizing she never actually agreed.

She bites her lip for a moment. "You won't let me fall?"

"I won't let you fall," I promise.

She nods slowly. "Alright, how do I do this?"

I think the easiest way is to get as low as possible, then let her climb on, so I lower myself until my belly is in the dirt. It's an undignified position, but fuck if I care when Elise is climbing onto my back.

She's still wearing the dress she wore to the party, so it takes her a second to get settled. "Let me know if you get too cold," I tell her, wishing I'd stopped for her coat.

"You're basically a furnace. I won't get too cold." Maybe not now, but a few hundred feet in the air, moving at the speeds I can fly at, the wind chill will freeze her. I'll need to be careful, and if she ever wants to do this again, find her some more appropriate clothes for the occasion.

"Hold on tight," I instruct her. "We won't be going far or too high—it's too cold and I can't risk us being seen."

"I thought you said you had magic for that."

"Magic that prevents humans from seeing me. Seeing as you're a human and will be in the air, I'd prefer not to mess with your mind."

"Oh, shit. That can happen?"

In truth, I have no idea. I've never tried to exclude a human from the effects of my magic before. "I'd prefer not to test it for the first time mid-flight."

"Yeah, I—yeah."

"Hold tight," I remind her, and I feel her fingers and thighs gripping me as I beat my wings once, using my back legs to push us towards the sky.

There's nothing quite like flying. It's a reminder that, whatever else changes, however else the world moves on, the dragon will always be king of the sky.

"Holy shit," Elise murmurs, her voice carried away by the wind so I can barely hear it. Her heart thumps rapidly in her chest, but I don't think she's panicking.

She starts to laugh. First a little, just a small chuckle, and then a moment later she's laughing so wildly that her whole body is shaking, and I'm worried for a split second that she'll lose her grip on me. But I can't quite tell her to get herself under control—she sounds free.

Testing my theory, I climb a little higher, waiting to see what she'll do. Her thighs tighten around me, her hands dig into my scales, and she leans forward, as if urging me to go faster. Naturally, I give her what she wants.

It's a beautiful night, with clear, star-filled skies, and I think I could fly like this forever. It's been so long since I've truly stretched my wings, and the dragon's instincts inside me are rumbling with contentment, purring with satisfaction. I have the skies and I have my mate: what else could a dragon ever ask for?

I could let those instincts win and fly all night, but I'm still conscious of Elise's human needs. And she's not showing it, but I'm sure she's cold.

I circle back towards where the car is, carefully negotiating the landing to help Elise keep her seat.

When we're firmly back on the ground, I lower down to the ground, enabling her to slide off of me easier.

Once she's on her feet and has adjusted her dress, she walks right over to me and rests her face against mine once more. "How easy is it for you to change back and forth?"

"Easy enough if I have space," I say slowly. "Do you want me to change back?"

"Please."

So I do, watching her with trepidation. I thought she enjoyed flying enough that I might have won her over, but perhaps her wanting me to change back so desperately is a sign that my dragon form is disturbing to her.

As soon as I'm back in my human form, Elise lunges forward and grabs me, pulling my face down to hers for a kiss that makes my whole body catch fire.

I kiss her back, holding her around the waist to pull her close. "What was that for?" I ask after a minute, ghosting my lips down to her neck, pressing a series of kisses along the soft skin there, delighting in feeling her shiver under my touch.

Her fingers have moved from my face down to my back, the tips of her fingers pressing into me like she's afraid I'll bolt. Which is ridiculous, because I doubt anything on this earth could actually get me to move from her side, but I'll let her hold me as hard as she wants.

"Do you always purr when you fly?" she asks instead of answering.

"I do not purr."

"You do," she says. "It's kind of like a low rumbling, I guess. A vibration." She shivers, and I don't think it's just from my lips on her skin this time.

"Elise... did I turn you on?" I ask, delighted by the revelation. Whether it's the vibration of my apparent purring, or the freedom of flying, or any and all combination of the above, I don't care. Elise not only accepts the dragon side of me, but she's actually turned on by it. "Do you want me to make you come, Angel?"

Her head tilts back, and I take the opportunity to suck at her collarbone. "Please," she whispers.

"Happy to be of service," I say, and then I scoop her up, encouraging her to wrap her legs around my waist as I walk us to the nearby tree. "You're not too cold, right? We can go to the car." John might lose his shit if he smells that we fucked in his car, but I'm prepared to buy him a new car if that's what it takes to fuck Elise and ensure she's comfortable.

Her legs tighten on my hips. "You're so warm, Marcus. Keep me warm."

With an invitation like that, how can I resist?

I still have my suit coat on, so I shed it quickly, dropping it unceremoniously onto the ground before lowering Elise on top of it. I'm sure my jacket doesn't do much to insulate her from the cold ground, but like she said, I can keep her warm.

"You liked how it felt to ride the dragon?" I ask her, my voice a low rumble I barely recognize, the dragon peeking out of me even in this form. "You like knowing that creature is obsessed with your pleasure?" I kneel between her spread thighs, rucking up her dress, then staring at the tantalizing panties covering what I'm so desperate for.

She smiles and spreads her thighs wider for me. "Marcus—"

"Yes, Elise?"

"I want to ride the dragon," she says, enunciating each word clearly.

I'm on my back in a second, not caring that I'm lying right in the dirt. I tug her on top of me, and she goes easily enough, laughing slightly when my grabbing hands pull a little too hard, a little too desperate.

"Can I take this off?" I ask, playing with the dress I've bunched up around her hips. Instead of answering me, she pulls it up over her head, tossing it aside.

She's not wearing a bra, and I'm left absolutely breathless, staring at her hard nipples pebbling in the cold air, hungry for the warmth of my touch. Holding her hips to ensure I don't dislodge her, I sit up, keeping her in my lap. When I'm at eye-level with her, she opens her mouth to protest the new position, but I just smile and bend my head, determined to keep those beautiful tits warm with my tongue.

Judging by the tight grip she has on my hair, she appreciates my efforts. "Marcus—" I don't stop, don't dare to move my head back, just suck and tease and feel her wiggle on my lap. My cock aches for more, and I imagine her pretty cunt is all slick and ready for me, but I continue to tease us both, keeping us on the edge, determined to see what she'll do next.

CHAPTER 36
Elise

I begin to rock my hips with purpose instead of just desperation, determined to see if I can make Marcus as needy for me as I am for him. His fingers dig into my waist, his tongue teases my breasts, and his cock grows even harder under me, but he doesn't break.

Fuck, this man does things to me I didn't know were possible. Maybe it's the supernatural creature in him—it was his dragon form acting like the world's largest vibrator that put me here after all. Then again, my last lover was also supernatural, and it certainly felt nothing like this.

Marcus rocks up into me, a groan escaping from his mouth. Right. No more thinking about Ethan. I'm here with Marcus.

Marcus, who I was pissed at a few hours ago. Fuck, that already feels so long ago, the events of tonight a jumbled mess.

My boyfriend can fly. He can fly and he took me flying, made me feel things I've never felt before. And I'm not just talking about how wet I am right now, although maybe that's part of it. But what I felt when we were in the air together—that's something I've never felt before, and could never have imagined.

I tug on Marcus' hair a little harder, trying to draw his head back. He responds, looking up at me with those eyes, the ones that I now recognize as more dragon than human. They burn with the fire behind them, and it might be a bit conceited, but right now, I think they burn for me.

Like he wants to prove me right, he licks his lips. "I ache for you, Elise. Please. What do you want?"

"I want to ride the dragon," I say again, and it somehow sounds less stupid this time. The way his pupils get impossibly bigger at the thought might have something to do with it.

"Whatever my mate wants, she gets," he says, his voice barely a rasp. He goes to lie back again, but not before he sneaks in a squeeze at my breasts. "Can't believe you went all night without a bra."

"The structure of that dress..." I begin, but he rolls his hips up to interrupt me.

"Angel, I'm not complaining about the dress, or your tits, or anything else like that. Just can't believe I didn't know. It would have consumed my every thought." Now lying on his back, he reaches up and lightly pinches my left nipple, sending a shudder through me.

He makes a show of laying his hands by his head in the dirt. "Well, come here. Ride your dragon."

My stupid panties are still in the way, and he's clothed except for his suit jacket. I suppose there's some sort of magic that protects his clothes, and I might be interested in learning about it later, but right now I wish his clothes were gone.

I stand up enough to push my panties down my hips, kicking them away, and say to him, "Get undressed for me, Marcus."

"Yes, ma'am," he responds. He physically rips his shirt off his body, sending buttons flying. I'm sure that shirt cost more than I want to think about, but I'm also sure I would have done the same thing if I had the strength. Then he arches his hips, pushing his pants down and kicking until he forces shoes and pants off his feet.

I go to straddle him again, but he makes a sound. "If you're going to ride the dragon," he says, "you might as well do it properly."

I'm inches away from his cock and raise an eyebrow. "Properly?"

"I know you want my cock, and you'll get it. But first—let me taste how wet riding me like that made you."

Fuck. "You want me to...?"

"Sit on my face, Elise," he growls. "Sit down and ride me until you come all over my tongue. Please. I'll beg if I have to."

"I know you're supernatural and apparently don't worry about the things us mere mortals do—"

"—You're not really a mere mortal anymore, Elise, not that you could have ever qualified as mere anything—"

"—But surely you still need to breathe."

"I need to breathe in the sweet scent of your cunt," he says, eyes smoldering and voice low and serious, which only makes my pussy even wetter. "Sit on my face, Elise. Give us both what you need."

"I'm serious, Marcus, I could—"

Apparently done waiting for me to give in, he grips my waist and drags me to his face, sending me tumbling to my knees. His firm grip on me keeps me from going completely flat on my face, but I end up on my hands and knees, hands just over his head and cunt so close to his face that I can feel him breathing on me.

"That's it," he croons. "Sit down, Angel."

He's made what he wants clear, and if I hurt him—well, I just have to trust that he knows what he can handle. Delicately, I press a bit of my weight down.

He growls and squeezes my hips again, this time pressing me to his face like he truly wants to smother himself in my pussy. "Marcus," I practically squeal, but then it's immediately drowned out by a groan of pleasure as his tongue licks along my wet folds.

The sounds of how wet I am shouldn't surprise me. But it's so loud, so obvious, that I flush before I hear his inhuman groan, his desperation as he drives his tongue into me, squeezing me like he can somehow force us even closer.

"Careful," I mutter, still conscious enough to worry about hurting him.

He bodily lifts me, holding me a few inches above his face with just the strength of his arms. "Stop worrying. Ride my face and make yourself come. Trust me." And then, like there can be no argument with that, he lowers me, squeezing me to his face, and dives back in.

If he's not worried, I suppose I don't need to be, either. He's clearly strong enough to force me off of him if he needs me to move. I rock against his face, moaning as he expertly drives me higher and higher. Completely forgetting my earlier fears, I grind against his face, finding that just-right angle, and let him push me over the edge.

My legs shake, my pussy spasms, and I let out a high-pitched keening I've never heard from myself before, letting the after-shocks roll through me as he refuses to stop licking at me.

"Marcus," I moan. His tongue circles my clit in answer. "Marcus, please, I need—" He doesn't let me finish the thought, licking me like I'm an ice cream cone and he's desperate for the taste. "I want to come on your cock!" I manage.

That seems to draw his attention. He slides me off of his face, sitting me on his chest while he watches me. His face is obscene, with blown pupils and my wetness smeared all over his jaw. He licks his lips, looking even more debauched. "My mate gets what she wants," he rasps. "But I want you to know you can ride my face whenever the desire strikes you. Consider it a personal favor to me."

I don't think I'm quite there yet. I don't know if I'll ever get to the point where I'll just brazenly straddle his head without his coaxing, but the way he's looking up at me somehow makes me want to.

"You're wet and dripping for me," Marcus murmurs. "Climb on. Take what you need."

I slide down his body, positioning myself over his cock. A hot flush of embarrassment floods my veins when I see that I've left a trail of my own wetness down his torso. When Marcus sees what I'm looking at, his mouth falls open and his eyes go even wider. He trails a hand down his chest, running a finger through my come before bringing it to his mouth, and groans as he sucks his finger clean.

He sucks his finger like it's a delicacy, and I get the sudden realization that he appreciates my cunt more than he's ever appreciated anything I've cooked for him, which is really saying something, considering how complimentary he is towards my cooking.

I position the tip of his cock at my entrance, feeling the piercing rub against my sensitive skin, and then stop, another thought striking me.

"You said your come literally changes me." It sounds so ridiculous to say.

He goes very still. "Yes?" he says, phrasing it like a question, like he knows he's treading on dangerous ground.

"That when you come in me, you're essentially making me immortal." That sounds somehow more ridiculous.

He just nods this time.

I dig the nails of my free hand into his chest slightly, leaving little half-moon marks on his skin. "I think I want that. To have that with you." I feel like I'm diving headfirst off a cliff, hurtling into this without knowing what's at the bottom. At the same time, I know there's no stopping me. I already started the dive. I've committed, and I don't regret it yet.

Then, before he can answer, I sink down on his cock, taking him in me all the way to the base.

"Oh, fuck," he mutters, and I'd echo the sentiment if I could talk, but he stretches me so wide it's like all the air is pushed out of my lungs for a moment. I'm so full, every inch of him filling me, touching every spot inside me—

I squeeze around him experimentally, and he groans.

"Elise, please—"

Riding him is worth it for that sound alone, that gentle begging. I'm determined to make him do it again, so, with one hand still digging into his chest, I rock my hips.

I just came, and yet there's something about Marcus that has me almost on the edge again. I experiment slightly, trying to find the angle to rock my hips at that will push him the furthest, but right now, it seems like everything is making him crazy. He's thrashing beneath me, rocking his hips as best he can to drive even deeper into me. Even so, he holds out.

"You need to come in me," I whisper to him, twisting my hips in a way that has him gripping my thighs. "If you come in me, this is real, right? I'm your mate, and we're together forever, and—" I don't know half the bullshit spilling out of my mouth, except I somehow know it's all real. Forever is a big word for such a new relationship, for someone like me who should be cautious, but I say it anyway, and I mean it.

Marcus growls, and then before I know what's going on, I'm on my back and he's folded his body around mine, dragging my thighs around his hips, hovering right over my face. "You're mine," he says as he thrusts into me. "Whether or not I come in you. Whether or not you give me that now or later or never. Nothing can change that you're my mate and I'm yours and please, Elise—"

The begging does me in. His eyes are wild as he pounds into me with powerful thrusts, like he has to fuck this truth into me, like the dragon instincts can somehow be forced into me. And it's somehow working. I might not see *mate* when I look at him, but I do see forever. I do see mine.

I work one hand into the hair at the base of his neck and pull, squeezing my thighs and my pussy around him. "Marcus, I need—"

I don't get to finish my thought, because Marcus is already working a hand between us, finding my clit and stroking. "Play with those pretty tits for me, Angel."

I do, and he pulls back far enough so he can watch me, groaning at the sight. "Goddamn perfect," he rumbles, and his thrusts somehow become even more intense, like he's completely lost control now.

Good. I think I like him like this. I like his eyes, intense and wild and focused entirely on me, giving me a glimpse of the creature underneath. I like his hand on me, playing my body just right, and the way he thrusts in me like he's chasing some impossible high. I like the deeper timbre of his voice, his desperation, and how ready he is to fall apart completely at the seams.

I can't resist, can't hold back any longer, so with his name on my lips, I arch up against him, falling over that edge and coming so hard my vision whites out at the edges.

Marcus growls, animalistic and low, and then he's coming too, filling me completely as he desperately rocks into me. "You're fucking perfect," he gasps before burying his face in my neck.

I experimentally stretch my limbs underneath him, trying to bring feeling back into them. I'm still so deliciously full, and I can feel his come leaking out around the cock still stretching me wide. Once upon a time, that might have felt gross, but I suddenly have a new appreciation of it.

Marcus starts pressing kisses wherever he can reach, down my neck, across my sternum, across my breasts. "You are amazing," he whispers against my skin. "Mine, fuck, no dragon has ever been so lucky, I can't—" He cuts himself off, trying to reach down to press kisses on my stomach, but can't make it work while still inside me. He makes a discontented little noise that nearly makes me laugh, and then he pulls out of me, sliding down my body slightly so he can press kisses to my belly.

I squirm. "Marcus, I can't go again." I'm not actually sure that's true—I think Marcus' talented tongue could make me do just about anything—but I know if I let him start again, I'll end the night impossibly sore and exhausted beyond belief, and I don't want that.

We have a long drive back to the apartment, after all. And just because I'm apparently all in on this doesn't mean that I don't have questions.

"I know, I know," he reassures me before pressing an open-mouthed kiss just above my belly button. "Just let me touch you. Nothing else. Please?"

It's those eyes that get to me. He looks up at me pleading, and I let my head fall back. "Can't resist those eyes."

His hands find my thighs and stroke over the skin there. It's meant to soothe, not titillate, but he's still desperately close to my still-dripping pussy, and I can't forget that. "You know that my eyes scare everyone but you?" he asks.

I nearly choke, the whiplash of his gentle touches and the tease of how close he is with his serious conversation too much to handle at once. "What?"

"Dragon's eyes," he explains, his breath tickling my belly. "It's some sort of long-ingrained prey instinct. Because if the dragon was hunting you and set its sights on you, that was it. Almost no one could hope to outrun the dragon. Creatures like me, humans, animals, they all have that instinct somewhere. But not you."

I work shaky fingers into his hair. "You wouldn't hurt me."

"Never," he agrees immediately.

"Does the dragon want to hunt me down?"

He looks up and grins. "Tonight aside, I admit I'm not really one for rough-housing in the woods. But if you want the dragon to chase you down, all you have to do is say."

There's a stick poking into my back that was easy to ignore when I was practically high on pleasure, but the slight pain of it is persistent now, which makes me think sex outside isn't something I'm interested in repeating soon. "Let's put a pin in that," I say, but I can't quite suppress the shiver, anyway.

"I should get you home. Somewhere warm and somewhere clean," he says, apparently now fully aware that we fucked right out in the open, in the dirt. The night is cold, but I was serious when I said I knew Marcus could keep me warm.

He helps me to my feet like a proper gentleman, and then we're left to try to get our clothes back on. My dress is fine if messy, but my panties are dirty in a way I don't want against my pussy. Marcus' shirt is ruined, but his pants seem to be salvageable.

"Hope we don't get pulled over on the way home," I mutter, thinking of what an obvious tableau we make.

"Afraid people will know that I'm so absolutely crazy for you that I couldn't help myself?" he teases, opening the passenger side door for me.

"I think I jumped you, actually."

"And I was a more than enthusiastic participant, trust me." He shuts my door gently, then moves to the driver's side. "Are you ready to go home?"

Home. It's been that for a while now, hasn't it? I know we've both said it before, but it feels somehow more permanent now.

I'm not some passing fancy to Marcus. I'm not something he'll move on from as soon as he finds out he can have better. He's apparently been doing whatever possible to tie the two of us together forever. He sees us as eternal.

From anyone else, it would sound like a line. From Marcus, who can turn into a great big dragon and literally take me flying and show me things I didn't even know were possible. This is real.

"Let's go home," I say, mind whirling. "Can I ask you questions while you drive?"

"You can ask me questions whenever you want," he promises. He starts the car, then puts it in drive. "What do you want to know?"

I don't even know where to start. "Everything."

He chuckles. "I'll tell you everything, Elise. That's a promise. But I might need a place to start. I'm old; there's been a lot."

"How old?" That seems like an important enough question to start with.

"A few thousand years. Back then, there were more dragons."

A few thousand years is an absolutely impossible number to wrap my mind around, so I focus on the second half. "Are there not a lot of dragons left?"

He shrugs. "A few dozen, I'd guess? We're not especially social creatures. Actually, we're downright territorial, so no one is collecting a census. But as humans became more... just more, it became harder to be us in the open. If you didn't have the magic to hide yourself and the smarts to use your human form wisely, you died out. Survival of the fittest, and all that."

"I'm sorry."

He shrugs again. "Like I said, we're pretty solitary. Dragons don't typically interact with each other out of their immediate family units and their mate. I speak with my father sometimes, but that's it."

"Your mother?"

"I told you the truth when I said she'd passed on."

"I'm sorry." I am, too, because that sounds miserable, to live so long without someone. I wonder how his father is handling that, if Marcus' parents were mates. But then another thought strikes me.

"I'm going to outlive my mother too, aren't I?"

His hand tightens on the wheel. "Most people do outlive their parents, Elise."

"You know what I mean."

He nods. "If we stopped having sex, you'd go back to normal. It would take a little bit of time—it's not instantaneous—but it would eventually happen. So I suppose if you want a mortal lifespan, then you can make that decision."

"And what would happen to you?"

"Don't worry about me."

He can say that all he wants, but I do worry about him. "I think it's safe to assume that I want this," I say cautiously, thinking back to how I was practically ready to jump him while he was still in dragon form.

"Sleep on it, Elise. You're allowed to change your mind." I know he feels like it's the right thing to say, and I appreciate him saying it, but I also see that he can't help a pleased smile when I say that I want this with him.

"So, let's say we do this. What does this look like to you?"

"What does it look like to you?" he challenges.

"I asked first."

He chuckles slightly. "Alright, alright. To me? I'd love exactly what we have right now. You in our nest, us having a life together. Getting to hold you, love you. Maybe you'd actually let me spoil you."

I sputter. "You have done nothing but spoil me since the day we met."

"Oh, Angel. If you think that's spoiling, then you have another thing coming. Dragons live to spoil our mates. It's half our purpose in life."

"That's a little overdramatic," I tease, but he doesn't crack a smile.

"Dragons like stuff. Possessions. We are collectors and eagerly acquire whatever catches our interests. But the whole point is to have a mate to share it with. You are mine and I am yours and so is everything I have. I want to give you everything."

I sputter. "You're saying you're rich because of me?"

"I'm saying I never would have worked half as hard as I did if I wasn't motivated by the idea of someday sharing it with you." He takes his eyes off the road long enough to look at me. "Will that convince you to let me spoil you now?"

He's saying that, over several thousand years, he's worked to build some seriously insane wealth just to give it to me. Absolutely unbelievable. "Maybe sometimes," I manage to concede.

"I'll take what I can get. And I'll convince you. Anything in the world you want and it's yours. I told you what I imagine for our future, but I am open to any adjustments you want. If you want to spend the next three decades traveling the world, tasting everything it has to offer, then that's what we'll do. If you want to live in a castle in France, then I'll find us a castle. If you want to move back to your hometown and live next door to your mom for the rest of her life, then I'll look for real estate."

I make a face at that. "My mom and I have a call each other once every few months or so type of relationship. We're not becoming neighbors."

"Okay, so that's one thing off the list. For now, though. Feel free to modify it at any time. You might want that, later."

When my mother gets old and I don't, I hear even if he doesn't say it. I don't want to think about that yet.

"We also are not moving into a castle in France," I say sternly, just in case he takes me not immediately shutting that idea down as permission to start going castle shopping on my behalf.

Fuck, I have the type of man who knows how to go about buying a castle. I knew that objectively before—there can't be that much difference between paying for a castle and paying for a penthouse like his—but it's mind-boggling to actually discuss it like this.

"Would that make you the princess the big bad dragon is holding hostage?" he muses, grinning to himself as he drives.

"You're showing me some interesting fantasies today," I tease him, relieved to move on to lighter topics.

"You're one to talk, Ms.-let-me-ride-the-dragon."

I flush. It sounds even more sordid when he puts it that way. "Are you complaining?"

"Fuck, no. Ride this dragon whenever and wherever you want." He takes one hand off the wheel to squeeze my thigh, my bare skin somehow even more sensitive to his touch than usual. "And for the record? I want to hear all your fantasies."

He'll be sorely disappointed, because I don't have a deep well to draw on. Then again, Marcus is an inspiring man, and I somehow know I'll come up with something.

Chapter 37
Marcus

E lise asks me questions the whole way home, like where I was raised—a truly impressive cave system in the Andes—and if I was hatched from an egg or not. I laugh at that one, reassuring her there were no eggs involved, and there won't be if she chooses to have children with me someday, either. She blushes when she asks me if our children would be more like her or me, and doesn't seem satisfied with my explanation of "magic" when I explain that they will almost certainly be dragons.

These hypothetical babies would be dragons like me, but I can't help but hope they are more like their mother in every other way. Not that I'm asking her for children anytime soon, and I reassure her of that—we have forever, after all, and even if our nest is only ever for the two of us, I will truly still be the happiest dragon to ever live.

As we get closer to the city, her questions taper off, and I look over to realize she's fallen asleep, looking adorable with her hair a sex-induced mess, her dress barely holding together, and her legs spread slightly.

When we get back home, I pull into the parking garage we never use, then carefully lift her out of the car and carry her upstairs.

"Marcus?" she asks me, voice groggy with sleep, as the elevator starts to move.

"Shhh." I hold her closer. "Keep sleeping, Angel. You're okay."

She looks at me for a long moment, then lets her eyes fall closed again and snuggles into my chest, and I feel like the greatest, strongest man alive that she trusts me like this.

When we make it upstairs, I bring us straight to our bedroom, laying her down on the bed. She doesn't wake again. I take a moment to assess, kneeling down to unstrap the shoes that somehow seem to be the only clothing item to escape tonight entirely unscathed. Once they're discarded, I eye the dress, wondering if it's better or worse to leave it. Ultimately, I decide it has to go, considering the amount of dirt on it now, and that zipper in the back can't be comfortable to sleep on.

We have dirt on us, dirt and sweat and come. But a shower can wait; she looks so peaceful in sleep.

I find one of my t-shirts and slide her into it, moving her like a rag doll. Then I quickly shed my own pants, leaving me in just my underwear and slipping into bed with her, pulling her close.

I kiss the top of her head, taking a long moment to just breathe her scent in.

"Goodnight, Angel."

She doesn't respond, just snuggles closer, warm and soft against me, and with her skin pressed against mine and her scent surrounding me, I fall asleep.

I wake up alone. It's not my favorite way to wake up, although I'm getting used to it by now. Elise is a morning person.

The smell of baking cinnamon wafting through the apartment is a decent consolation prize. I get out of bed, taking a moment to use the bathroom and brush my teeth before going to find Elise.

The scent gets even stronger, and I find Elise leaning against the counter, a bowl next to her elbow and the oven baking away.

She's so distracted by her phone that she doesn't even notice me coming in. I move behind her and wrap my arms around her, kissing the top of her head. She startles for a second, but then settles into my arms. "Good morning, beautiful."

"Marcus, I—" She seems almost lost.

"What's so interesting to you, there?"

"My blog gained twenty followers overnight," she blurts out. "And a shit ton of comments. Someone asked if I'd do videos."

I lean over her shoulder to see her phone. "Oh, you met her last night," I tell her, looking at the name on the comment. "She works in acquisitions, remember?"

"Yeah, but..." she shakes her head in amazement. "I spoke with her for like twenty minutes. I just mentioned the blog in passing, and only because you said something first."

I squeeze her again. "You make an impression on people," I murmur. "Don't be surprised that people are interested in you."

She just stares at her phone for a moment. "Pretty much no one has been before," she mutters.

I could tell her that's because Ethan demanded every ounce of her attention, every morsel of her wonderful personality he could grasp. I don't say it, because I don't want to ruin this moment for her.

I don't know if she realizes that I did a background check on her when I first hired her, so I'm hesitant to bring up any information she hasn't told me herself yet. But in my own mind, I can put the pieces together. She came to this city with a dream and no support, with a mother who she perhaps loves but isn't close with. Her only friend, Lacey, is someone she saw sporadically at best, and their relationship seems to be almost entirely rooted in work these days. Ethan had chosen his target well, and then done everything in his power to continue to isolate her.

But now, free of Ethan and his control, she's blossoming. She's so likable and kind and brilliant, and this is just proof of that. I certainly didn't make my employees check out her blog or send her kind messages. I'm not above doing something like that, but I doubt I'd ever have thought of it, and I was far too distracted last night to do any such thing.

No, she did this all on her own by being as wonderful as she is. "So, are you going to film a video?" I ask.

"Who would want to see that?"

I shrug, bending further to press a kiss to her shoulder. "Seems like several people, Elise. Have faith in yourself." I stand upright, reluctantly releasing her. "At the very least, let me help you take some pictures of breakfast."

She has better photography equipment now, so she really doesn't need my help anymore, but I hope she'll let me pretend.

She glances at the oven timer. "Five more minutes, but then I need to ice them."

"Cinnamon rolls?"

"I was looking for something a little sweet this morning," she says, then shifts from foot to foot. "Can you just tell me: I didn't hallucinate last night or anything, right?"

"If what you remember is riding my dragon form on your first flight and then literally riding me into the ground, then no. No hallucinations."

She rubs a hand over her face. "Alright. Didn't think so."

I watch her closely, looking for any signs of distress. "Are you upset about that?"

"No," she says after a quick pause. "I'm not. Just still in shock a little, I guess? It's a big change, Marcus."

"I know," I reassure her, and my arms feel empty. "Can I hold you?"

She opens her arms in invitation, and I pull her close without another word.

After a long minute of inhaling her scent and steadying the both of us, I clear my throat. "I hate to bring up upsetting things, but Ethan did hunt you down last night."

She tenses, and I rub between her shoulders, hoping to ease her fear. "It's probably a bad sign that I nearly forgot it after everything."

"Lots of things happened yesterday," I tell her soothingly. "And you don't need to worry about Ethan."

"After what I saw yesterday and what you told me, I am worried about Ethan, though."

"Don't be. After you accepted our mating bond, I have no need to fear anything anymore. They can investigate to their heart's content; you're my mate and they can't tell you anything you don't already know. They can't separate us. The laws of nature are against it. So if Ethan comes near us again, I'll kill him."

"I don't..."

I kiss her hair just as the oven timer goes off. "Leave it to me, Angel," I promise. "You don't have to do anything but know you're safe."

She squirms out of my arms to get the cinnamon rolls, and she turns on the lights to get a picture of them without icing before setting to work. "Can I help?"

She doesn't need me to hold a flashlight anymore, but I'll take any excuse to be part of the things she cares about.

She hands me a spatula. "Ice half," she instructs, then turns back to her task. I practically beam at being included in this with her.

Does she need me to do this? Hell no. But, I like that she makes room for me anyway.

The little swipe and pat she does to get perfectly even, aesthetic icing is impossible. Mine look like I just dumped the bowl over the top despite my efforts, and my hands unfortunately don't look much better.

Elise turns to look at me when she's done and laughs. I suppose I do look ridiculous, covered in icing up to my wrists and frowning over a damn cinnamon roll like it holds the secrets to life.

"You have a little..." She gestures at all of me.

"Don't laugh," I grumble, but then laughter is the last thing on either of our minds when she takes my hand and, keeping eye contact the entire time, sucks two of my fingers into her mouth.

Goddamn. I'm hard in my pants almost instantly, blood rushing away from my head, and all I can do is stare at her as those dark eyes watch me, bright with mischief.

"Elise," I manage to grit out. She makes a humming noise around my fingers in acknowledgement. "If you want pictures of them all pretty, take them now. I think we have plans before breakfast."

She reluctantly releases my fingers. "Not in the kitchen," she murmurs.

"Then you better hurry, because you are torturing me."

She takes a few quick pictures of her creations and then nudges me over to the couch and away from her clean kitchen. I go to tug her onto my lap, but she shakes her head and then sinks to her knees.

"You wanna suck my cock, Angel?" I ask, already a little breathless.

She looks up at me, cheeks flushed but smiling softly. "Just don't make a joke about icing, alright?"

It hasn't even crossed my mind, but I do realize my hands are still covered in the stuff, and that she'll probably be upset if I get it in her hair, so I hastily wipe it on my pants.

She barely gives me time to get that done before she's working me out of my pants and wrapping her lips around me. I last an embarrassingly short time, barely able to restrain myself from rocking into her throat while she teases me right to the brink.

"Angel, I—"

She uses her tongue to tease at my piercing, and I'm lost, completely lost to her, spilling down her throat before I can even warn her, then left gaping at her when she licks her lips clean, smiling up at me.

"Come here," I say, my voice practically a growl, determined to have my turn tasting her too.

I check her blog later in the day, and she posted the cinnamon roll pictures, my wonky ones right next to her beautiful ones. She's even written a little caption about how cooking can be a powerful activity with loved ones, and I can't help but grin.

CHAPTER 38
Elise

"What did I do to earn such a delicious reward?" Marcus breathes, licking at my neck as I wake up slowly, stretching into his arms.

"Reward?" I ask groggily, eyes still closed as he strokes my skin.

He chuckles. "You're still in bed, Angel. That's a rare treat for me."

"What time is it?" I ask, forcing my eyes open so I can find a clock.

Instead, Marcus just kisses me, distracting me from my quest. "Marcus," I murmur, turning my head. "I have to—"

He kisses the corner of my mouth, then my chin. "You have to nothing," he murmurs. "Be here with me."

And that sounds so damn good. I can't come up with any argument against it, so I sigh and relax back into the bed, turning my face back and seeking his lips.

He rewards me giving in by kissing me slowly, lazily, like we have all the time in the world to lie here in bed.

Just when I'm about to demand more—I always want more, even though I'm still a little sore from how good he fucked me last night—my phone rings.

"Ignore it," he mutters.

I squirm. "Like four people have that number. I have to check."

He sighs, giving me just enough space to grab my phone. MOM flashes on the screen, and I hastily pick up before she gets sent to voicemail. Marcus, sensing defeat, settles onto the bed, resting his weight on his elbow so he can prop himself up to watch me.

"Hi, Mom."

"Hi, baby," she chirps. I can hear voices, then a car rushing by. She's out and about then, calling me during her errands. "How've you been?"

"Fine." I have a moment to realize that I'm never going to be able to tell my mom the truth of my life again. Dragons and magic and flying—there will always be this invisible barrier between us now.

But then again, I put up that barrier years before I even met Marcus. I'd moved away for a reason, after all.

Before I can feel bad about it, she starts talking again. "I was wondering what your plans are for Christmas."

I frown. I never go home on Christmas. Marcus tilts his head, mouthing *invite her?*

I shake my head. No, definitely not happening. I want her to meet Marcus someday, I suppose, but next week is definitely not the time.

"Uh, I have plans here," I fib. "Why?"

"I have someone for you to meet." She takes a deep, audible inhale, and I know she's bracing herself for my reaction. "His name is Jackson. I think you'll like him."

I know she's waiting for a reaction, and maybe once upon a time I'd have given her one. Pre-teen me definitely had a *he's not my real dad* phase. But the truth is, these days I don't care who she dates as long as they don't hurt her. I know they won't last that long.

"Maybe some other time," I tell her. "I want to, Mom, but Christmas just isn't convenient."

"You and Ethan haven't been down here in ages," she complains.

I swallow around the lump in my throat. "Ethan and I broke up a bit ago," I admit. I should probably feel bad that I didn't tell her, but I can't quite make myself. "I'm actually seeing someone new."

There's silence on the other end, and I'd worry that the call dropped if I couldn't still hear traffic. "Is he good to you?"

Marcus watches me with patient eyes. I know he can hear every word, but he doesn't say anything, doesn't push me. "He's great."

"Good, baby. That's all I ever wanted for you. You'll have to bring him soon. You, me, Jackson, and him. We'll do something nice."

I can't quite picture Marcus in my quiet little hometown, but at the same time, I know he'll go if I ask. "That sounds good, Mom," I murmur. "Hey, I need to go. Work."

"Of course, Elise. Talk soon?"

I'll call her on Christmas, I'm sure. That's what we do. Then after that, who knows? But I say, "Yeah, talk soon. Love you."

Marcus takes my phone from me gently when I hang up. "You okay?"

I manage a smile. "I'm fine."

"Seriously."

"Seriously," I assure him. I'm always fine when it comes to my mother.

"You could have invited her here for Christmas. Or we could go to hers."

I do like that he says we, like it's a foregone conclusion we'll be going together. I like it so much I lean in to kiss him.

Marcus eagerly accepts my kiss, conversation forgotten, and tries to roll me onto my back. Unfortunately for him, I'm fully aware of what time it is now, and I wiggle out from under him. "Come back here," he pouts as I get out of bed.

"It's time to start the day, Marcus." I have things to do today, starting with feeding the both of us.

"I can help you start the day," he offers, flopping onto his back.

I grab his shirt from yesterday off the top of the hamper. "I'm going to go cook breakfast," I say, slipping it over my head. "You're welcome to join me."

As I expected, I hear footsteps following me before I even reach the door.

I wait for Marcus to close his office door, grumbling about a boring video call, before I even contemplate starting the video.

Honestly, I could have stayed in bed with Marcus for hours, could have let him help me forget all about the phone call from this morning, if only I hadn't already promised myself that today is the day I try to tackle the request for video recipes on my blog.

They're probably just being nice when they comment on my blog. Or they figure that the best policy is to suck up to the boss' girlfriend. But on the off-chance that they actually want to see the steps in a little more detail, then it really isn't that hard for me to do.

Of course, reality quickly proves me wrong. I have this vision of focusing the camera on my hands and just explaining what I'm doing, but I quickly realize how often I move around the kitchen when I work, how some of the angles are impossibly bad, and just saying what I'm doing leads to a lot more swearing than I'd ever be comfortable posting on the internet.

"What did the kebabs do to you?"

I don't even jump anymore when Marcus surprises me. For a man who turns into a dragon as big as a house, he's shockingly light on his feet. "This is harder than I thought," I admit.

"The kebabs?"

"The filming. Not the kebabs." I glance at the clock. He's out here because it's lunchtime, and I've spent so much time trying to take footage that there's no lunch for him. "Shit! I'm sorry, Marcus, I'll—"

He rolls up his sleeves. "Put me to work, boss."

I bite my lip. "I'm so sorry, I should have lunch—I won't do this again, I swear. All stupid filming endeavors will be fully off the clock."

"Elise, you know I don't care," he says, his voice annoyingly calm. "And if I had my way you wouldn't feel like this is a job anymore." He pauses for a second. "Then again, I also don't want you to feel like I've brought you here to cook all my meals for free, so neither option is great. But I do want you to consider yourself entitled to do whatever you want. Buy whatever ingredients, take your time making it, film every step of the process. Ask me to hold a camera, or tell me to order pizza and leave you alone because you don't feel like cooking at the moment. All are valid options."

How does a man like this even exist? Is this some result of some crazy dragon magic I can't understand?

I run a hand through my hair, accidentally knocking several strands loose. "How hungry are you and when's your next meeting?"

"Meetings can be rescheduled, and I can wait for food. Or I can order something if you're hungry, and we'll eat the kebabs for dinner."

"You can't just reschedule meetings, people are relying on you."

Marcus uncrosses his arms and walks over to me. "That's the benefit of being the boss. Things are rescheduled because I say they are all the time. And believe me, I've already made my money. I work because I like keeping busy. But I would much rather be busy with you." The words sound like a come-on, but the tone is so sincere it makes my throat ache. "Pizza or Chinese?" he asks after a moment, reaching up to push those loose strands of hair off my face.

I swallow, giving myself a moment. He's too much sometimes, but I think it's in the best of ways. The ways I'm not used to, the ways I don't know what to do with. But I fight my knee-jerk reaction to shut this down, and say, "Chicken wings?"

So we eat chicken wings standing right at the counter while Marcus pulls out a business legal pad and a blue pen. "Figure out what you need for the video," he instructs me. "So that way we can know what shots you need."

I have sauce on my hands, so first I have to hunt down a napkin, and then think about the steps of making kabobs.

Writing my recipes on the blog has trained me to break down what is often instinctual to me to manageable and clear steps for others to follow, but I've never had to think of what a camera might need to pick up. When I'm taking pictures, I think of it as endpoints—people want to see the finished product and maybe one or two steps along the way. But now, people want to see how I go about cooking, and what goes into the meal.

Marcus looks over my list and nods. "I'll hold the camera," he says, setting my tiny little tripod aside for now. "And focus on what you're doing. Your show, Elise. Direct me."

I'm pretty sure that the guy with the camera should be the director, but Marcus is surprisingly flexible and doesn't complain when I do four takes of mixing up my marinade. We eat an early dinner of kabobs, then retreat to the couch, him with a mystery novel and me to solve the mystery of how to edit and post a video like this.

When Marcus sees that I'm done for the night, he leans over and kisses my nose. "I'm proud of you for trying this, you know that?"

I try to brush it off, but the thing about Marcus is that he's persistent. "I'm serious," he murmurs, now using his thumb and index finger to tilt my chin. "Starting something new is hard, Elise. And you're trying it."

He's not wrong. How long has it been since I tried anything new? For someone who prides myself on creativity and always keeping it fresh, it's so easy in hindsight to see how stale my life was before Marcus.

"We'll see if it's any good," I say, because I can't quite handle this right now. But I know he's right.

"It'll be great."

"You're so optimistic," I tease, reaching up to stroke my thumb over his cheek.

He chuckles. "That is something no one has ever accused me of before."

"And yet you're probably the most optimistic person I know."

He's very quiet for just a moment. "Angel—that's you. I've waited millennia for you. And you're here, and you're amazing. I'm in awe of you every day, and you're right: I'm nothing but hopeful for our future."

He's waited so long, and he got me. And I'd think that would be a disappointment, but he's looking at me like he truly thinks that he's the luckiest dragon in the world.

He strokes my hair out of my face. "Now, do you have anything else to do?"

I do, actually. I need to learn how to post a video, which I'm sure involves time setting up a channel and then learning how to integrate that with my blog.

I put my phone and computer aside. "Nothing that can't wait until tomorrow," I decide.

Marcus grins, then scoops me up without warning, making me laugh as he carries me to our bedroom.

CHAPTER 39
Marcus

A conversation on a video call reminds me that Christmas is in just three more days. I glance at a calendar to confirm and, fuck, they're right. Christmas isn't usually something I care much about, beyond doing the bare minimum to seem like a normal human to blend in wherever I happen to be, but this year is different.

For one thing, Elise absolutely deserves to have the perfect holiday. For another, it's a ready-built excuse to spoil her, and one she can't deny me.

I reschedule my calls for the rest of the day and wonder, not for the first time, if I should resign. It's not like I need an income, and there's plenty of people who can run the company as well or even better than me. It'll be there for me if I want to go back in a generation. But for now, Elise should be my priority.

I'm not exactly experienced in relationships that last longer than a night or two, but I'm fully aware that it's not healthy for couples to spend every waking minute together. People are supposed to have hobbies. At this stage in our mating, I want

Elise at my side at all times, but I know I have to be careful not to stifle her.

I'll ask her about it after the holidays. But for now, I have things to do.

Elise is taking pictures of something in the kitchen when I emerge. I walk over to give her a kiss on the top of her head, looking over her shoulder to see chocolate chip cookies. "One of these for me?"

"Spicy or regular?"

"Spicy cookies?"

She hums. "Yup. Someone made a comment on the cinnamon rolls, asking for a few more baking posts. So I did regular chocolate chip cookies and spicy ones for people ready to try something new."

"Can I have one of each?"

She nods, so I scoop up a cookie from each cooling rack, decide to be surprised on which is which, and shove one in my mouth.

It's the spicy one, a delicious, warm heat that really goes perfectly with the bitter chocolate. "Excellent," I tell her as soon as I swallow and before shoving another bite in my mouth. "I hate to eat and run, but I need to go out."

She tilts her head for a kiss, which I eagerly give her before I go out to locate appropriate gifts.

It's Christmas. Surely she has to accept gifts on Christmas, right?

The car service is damn convenient, dragging me all over the city and allowing me to pile in package after package.

Elise isn't easy to shop for in the way some people are; I'm not particularly known for giving presents, but I know most people can be won with something flashy and expensive. Elise isn't like that. Even so, I have the time of my life shopping for her, walking through stores and boutiques and deciding what she'll like best.

A cocoa mix that supposedly makes the best hot chocolate she'll ever have. A basket of luxury bath products, because she needs to relax more. A new video camera so she can film her videos, and a microphone to go with it. A ruby necklace, because the dragon in me can't quite resist something shiny. I'd honestly buy out the entire jewelry store, but I think she'd kill me, and anyway, there's something more appealing about going into the jewelry I've acquired over the centuries and picking out what pieces would suit her best.

She tells me repeatedly that she has everything she needs for the kitchen, so I leave that alone. Plus, buying her cooking items feels uncomfortably close to giving her additional work for Christmas, and I'd like to avoid that.

Someday, we'll have to sort out this job she has. Maybe we'll reach the point where she truly believes that being my mate means she's entitled to my everything. The first day she uses that credit card I gave her for more than the bare essentials, I truly will throw her a party.

Instead, I head to the bookstore, finding her a few novels because I've seen her pick through some of mine and I hope I have a grasp on which ones she enjoys now. Then I go to the travel section, searching through the stacks until I find what I want.

There. Six books about the best food tours of the world. And while any trip we take isn't being booked by a run-of-the-mill tour agency, this will be a good start.

I leave all the bags in the hallway outside the penthouse door before peeking my head inside. As expected, Elise is still at the kitchen counter, this time messing around with a marinade for the dinner she's making.

"You work way too hard," I tell her, walking over to her for a kiss.

"You're one to talk."

I snort, because I've done very little work today. And I could quit tomorrow and find happiness in my life, but I'm not sure the same could be said for her. "You deserve to relax, Elise."

"I am relaxed." She relaxes into my arms, but far from convincing me, it tells me just how tense her muscles are.

"Nice try." I get a bright idea, pressing a kiss to the top of her head before telling her, "Meet me in the bathroom? I have an idea."

She raises an eyebrow but nods, and as soon as she turns away I head back to the hall to find the luxury bath products. There's no rule that says she can't have a gift early.

She gives me an accusing look when I enter the bathroom, brandishing the basket in front of me. "You did not just have that lying around."

"I went shopping today," I admit without shame and a touch of pride. Call it residual animal instincts, the things that harken back to eons before even I was born, but the dragon inside of me is insufferably proud to have gone and hunted for something that pleases our mate. "I hear that's the appropriate thing to do in this season, after all," I add, just in case she's going to try to reject yet another gift.

Her eyes narrow. "This was meant to be my Christmas gift?"

"One of many," I reassure her, because I don't want her to think that I'm spoiling her Christmas present. "Don't worry about that."

"I'm worried you went out gift shopping! Marcus, I haven't got anything for you, and—"

"You're here, with me," I interrupt. "What greater gift could I ask for?"

She just rolls her eyes. "Marcus, that's sweet, but really; I already feel weird about the fact that you let me stay here for free and pay for my work and have bought me so much stuff, so this is too much."

"It's a bath, Elise," I tell her. I maybe had visions of presenting the basket to her and picking out the products she wanted to use together, then sliding into that tub with her. It's plenty big enough for two. But I can guess that won't be happening. She's too worked up to think about having sex right now.

It's not that I didn't know that she had these insecurities, these fears. But I didn't think a Christmas gift would be the straw that broke the camel's back.

"Tell you what," I tell her. "Let me cook Christmas dinner with you."

"That's not a gift," she protests.

"It is to me," I tell her, then push the basket more insistently at her. "Now, you're going to relax, please? You deserve a break."

She eyes the basket, then me. "Is this going to be a thing, Marcus?"

I don't know why she's surprised. "Dragons love giving gifts," I remind her. Mated dragons love showering their mates in presents. Wars have been fought in the past to find the perfect gift, and while I doubt Elise wants wars fought in her name, I can't deny that if she asked me for something and raiding an enemy stronghold was the only way to obtain it, I'd go to battle, no questions asked.

She sighs, and I think she's going to argue more, but then she reaches for her shirt. "Let's test this one out then," she says, shirt covering her face, and I grin.

Looks like I'm invited to her bath after all.

CHAPTER 40

Elise

After breakfast, Marcus kisses me and then heads to his office. "Last day," he promises.

"Last day for what?" I ask, already loading our dishes into the dishwasher.

"Work. I'm taking tomorrow through the New Year off. Most of the office is. So, start thinking about what you want to do with that time." Then, just to cement how perfect he is, Marcus kisses the top of my head before going to work.

After yesterday's dragons love giving gifts conversation and the plethora of moments where he's insisted on spoiling me, I have a feeling I could ask to go to the moon and he'd somehow work it out.

I don't want the moon, but I'll be grateful for the time. It might be nice to go see the Christmas tree at Rockefeller Center. Maybe go ice skating or to a holiday market. I've lived in this city for years now, and I've never done any of that.

I'd assumed that Marcus wasn't invested in Christmas. We'd gone to his company Christmas party, but I'd assumed that had more to do with the image he'd like to project to his employees than any real desire to celebrate the holiday.

The revelation of his age had been a shock of course, but it had also cemented the idea that he wouldn't care about Christmas that much. And that relieved any of the anxiety of having a perfect holiday together.

Except here he is, sneaking out to go shopping for gifts. As in, plural. And now he's taking over a week off of work to hang out and do whatever I want to celebrate the holiday, and all he's asking in return is that I let him help cook Christmas dinner.

I'm not an idiot; I'm fully aware that Marcus knows my financial situation will never match his. He can say what he wants about his money being my money. In his mind, I think that's even true. But that doesn't mean he and I can go gift-for-gift, and he's just trying to soothe the sting of that for me.

Well, fuck that. Yeah, I'm not going to be able to match whatever gift-buying spree he went on yesterday, but I'm not broke. I can buy him something nice; let him be the gift-receiver for a change.

The crisp December sunshine feels great on my skin. I look up, letting the rays bathe my face, and set off down the sidewalk.

I probably should have thought about what someone like Marcus likes before I left the apartment, but I'm not turning back now. I'll just have to think while I walk.

He likes art, but I'd hazard a guess that there's enough on the walls. He seems to like wine, but I don't even know where someone would go to buy the types of bottles I know he has.

Books. Marcus likes books, has plenty of them, and books I can do. I turn on the next corner to get to the bookstore. It's perfect: personal, not so overly expensive that either of us will feel weird about it, and something well within my ability to choose for him.

"Out without your new boyfriend." The voice sends a cold chill down my spine, causing my muscles to lock up as someone falls into step beside me. "Did he decide you're not worth it and cut you loose, Elise?"

Ethan. I stop walking, frozen to the sidewalk. "He'll kill you if you touch me," I mumble, trying to sound firm even when my heart is pounding a mile a minute.

He reaches out and touches my face, a gentle mockery of touches we once shared. I flinch back, but then his other hand is there, grabbing the back of my neck and stopping me from recoiling. "Humans just aren't worth defending like that, babe," he says, whispering it like it's a secret he's confiding in me. "I claimed you first; laws of nature say you're mine."

"I'm not a fucking piece of furniture, Ethan," I manage to snap.

His grip on my neck tightens, and then he's dragging me into an alley like I weigh nothing. My whole body shakes when he slams me against a wall, and I can't get my breath.

His hand slides around to the front of my throat, squeezing lightly. I scrabble at his hands, trying to push him off, but it's no use; he just digs his fingers in and keeps squeezing. "No," he agrees. "You're food, Elise."

I try to kick at him, but he completely ignores the attempt, acting like he doesn't even notice when my foot connects with his shin. I throw my weight down, trying to squirm out of his hold, but his grip doesn't loosen and I grow more and more light-headed.

And then the world goes hazy before my eyes slide closed.

CHAPTER 41

Marcus

I don't know anything is wrong until lunch, and I'll never forgive myself for not knowing for so long.

When Elise isn't in the kitchen when I leave my office, I force myself to stay calm. There's a lot of places she could be, lots of things she could be doing. I check our bedroom and our bathroom and even her old room. I check the gym down on the first floor of this building, just in case she got a sudden desire to lift weights. No luck.

"Did Elise go out?" I ask the doorman. I shouldn't have waited so long. People always check the obvious places before escalating problems, but that wastes valuable time if there's an incident. Anything can happen in that time. Elise could be anywhere.

"Sorry, sir. My shift started fifteen minutes ago. I have no idea if anyone left."

My panic makes it hard to breathe. I should have planned for this, should have anticipated a moment like this. I never wanted her to feel like a prisoner in our home, but now I'm regretting not telling the doormen to call me if she leaves.

I make myself nod to the man and walk outside, taking a deep draw of air. My mate's scent, always like freshly baked bread and rosemary and home, lingers on the air, but it's hours old, and I can barely detect it around the thousands of other scents.

Did she go to the grocery store? We always go together lately, and after Ethan's brazen attack last week, I assumed we'd continue until the issue is dealt with. But she's gone. She's left for some reason, and I can't find her.

Panicking, I call her phone. It rings out until it goes to her automated voicemail message. I try again, then a third time. On the third time I leave a voicemail, begging her to call me back as soon as possible.

Just in case she can't call, I text too, begging to know where she is. Nothing.

Anything could have happened to her. She's out in the world and she's not answering. Maybe she's busy. Maybe human problems waylaid her—best-case scenario she's on a train delayed underground, worst case she got hit by a car or otherwise injured. Or maybe, as the dragon inside me fears, something from my world got to her.

Ethan. I should have told everyone I know to hunt him down. I should have led a hunt myself. I should have ripped his innards out and strung him up by his intestines to make an example of him.

I'm becoming more and more convinced that Ethan got to her. That she's in the most dangerous hands I can think of.

I try to track her by her scent, but my senses aren't good enough, not with the time that's lapsed, not in the crowd of this city.

I go still. I might not be able to sense her all the way across the city, but I know some people who can.

I avoid Lucius Lawson and his guard dog almost pathologically. I don't have anything against the rules of conduct they enforce for our kind, and they know better than to tangle with a dragon who isn't a threat to them. We have no need to interact. But that doesn't mean I don't know how to get in touch with them.

They'd never lift a finger for a human. But for a mate, would they?

Would they do it because they fear what I'll turn into if I lose her?

I don't care what I have to promise them. I'll pay any price. And when it's done, they can witness me tearing Ethan to shreds. We're not supposed to kill our own, but even they'll have to forgive me when I do it for my mate.

It takes me three tries to dial correctly, my fingers are shaking so badly. "Lucius Lawson." His voice is clear, crisp, and disinterested, but I get the feeling that he knows who's calling. He picked up himself, after all. Don't governors usually have staff meant to do that for them?

I should say something polite, or at least something more formal. But all I can work out is, "He took her. My mate."

Lucius is quiet for a long moment. "Are you at home?"

"Close," I manage to say, my brain very far away from this phone call and the question Lucius is asking.

He's quiet for another moment, and I get the feeling I've been put on mute. I pace in the street, not caring for the passers-by staring at me. I can't be the weirdest thing they've ever seen in this city, and I don't give a fuck what they think about me.

"Max will be there in an hour," Lucius says. "Wait for him." He hangs up before I can respond.

Maximus throws his car into a spot of questionable legality fifty-four minutes later, then jumps out of the car. I've been waiting in the lobby of my building, wanting to be where he can easily find me.

"He took her. I don't know how many hours ago," I say instead of offering any sort of sensible greeting.

Max, to his credit, doesn't seem at all bothered by my lack of manners. "Give me the basics, Marcus," he says, and for a big rough and tumble bruiser, an infamous killer, his voice is surprisingly gentle. "We didn't even know you had a mate."

"Recent," I manage to say. "And I didn't... she's human, and the situation was delicate, so I didn't..."

Marcus nods, though. "Trust me, I get it." I glance downward to see the tattooed wedding band on his finger. It's been years since I've seen Max, and that certainly wasn't there last time, but I don't have the presence of mind to ask about it now.

"Her ex, he's an empathic demon," I manage to say.

Max hisses. "Parasites."

All I can do is nod. "Should have killed him, but at first she was too human for me to risk it, and then I was too busy spending every damn second with her." I was too busy being absolutely in awe that she agreed to be mine. I was basking in her glory when I should have been out there protecting her.

"You said she was too human. Is she not anymore?" He's all business when he asks, a man just trying to understand all the variables. His calmness is almost as infuriating as it is reassuring.

"The mating process with a dragon, it brings about some changes. She's mostly human. You wouldn't be able to tell the difference."

He looks at me for a second, perhaps concluding how those changes come about. "I don't want to know more. Alright, you think the ex found her?"

"I don't know, but she's gone and she won't pick up her phone and he's a threat to her and—" I take a deep breath. "Every moment he has her is a moment too long."

Max doesn't say a word about how this could be an ordinary human thing, that she could be with friends and declining my calls to get some peace, that I could have somehow upset her and she left, that she could have a very normal and human emergency. I think I'd fully lose my shit if he did, that the dragon would burst out of my skin without me summoning it, and all would be lost. Maybe that's why he keeps the thoughts to himself.

Or maybe he's as protective and paranoid as I am. I think about that wedding band again.

He nods. "I can find her," he promises. "My sense of smell is stronger than just about anyone's."

"That's why I called. If you need something with her scent on it—" I begin, but he raises an eyebrow and cuts me off.

"I can smell her on your clothes already, Marcus," he interrupts, smirking slightly. "It's natural. We start to smell like people we spend time with."

I wait until his back is turned to give what is hopefully a subtle sniff. My senses aren't as good as his, but he's right; there's a woman on his clothes and skin, even in his hair. If he's anything like me, he wears that scent like a badge of honor.

Fuck, when I get Elise back—and it is *when*, I refuse to think of any other options—I'm going to bathe myself in her scent.

We're not getting out of bed for days. I doubt I'll be more than an arm's reach away from her for weeks.

Max starts walking, no comment or indication that he's caught her scent. He really does look like a bloodhound like this, determined and entirely focused.

He stops on the corner, and I catch up, waiting for him to pick a direction. He gives me a quick glance, an apology, I think. "It works better in my other form," he says quietly, mindful of the pedestrians around us. "But that would stick out here. I'm too big for you to convince anyone I'm your pet, and I'd probably rip your arm off before letting you put a leash on me."

Fair. He picks a direction, walking off again, and I stick close behind him.

We get to a spot that seems the same as any other to me, but Max stops. "She was here for a while," he says. "There's another scent. Yeah, that's an empathic demon, alright."

The dragon in me roars, loud enough I think my brain might break. It rattles my skull, and while the roar never leaves my own head, a growl escapes. Max looks at me. "You were right. Now let's go get her."

"When we get there, he's mine."

Max doesn't argue. He just takes a moment, turns on his heel, and starts bringing me in the right direction, closer to my mate.

CHAPTER 42
Elise

I wake up tied to a chair, with a gag in my mouth and rope cutting into my wrists and ankles.

Ethan reclines in what is, as far as I can tell, the only other chair in this shitty apartment. There's one bare overhead light-bulb and no natural light. Are we underground?

Ethan reclines like he's the king of the world, like everything is going perfectly for him. He's lost weight since I ran from our apartment, and he has dark circles under his eyes, but he's watching me with such a self-satisfied smirk that you'd think everything has been going his way the entire time.

"Just you and me now, babe," he croons as soon as he sees I'm awake. "Be honest, this is what we needed, hm? Some time to focus on just us."

He says this like he's completely unaware of what's gone down between us, like he didn't terrify me that night in our apartment, like he didn't assault me at the Christmas party, like he didn't just kidnap me. He's not unaware, though. As light as he's keeping his voice, I can see the cold intent in his eyes.

I rock in my chair, tugging at my bindings.

"None of that, now," he scolds. "You'll hurt yourself."

I don't really give a fuck if I do, if it would get me away from him. But I stop for a moment, knowing it's not worth wasting the energy, knowing I need to be smart about this.

Marcus will come for me. I should have been smarter and left a note or told him I was going out or literally anything so he'd have a place to start. I should have understood how much of a threat Ethan was. Even so, I know Marcus will come for me. But in the meantime, I need to keep myself together and safe.

The gag is cutting into my face, and trying to talk around it isn't helping. Ethan clicks his tongue at me. "You don't need to say anything. You just need to listen for a minute."

I'd rather lick the floor of a subway car than listen to him, but unfortunately I don't have much of a choice in this position. Ethan stands up, looming over me so my whole view is of him. "I think you might have heard some things about me, Elise."

Yeah, like he's a damn parasite who literally fed off of me, but honestly, I didn't need a dragon to point out to me that Ethan is bad news. If only I saw it earlier; I could have avoided years and years under his thrall.

"I'm here to promise you that it's not like that," he continues. His voice is almost gentle, almost soft, but there's a hardness underneath it that he can't hide. He's playing nice, but he's just as happy to drag me where he wants kicking and screaming if that should fail.

343

"We were good for each other," he murmurs, sinking to a crouch in front of me, bringing us to eye-level. "We were great for each other. You were my whole world. Remember that?"

He reaches out to tilt my chin, forcing me to look at him. He watches me unblinking for a long moment, practically staring into my soul. He looks away first, huffing before standing.

"That used to work."

My insides freeze over, everything going very still. So he did use his creepy, invasive magic on me when we were together. I want to throw up.

"Do you even know what that boyfriend's done to you?" he asks, then shakes his head like he's dismissing it. "It's fine. From what I understand, it wears off. And I have all the time in the world."

If he's talking about my immortality, then it does wear off. Marcus told me that, promised me that I could go back to a normal human life if I chose. And Ethan apparently plans to keep me here long enough for that to happen.

He watches me for a long moment, then abruptly asks, "You thirsty?"

I am. I have no idea how long I was unconscious, but I feel like breakfast was ages ago. Hesitantly, I nod.

He grabs a water bottle and walks up to me. "Got to take care of my human," he says lightly. "Humans are fragile, after all. And I always took care of you so well, didn't I, Elise?" He crouches down again to look me in the eye. "If you scream, I'll knock you out again, and I won't take the gag out again until the filth is out of your system and you're ready to be mine again. Got me?"

I want to spit in his face, to scream that I'll never be his, to shout my head off. But he's absolutely serious and I know it. I have to be smart about this.

I nod, holding perfectly still while he pulls the gag out, and hate myself a bit for it.

Chapter 43

Marcus

"He had a car," Max says the third time he stops entirely. "And mechanical transportation is the biggest pain in the ass in human history. But I'm very good at this." He pauses, then starts walking again. "And he didn't go that far. Stupid fucker," he adds. "Should be halfway across the country by now if he didn't want you coming after him. Even I know dragons will literally tear the world apart for their mates."

"Always," I say through gritted teeth, because Max is understating the problem significantly. The dragon is two seconds from bursting out of me, ready to raze the city to the ground in order to find Elise.

Knowing that Max would put me down for that—or at least give it his best try—isn't enough of a deterrent. Only knowing that an enraged dragon is a threat to Elise keeps me in control.

The dragon would never hurt her, but if I rip buildings down with fire and claws, I might inadvertently put her in harm's way, and I could never risk that. Plus, I doubt Elise would be happy if I left the city she calls home in ruin.

Max stops to look at me. "You okay?"

"Fine," I say shortly.

"Turn here." I follow him, then almost run into his overly large back when he stops again. "This fucker is annoying," he mutters. "You should have killed him when you had the chance."

"I was distracted by taking care of my mate," I say, but I know he's right. "I didn't think you and your boss endorsed that type of extra-judicial killing, anyway."

Max shrugs. "Don't look at me. I'm the one who deals out the judicial killing, and I dealt out plenty before that, too. I'm not here to judge."

Lucius probably would have. But he sent Max here to help me, all because I broke down about my mate and nearly begged. Surely he respects the mating bond enough to excuse a little murder.

"But also, I would rip the world apart for my wife," Max continues, taking a left. "So I have no room to judge either way."

Max's steps pick up. "Got you, fucker," he mutters, and charges towards a dilapidated-looking building, me hot on his heels.

CHAPTER 44
Elise

I drink the water greedily, and Ethan doesn't re-gag me when he steps back. I keep quiet, just in case it's an oversight; I don't want him to change his mind.

"Snack?" he offers unexpectedly.

I half expect it to be poisoned, but no. He wants to keep me, to own me. He wouldn't hurt me.

Hesitantly, I nod. He steps close again, bringing me a pouch of squeezable applesauce for small children. Then he holds it to my mouth and feeds me, gripping my chin like I'm an infant. I flush in humiliation, but I can't move out of his grip.

"You're going to be okay, Elise," he abruptly promises me. "I'll take care of it. You used to love me, remember? You're going to be okay."

"You kidnapped me," I remind him, moving my mouth away from the stupid applesauce. It's not even good applesauce, bland and watered-down. "I was okay before you knocked me unconscious and tied me up."

His mouth presses into a thin line. "I'm not going to hurt you. I put so much time and energy into you, making us perfect together; I'd never hurt you."

"You already have," I point out. "Multiple times."

"You're telling me the dragon doesn't get a little rough with you?" he asks disbelievingly. "You have a type, babe."

I don't know what's more insulting: the implication that abusers are my type, or him calling Marcus one. "He's never hurt me," I tell him.

"You seen the giant beast yet?"

"I have."

"I don't know if he told you. I doubt he did; it wouldn't put him in the most flattering light. But dragons are violent, obsessive creatures. It's only a matter of time until he hurts you."

Obsessive? That's definitely true. But violent? I have no doubt Marcus is capable of violence. Ethan will learn all about that part of him soon enough. But not towards me. Marcus is perfectly gentle with me.

"I'm just looking out for you, Elise," he continues. "I love you. I can't stand to see you misled and hurt."

"You don't love me," I correct. "You feed off of me, Ethan."

"They can be mutually true," he says, and for the first time his eyes are earnest. "What did it matter, Elise? It didn't hurt you. I loved you and I needed you. That sounds like true love to me. We were made for each other; I needed you, and you were

349

perfect for me. Just the right type of devotion. That sounds like that kind of forever, binding love you always wanted."

I flush at the reminder of how well he knows me, that he met me when I was a desperate kid trying to make something of myself. That he knows all of my insecurities, all of my fears, and how desperate I was to be loved back then.

"I can give you that type of love," he persists. "What does it matter if I need you for energy? It doesn't hurt you. Really, it just means we love each other."

And maybe that could be true. Maybe there is a world where someone like Ethan could be fed by a devoted, consenting partner. Maybe it could be love.

But Ethan put his hands on me not once, not twice, but three times. And I don't want him anymore.

I look him straight in the eyes. "We're over, Ethan. Accept it and let me go. Maybe it could have been like that, but it's not now and it won't be again. You ruined it."

His face goes cold and as hard as stone. "You're making a mistake, Elise." Then, like he's driven by some forces outside of his control, he closes in on my space again, raising a hand. I flinch, bracing myself for the blow, but it never comes.

Instead, he strokes my hair back from my face, an oddly gentle gesture that forces me to remember our past. I have to keep my hair up when I work, so I was always taking it down when I got home, and Ethan was always pushing it out of my eyes.

I can't help but remember those days with a soft brush of nostalgia. But before I can say anything, he pulls back with a look of disgust. "That always used to work."

My stomach drops. I see how it is: I was a vending machine to him. Insert basic care and affection, receive the cocktail of love and adoration he requires. God, was anything at all real between us?

I force myself to bury the turmoil. That doesn't matter, not really. I'm done with him and the past is the past. "You're delusional if you think I'll ever give you what you need again," I tell him. "I hear you need devotion, and I already wasted too much of that on you. I've moved on."

"You moved on awful fast," he sneers. "Ready to latch onto whoever will provide for you, hm, whore?"

My entire brain goes empty. After everything else he's said and done, calling me a name should not be the final straw. But somehow it shocks me to my core, leaving me open-mouthed and speechless.

I don't have to figure out how to reply to that though, because the door bursts inwards off its hinges and Marcus comes storming in, a picture of pure rage with clenched fists and powerful, quick steps.

He looks at me quickly, but rather than coming over to me, he only grows more wrathful, advancing on Ethan. He doesn't say anything, becoming somehow more intimidating for not issuing a single threat.

There's suddenly a pressure on my wrists, and someone is untying my hands. "Let's get you out of here," a deep voice says. "You don't want to see this. Trust me. I hear dragons can be vicious when their mates are threatened."

The rope gives way, but I don't move. "Who are you?" I demand, because I'm not about to walk off with a total stranger. I've already gotten myself into enough trouble for today.

"My name is Max," he tells me. Then, without waiting any longer, he grabs me by the hips and lifts me up and over the chair like I weigh nothing, setting me back on my feet. I'm unsteady, looking up at a truly massive man, all brawn and looking like he could comfortably rip me in half. He gives me a smile I think is meant to be calming. "I'll tell you whatever you want, but you don't want to be in here."

I hear a disgusting ripping behind me, and a scream, and deliberately don't turn around. Perhaps Max is right.

I follow him into the hall, and Max tries to prop the door back in the doorframe like that's going to do anything. I can still hear the screams, and Max just frowns at the door. I look around and see we're in an illegal basement apartment; the dark hallway is run-down past the scummiest landlord's standards. I don't want to touch anything or even step on the ground.

Max gives up on the door, leaving it only half covering the opening. He purposefully steps in front of it, like he can some-how keep me and the violence inside separated with just his body, and then turns to me, arms crossed over his chest. "Did he hurt you?" he asks.

"Just knocked me out and tied me up," I tell him, touching the new cuts on my wrists from the rope. "Nothing serious."

Max opens his mouth, but a cut-off scream from inside the apartment tells us both how seriously Marcus takes it without Max having to say a word.

He sticks out a hand. "I'm Max," he says again. "Nice to meet you properly."

I shake it wearily. "Are you a friend of Marcus'?"

"I'm not sure your boyfriend there really has friends," he muses, then shrugs. "Not that I get to judge. Creatures like us, it's not exactly easy."

"Are you a dragon too?"

"Wolf shifter. I'd be tearing that shitstain apart with my teeth if your boyfriend wasn't taking care of it."

"If you're not his friend, why do you care about this?" I ask him suspiciously, because what I've learned by now is that nothing in life is ever free or easy, except maybe when it comes from Marcus.

He huffs. "This is my job, Elise. I handle creatures who step out of line."

I raise an eyebrow. I might be about to fall over, but I'm not stupid. "Marcus said you people wouldn't give a fuck about me, because I'm human."

353

"Not so human anymore. And even if I didn't give a fuck about protecting humans—and I'm not saying I don't—it is my job to keep our kind under wraps. And a dragon losing his shit and rampaging through the streets in full dragon form would not do that, and that's exactly what would happen if Marcus lost you. So, here I am."

A particularly loud scream comes from behind the door, and I flinch. Max raises one of his truly giant hands, touching my shoulder and gently rubbing through my shirt. "Almost over now," he says, and I don't want to ask if he recognizes which screams mean death is near, or if he can sense something through the door that I can't.

He must see that I don't find that as reassuring as he wants me to, because he gives me an awkward smile. "I think you'd like my wife."

I twitch, his words successfully drawing me out of listening to whatever is happening in the next room. I guess I didn't expect a big burly bruiser—who already admitted he kills people for a living—to have a wife his voice goes all soft over. But a quick glance down shows a dark band on his ring finger. "Based on what, exactly? You don't know me."

He shrugs. "She was born human, too, and doesn't really have any female friends who understand straddling the two worlds. I mean, I was born human too, but I don't remember it, so I can't really commiserate there, hard as I try. And I think there's just something about women being friends with other women that's different."

It's probably true, although I don't have much of a basis for comparison. I like to think that Lacey and I are friends again, but she's the only one I have.

And he's right about me needing people who can understand this former human thing. I don't know if I really consider myself former, or know what I am now. But Ethan's tricks don't work on me anymore, and I can't quite wrap my head around living practically forever, even if Marcus assures me it's true. "Is your wife like me?" I ask him.

"More like me. She turns into a wolf now. Cute as hell, too," he says, his smile soft, like it's normal to call a wolf cute. "But she gets the whole thing with being a human before. You'd like Casey."

A scream rips out from behind us before I can respond, and then, perhaps more alarmingly, cuts off. Then the door comes tumbling down, and before I know what's going on, I'm in Marcus' arms. I rest my whole weight on his chest, burying my face there and inhaling that bonfire scent.

"Are you alright?" he breathes against my hair.

"I'm okay." It's close enough to true. It'll take me time. But I'm not hurt, not really.

He pulls back. "He'll never hurt you again," he promises, which feels a bit redundant. We all know what he did to Ethan.

Max clears his throat. "You under control?"

Marcus' hands tense on me at the reminder that we're not alone, but he lifts his head and nods. "The dragon is satisfied," he says, sounding grave.

"Good. I'll take care of the clean-up, then. You should get her home." He looks at me. "And think about what I said, Elise." Before we can say anything, he pulls out a cell phone and starts dialing as he walks into the apartment.

"What did he say?" Marcus demands.

"He wants me to meet his wife. Says we'd have something in common, both being former humans."

He raises an eyebrow. "I wasn't aware other creatures could do that. I thought dragons were rather unique in that regard."

"I didn't ask for details, Marcus."

"No, of course not." Without warning, he scoops me up under my knees, holding me like a princess. I don't resist, collapsing into his chest again. "Let's get out of here."

"We're still in the city?" I check, not having seen the outside world since Ethan knocked me unconscious.

"Mhm. I'll get us a car." He pauses a minute, clearly realizing that his hands are occupied. "You can call us a car."

"I don't have my phone. I don't know what Ethan did with it."

"Back pocket."

So I grab his phone, then use his face to unlock it before finding a ride-share for us.

The ride home is achingly quiet, and Marcus doesn't let me go once. The driver should probably say something about seatbelts, but something about Marcus keeps him quiet.

The doorman at our apartment doesn't comment on Marcus carrying me either, just welcomes us home.

At last, we're alone in our apartment, and Marcus brings us both over to that comfortable couch, sitting down and positioning me so I'm on his lap. "Do you need anything, Angel?" he asks, looking me up and down as if there will be a sign that tells him exactly how to care for me.

I need food, and more water, and I'd love a shower and I need to sleep for three days. But even more than that, I need Marcus to keep holding me. "Just this."

He nods. "Alright then. Do you want to tell me what you were doing out there, then?"

CHAPTER 45
Marcus

S he goes very still and then her eyes tear up, and my heart nearly wrenches right out of my chest. I almost take it back. It really doesn't matter, not if it's going to make her sad.

"I wanted to buy you a Christmas present," she mumbles, and I wouldn't be able to make out her words at all if my hearing wasn't so good.

"Did I lead you to think that I needed a Christmas present?" I press. I don't need things from her, and if I in any way implied that I did, then I need to change that immediately.

She rolls her eyes, an interesting effect with the tears still leaking out of the corners. "You don't need to say it, Marcus. You went on a crazy shopping spree for me, and I just wanted to be an equal in this relationship."

I straighten up. It's time to clarify some things for her before she feels any worse about herself, or puts herself in further danger. Not that I think there's further danger out there—Ethan is very much dead, and I don't know anyone else who would think risking my wrath by coming after her would be a good idea—but I need her to understand, regardless.

"I don't care about gifts, Elise. You're my gift." She scoffs slightly, reaching up to wipe her eyes. She can scoff all she wants, but that doesn't make it less true. "Elise. I waited millennia for you. I built up a hoard for you. I made a comfortable nest so I'd have a safe, welcoming place for my mate. The moment I realized how much I wanted to give you things is the moment I knew you were mine. I've never wanted that before, and I never will again."

"That doesn't make me feel better," she points out, voice very quiet now.

Maybe it doesn't, but she's thinking too much like a human. I can't fault her for it, but I need her to think like a dragon for just a moment. "I know I'm asking a lot, for you to understand my perspective on this. But I'm genetically hard-wired this way. I'll never not want to give you things. It fills me with a contentment I can't quite explain, knowing you're taking something of mine. That I provided it and it makes you happy or comfortable or content. The idea that it's ours now is the most powerful force in my world. Letting me give to you and you being here is a gift in and of itself, every time."

She stares at me for a long moment. "I'll try to understand that. But I have some rules."

"Alright." Rules? When was the last time someone imposed rules on me? It doesn't matter. I'm eager to follow wherever she leads.

She moves to sit up fully, giving me a look that's all business. "First off: I'm not comfortable getting my salary from you anymore."

I tilt my head. "I think I've made it clear that I never expect you to take care of me, and I'll certainly make sure you always are kept in luxury, no matter what. I'll call the agency after the Christmas holiday."

She's already shaking her head. "That's the other part. I'll respect that you have crazy money, and I'll try to remember that you genuinely like sharing it with me. But I'm not here to be kept, Marcus. I'm going to have a job."

I make myself hold still for a long moment so I don't say anything I'll regret. If I'm asking her to understand my dragon nature, then I need to understand her human mind. And humans don't like to be kept.

I hate the idea of her going to cook for someone else every day. Never mind the problem of her spending so much time away from me, which I recognize as selfish and hypocritical, but her food has always felt intensely personal. Like it was a gift just for me, and my dragon is way too possessive to share that with anyone else.

But this is about compromise, so I swallow down my first few responses. "What will you do, Elise?"

She shrugs. "Maybe I could find a new personal chef position. But Lacey's also looking for more staff, I think. That might be a tempting offer. I wouldn't get to cook whatever I want whenever I want, but I don't think any private clients would give me quite as much freedom as you do, anyway. And Lacey and I are friends again, I think. It might be nice to work with her."

"Why don't you take some time to think about it." She opens her mouth to protest, but I keep going. "What if we both took some time?"

She pauses, tilting her head. "What do you have to think about?"

"Transitioning to a full-time devoted house dragon?" I suggest, grinning and ducking my head to press a kiss to her cheek. "I have money, Angel. I don't need my job. I've liked being busy, but now, why don't I show you the world?" When she doesn't immediately look convinced, I say, "I'm not trying to object to your rule. You can do whatever you'd like with your time. Just consider this a brief intermission for both of us."

She opens her mouth, then closes it again, considering my offer. I appreciate her taking it seriously instead of immediately brushing it off like I know she would have done in the past.

"Like where?" she asks eventually.

"Make a list. We'll go everywhere you want."

"That could take a while."

That sounds so damn perfect to me. "I know, Angel. We have all the time in the world."

Her smile is nearly blinding. "I like how that sounds."

"Enough to go make a list?" I ask.

She looks at me for a moment, then grinds her hips against my lap. "Do you need that list right now?"

Fuck me. I look into her eyes, looking for any sign that she isn't okay, that fucking her right now would be pushing things too far after earlier. All I see is hungry eyes looking back at me, and my cock throbs in my pants.

"No," I say, pushing her shirt up slowly while I talk. "I think we can wait a little while."

CHAPTER 46
Elise
Christmas Day

"**N**o, Mom, I told you. I won't be around," I say, tilting my head further back so I can look out the massive windows while reclining on the couch.

It's snowing outside. It won't stick to the ground enough to call this a proper white Christmas, but it looks pretty for now.

All in all it's been a fantastic Christmas. Marcus woke me up with kisses along my neck and spine that hastily turned into Christmas-morning sex that lasted most of the morning. After we showered, he went to poke around at everything I bought for Christmas dinner while I called my mom.

He's even been good at not giving me an excessive amount of gifts. I'm trying to be more understanding of it and trying to appreciate what he wants to give me. It's hard, because I don't like feeling like I'm in debt to him, but I'm working on it. After all, he can't help it.

Plus, the man is taking me to Italy tomorrow, and that's just the start of a four-month travel extravaganza. Or should I say, the start of the four month planned travel extravaganza. Marcus has repeatedly reassured me we can always make our trip longer, and I've not only refrained from shooting him down outright, but I've actually considered it. So, clearly, I'm making progress at understanding what my dragon needs from me.

Mom is trying to bring up me coming to meet her latest boyfriend for New Years since Marcus and I didn't come for Christmas, but I'm not changing our travel plans. If he's still her boyfriend when we get back, then we can talk about driving down to Pennsylvania.

There's a clanging in the kitchen, and I resist the urge to look over at Marcus and find out what he's up to. I won't be able to resist the urge to go fix whatever he's doing, and I really should finish this call first. Apparently, he was serious about wanting to cook Christmas dinner together. Then again, after how Thanksgiving worked out for us, I suppose I shouldn't question his cooking decisions.

She wheedles one more time, but when I hold firm, she sighs and wishes me a happy holiday, and I know that this conversation has reached its natural end. "Merry Christmas to you, Mom."

"All done?" Marcus asks when I set my phone aside. He's significantly closer than I thought, and I jump.

"Your other form is a menacing, fire-breathing winged beast as big as a house," I complain. "How in the world are you good at sneaking up on people?"

He grins. "You could put a bell on me?"

I shake my head at his ridiculousness and reach up to pull him down to me for a kiss, and within a few minutes he's crawled over me, cradling my head with one hand and supporting his weight with the other.

"Mm, dinner?" I manage to ask, turning my head to the side slightly so I can think. I refuse to waste that food.

Marcus, not to be deterred, presses kisses down my neck. "Didn't start yet, Angel," he murmurs, his breath hot against my skin. "Thought we could use an appetizer."

It's a cheesy line, but I'm apparently into cheesy lines, because I can't get my hands back on him fast enough.

Marcus is wearing a set of silk Christmas pajamas. It's actually endearingly cute, especially for a man I'm relatively sure never celebrated Christmas before me, but endearingly cute isn't quite the look I'm going for right now.

I shove a hand into his pants, working them halfway down. As I expected, there's no underwear underneath, so his hard cock springs free, ready for me immediately.

My eyes are instantly drawn to his piercing. "Did you change your jewelry?" I ask dumbly, staring.

He tilts my head up, denying me a view of the red-and-green Christmas themed cock piercing, but giving me a great view of

365

those sparkling eyes and a mischievous smile. "Merry Christmas, Angel," he murmurs. "Want to test it out?"

Fuck yes. My entire focus is this man with a bedazzled piece of cock jewelry and a still tragically-on silk pajama shirt, both of which he bought just to make me smile. I shove at his chest, and he lets me flip him onto his back as I climb on top, my hands already moving to the buttons on his shirt as my pussy rubs against his cock, soaked and eager for more.

"Show me what you got," I challenge.

He smirks again, hands finding my hips, then my tits. It impedes my ability to take his shirt off, but I let him have his fun. "Always, Angel," he croons, voice low and full of promise.

Looking for more?

Want more?

For a special bonus scene of Elise and Marcus, sign up for my newsletter at www.addyjameswriter.com

Preview of Snowed In With A Werewolf

Snowed In With A Werewolf is Luc's story. If you've ever wondered why he's such an asshole, why he's so desperate for power, and what it takes to get a man like that to relax—then I have a story for you. Please be warned: Luc is a (light) stalker.

The robbers are expecting a quiet night and an easy score.

I saw a movie like this once. Two robbers staking out homes of families going away on vacation. No doubt they saw the small family drive away yesterday morning, the harried parents and two kids piling into the dented minivan. Then they saw the lack of lights, the back gate that can be shimmied open even when it's supposedly locked, and the outdated alarm system sign for a company that doesn't exist anymore, and thought they'd have an easy night. It didn't end well for the robbers in the movie, and it won't end well for these two, either.

I listen to them whisper outside the back door as I sit on the staircase, halfway between the woman I came here for and these robbers, waiting for whatever comes next.

So much for my quiet night basking in Penny's proximity. This is only the second night ever that I've had an opportunity to be inside the house, and these morons are going to ruin it for me.

When they get the door open, I push to my feet. Nothing good ever lasts.

I meander slowly into the kitchen, leaning my hip against the chipped linoleum counter. The house is so dark that I'm covered by shadow, and I doubt any human could see me. Just the way I like it.

When they finally make it inside, they split directions. One of them goes to the living room, where the old TV and gaming system are practically hidden among the pile of children's toys. The other heads for the stairs.

"I wouldn't." I step up behind him, silent as the grave with two thousand years of practice.

He jumps, turning towards me. "What the—"

"If you wake up my girl, we're going to have a problem," I tell him. "This is your one chance to get out of here unscathed."

I listen for a moment. Judging by the soft breathing, Penny is still asleep upstairs, completely unaware of what's happening in this house. This is the second night I've broken in, and she hasn't so much as twitched as I've walked around. She's always seemed like a heavy sleeper when I watched from a distance. Hopefully, that trend continues tonight.

"Who the fuck—"

"That's not the right question," I scold, stepping closer. "The question is, how smart are you? Because anyone with any brains at all would get out of here right now and save their own sorry skin."

His eyes flick up and down, and I know what he sees. It's the same thing everyone has seen when they've looked at me since I was a child: too scrawny to back up my mouth.

There's a scuff behind me. The other one thinks he's quiet, but my ears are sharp enough that I could hear a pin drop in the house next door. My muscles tense, and I resist the urge to squeeze my hands into fists. I have no doubt I could beat two humans in a fistfight, but that's not the way I win fights.

Not that my usual method will be much help here, either. Poisoning, tricking, and manipulating others into doing my dirty work is a little out of reach at the moment.

But I have a dirty trick I can pull here, and it's a big one.

And what can I say? They interrupted my night with my girl. I don't know how many of these I'm going to get, how many chances I'll have before someone catches on and I have to let this obsession go. I'm just mad enough to think that this is all a good idea.

"Last chance to leave," I tell him. I already know he won't take it. I can see it all, the next three, five, ten steps ahead. Like a chess game, I can envision every move coming down the line.

And I never lose at chess.

He swings. I duck, timing it perfectly so he knocks his friend sneaking up behind me in the face.

There's an echoing crash, one of them falling into the bar-cart and knocking over the bottles of cheap liquor. I wince, absently making a plan to replace those while reaching for one of the broken bottles.

Checkmate. It's always good when a weapon falls into my lap. I palm the glass, weighing up my opponents and determining the best place to strike.

When one lunges at me, I hold my position until he steps right into my range, then cut under his arm with my broken booze bottle. It won't kill him, but it'll hurt something awful and bleed a fair amount, which is all I need.

"There're easier pickings somewhere else," I tell them, because I'm not heartless. I really don't give a fuck what most humans do. Crime will never go away entirely, and I'm not going to pretend I can stop it.

But they crossed a line when they picked this house. When they picked this woman.

I can see them turning it over in their heads. The risk versus the reward. The threat that this skinny guy in front of them wearing a suit poses. The bottle in my hand. Whatever they've no doubt already spent the money they hoped to get on.

There's a way to end this quickly. Of course, the most effective way would be to have Max with me, but Max doesn't know about this place. For the first time in our long existence, we're leading semi-separate lives, and I was grateful for that before right now.

Ah, well. Needs must. I force a partial shift, letting the wolf take over my face. Teeth, eyes, and a snout—just enough to make these men practically shit their pants.

I'm dripping sweat under my suit, my muscles starting to ache. It's incredibly hard to hold a partial shift like that. I've practiced thousands of times, but even so I can't hold it long, having to make a decision to shift entirely or to take my human form back. I settle back into my human skin only to see that the would-be robbers have already turned tail and run.

Well, then. Now that that's solved...

There's a footfall behind me, and it's only then I realize the sound changed. The peacefully slumbering breathing from upstairs is gone.

Shit.

Also by Addison James

<u>Supernatural Christmas</u>

A Werewolf for Christmas

Snowed in with the Werewolf

<u>Crae Romance</u>

Callum

Bryce

Heath

Celia

Silas

Estrid

Standalones

The Heat Cure

Dragon's Treasure